AGGIE MORTON

MYSTERY QUEEN

AGGIE MORTON
MYSTERY QUEEN

PERIL AT OWL PARK

MARTHE JOCELYN
WITH ILLUSTRATIONS BY ISABELLE FOLLATH

tundra

Tundra Books, an imprint of Penguin Random House Canada Young Readers,
a division of Penguin Random House of Canada Limited

Library and Archives Canada Cataloguing in Publication

Title: Peril at Owl Park / Marthe Jocelyn.
Names: Jocelyn, Marthe, author.
Description: Series statement: Aggie Morton, mystery queen
Identifiers: Canadiana (print) 20190235071 | Canadiana (ebook) 2019023508X
| ISBN 9780735265493
   (hardcover) | ISBN 9780735265509 (EPUB)
Classification: LCC PS8569.O254 P47 2020 | DDC jC813/.54—dc23

Published simultaneously in the United States of America by Tundra Books of
Northern New York, an imprint of Penguin Random House Canada Young
Readers, a division of Penguin Random House of Canada Limited

Library of Congress Control Number: 2019955870

Edited by Lynne Missen and Margot Blankier
Designed by John Martz
The text was set in Plantin MT Pro.

Printed and bound in Canada

www.penguinrandomhouse.ca

1   2   3   4   5   24   23   22   21   20

Penguin
Random House
TUNDRA BOOKS

FOR ROBIN, CAT, AND EMMA,
NICK, AND KAREN,
BELOVED COUSINS

Marjorie Greyson

James Greyson

Beatrice Truitt

Lady Greyson

Kitty Sivam

Lakshay Sivam

Inspector Willard

Frederick Bolt

Annabelle Day

Sebastian Mooney

Stephen

Roger Corker

DECEMBER 23, 1902

TUESDAY

CHAPTER I

AN OMINOUS ARRIVAL

MY SISTER'S NEW HOME was named Owl Park, a manor house surrounded by gardens and woods that were possibly full of owls. Dotted among the gracious old trees were a gazebo and a maze and a pond where swans floated during the summer months. Marjorie's new husband was ever so nice, even with being a lord. James was the sort of person who liked having extra children come for Christmas. Not the sort of person who would invite a murderer on purpose.

James and Marjorie's wedding had been at Owl Park in September this year, but now was my first real visit, and Grannie Jane's as well. Despite being fairly ancient—more than sixty-six years old—Grannie had nobly offered to ride backward in the coach from the rail station, letting

Hector and me have a window each. She knew we liked to spy on the world, ever since our great cleverness in solving a mystery several weeks ago. She had become nearly as fond of Hector as I was, as he came for tea most days when his school was done, and made us laugh and showed off his good manners. Our teas were also more delicious than what he'd get as a boarder at the vicarage.

Snow began to whirl as our coach rumbled up the drive, dancing flakes making the stone chimneys and gabled windows look as if they belonged on a picture postcard.

"I wonder if the ice on the pond is thick enough for skating?" I said.

Hector blinked in alarm. "I am hoping not," he said.

"*You* needn't go skating," I assured him. "But some of us might like to try, if the pond cooperates. You needn't do anything you don't want for this whole week!"

Except for the one dire thing that I did not say out loud. Hector and I both would be having Christmas without a mother or a father beside us. Hector's parents and little sister, Genevie, were kept far away in Belgium by his father's work. My mother was at home in Torquay, flattened by sadness because my Papa, my beloved Papa, had been dead for nearly one whole year. She would finish full mourning in January, but it was not considered correct for a widow to travel or participate in merry festivities until the proper amount of time had gone by.

Hector stared solemnly out the window, one finger idly doodling in the condensation upon the pane. Was he feeling lonely? Was he nervous about staying in a fancy house, with everyone a stranger except for Grannie Jane and me? I would have my sister and James, but Hector would have only me.

"Lucy will be here too," I said. "She's not eleven yet, but very jolly and not shy at all."

Lucy's mother was my sister's husband's sister. That made us cousins of a sort, I was pretty certain. On the day when Marjorie married James in September, Lucy and I were flower girls, dressed like twins in white muslin dresses with wide sashes of blue satin. Marjorie had written that Lucy was *panting* to meet me again.

Our coach swung around in front of the arched and columned entrance of Owl Park.

"Well, well," said Grannie Jane. "A royal welcome."

The servants were in a formal line by the entryway, each facing forward like guards at Buckingham Palace. Marjorie and James waited on the flagstones next to the row of dark liveries and white aprons.

Marjorie began waving with both hands. I pushed up the window to wave wildly back.

Grannie Jane clucked her tongue and quietly scolded. "Your sister is behaving like a schoolgirl. No surprise that James's mother is attempting to adjust her deportment."

We'd had letters full of woe about Marjorie's efforts to become a proper lady of the manor, and mostly falling short of her mother-in-law's high standards.

"Only because I miss her!" I said. "We've not seen her for nearly two months, since just after Mrs. Eversham's murder. I expect she behaves like a lady most of the time." I fiddled with the door handle the instant the coach came to a stop. Grannie put a hand upon my arm.

"Do not blunder down, Agatha. Allow the footman to assist. For Marjorie's sake, you must show that you've had a tiny amount of breeding—"

A man wearing dark livery, with a nose pink-tipped from the cold, opened my door from the outside. I flashed him a smile, used his shoulder as a vaulting pole, and leapt to the ground to be scooped into my sister's arms. James was right behind her, adding his arms to the embrace.

Grannie Jane descended, more gracefully than I had, and then Hector hopped down to be welcomed by Marjorie and introduced to James. Every person I liked best in the world—except for Mummy and my dog, Tony—was standing right here in a circle.

"Come in, come in, let's get you out of the cold," said James, giving one arm to Grannie and the other to me. "Mother is waiting to greet you."

"Must the servants catch their deaths on our account?" said Grannie Jane.

"Don't worry about the servants, Mrs. Morton," said James. "They come from hardy stock."

Blue-lipped and shivery stock, I thought. *As cold as penguins cast away on an iceberg. As cold as explorers seeking the North Pole. As cold as puppies stranded in a snowbank.*

"I know it seems barbaric," said Marjorie, "but it's been done this way for centuries, to honor visitors. I'm afraid you'll find that we bump up against tradition rather a lot at Owl Park."

The door to the manor was held open by a gaunt man in a fine black coat, who gazed somewhere over our heads.

"Thank you, Pressman." James led Grannie in, as Marjorie slid an arm around my shoulder.

"Please appear to be sweet and docile with James's mother, if you can," she whispered in a rush. "To fend off her snippy rebukes."

I hardly listened because we'd arrived in the Great Hall and paused in front of an enormous crackling fire to see how Christmas had already come to Owl Park. A yew tree stood in the center of the hall, its boughs festooned with gold foil bows and paper cornucopias of nuts and sweets. Candles clipped to every branch burned like stars against the dark green branches.

The Dowager Lady Greyson waited beside it, with an indigo cashmere shawl wrapped tightly about her narrow shoulders. She looked nearly as old as Grannie

Jane, with a long nose and a mouth pinched into a button.

I'd practiced my curtsy all week and was pleased at how well I managed. But instead of a polite greeting, I found myself mumbling under her severe inspection. Hector, however, performed his expert bow, and Lady Greyson's face brightened as if she'd seen a butterfly open its wings. Lucy hovered beside her grandmother, trying to catch my eye and grinning.

"Do stop jiggling, Lucy!" said Lady Greyson, before turning to Grannie Jane. "Do you do stairs?" Her accent was the most imperious I'd ever heard. Rather like meeting the Queen. Except that Queen Victoria was dead now, and it was her son, Edward, who ruled as King.

"Slowly but surely," said Grannie Jane.

"I understand you've come without your maid," said Lady Greyson. "I believe we're meant to lend you one." She began to climb the steps as Marjorie swooped in for a whisper.

"Sorry, Grannie," she said. "She's a trial. But if anyone can stand up to her, it's you."

"I am not the one who needs to do that." Grannie Jane gathered her skirts for the hike up what looked like two hundred marble stairs. "But that is the topic of a later conversation."

"I'll come up with you," said Marjorie. "Lucy, you'll

look after Aggie and Hector, won't you? Perhaps a tour of the ground floor? There is just time before the dressing bell rings. Hurry when you hear it, and put on your best things. You mustn't be late."

I groaned. Getting dressed for dinner was one aspect of the holiday that I dreaded. Mummy had made such a fuss about me having proper dresses, and Gracious Manners to go with them.

Marjorie gave me a little push. "Count yourself lucky that James's mother has agreed that you may be at table with the adults this evening and not up in the nursery eating buns and hot milk."

"We'll be ready, Aunt Marjorie," Lucy said. "It's *fun* getting dressed for dinner. Grandmamma says I may wear her pearl necklace. I have a lovely neck, she says." She lifted her chin and swished her plaits over her shoulders so that we could appreciate her loveliness.

"Positively swan-like, Lucy," said Marjorie. "We have more visitors arriving any minute, so I shall be right back. Mr. Lakshay Sivam is a good chum of James from university. As it turns out, I knew his wife at school. No hijinks, I beg of you. They will be weary from their travels."

Lucy smiled as brightly as sunshine. "No hijinks before dinner, we promise, Aunt Marjorie."

Marjorie shot her a pretend glare and hurried after Grannie.

Lucy didn't pause to shake hands or be polite with hello-how-are-you. She threw her arms around me and squeezed until I squeaked, much friendlier than I expected after one day's acquaintance as flower girls. Finally, she let me breathe so that I could say, Hullo, this is Hector, and he made his little Belgian bow and said Enchanté, and Lucy stared. He was wearing a smart new coat that I'm certain the vicar's wife had purchased before our excursion, not wishing anyone to accuse her of neglecting the boy in her care.

"Aunt Marjorie said you were foreign," said Lucy to Hector. "I didn't know if that meant brown or peculiar."

"If this is the only choice," said Hector, "it is logical to deduce that I am peculiar."

Lucy clapped her hands. "Yes! Let's all be peculiar, shall we? Uncle James's foreign friend was born in Ceylon. He has just come back on a sailing ship from visiting there, though, really, he and his wife live in Hampstead like normal people. Won't this be a Christmas unlike any other?"

Hector raised an eyebrow and I tried to raise one back, a trick I had not yet mastered. It would indeed be a Christmas like no other.

"We're sleeping up in the nursery suite," said Lucy. "All the way at the top. It's not so babyish as it sounds because I'm here without my nanny, thank goodness.

There's a new baby at my house. His name is Robert Phillip Charles Chatsworth. I shall call him Robin. Or possibly Bobbo. My mother got sick after the baby came, even though she wishes with all her heart to be at Owl Park for Christmas. She let me come, though, because she hasn't much energy and says I use up most of it. Nanny stayed at home to help with the baby. She very likely may never be *my* nanny again! I am *free*! Utterly free!" Lucy spun in a circle and swooped her arms like a giant heron attempting a takeoff.

"My nursemaid is not here either," I said, without imitating a heron. "Charlotte has gone to visit her mother, in Scunthorpe." I imagined their Christmas would be wholesome and educational, alphabetizing spice jars or translating carols from the original German.

"Shall we not bring with us the luggage?" said Hector.

"Don't be silly." Lucy waved a hand. "The footmen will do that. This place is simply buzzing with servants, and Grandmamma hired extras for the holidays. She always does."

Hector and I exchanged another look. At the vicarage there was only a cook, and a maid for the rough work, laying the fires and doing laundry and such. It was the same at my own house, Groveland. After Papa died, it turned out that we didn't have enough money and had to let the servants go except Mrs. Corner, who still did our cooking, and Sally, who did everything else. There'd been a gardener, but he was gone now too.

Lucy watched as Grannie Jane's skirt disappeared around the curve of the staircase above us. "Old ladies are so slow to climb steps!" She turned to us with shining eyes. "Now!" she said. "Tell me every little thing about the murder."

A picture of the corpse under the piano flew across my mind, as it had too often since finding Mrs. Eversham. I could not fault Lucy for her curiosity. Being a person with what my mother called a Morbid Preoccupation, I'd have been agog to hear the tale if I hadn't lived through it myself. But it did seem a bit bold for our opening conversation.

"Perhaps," said Hector, gently, "such a story will wait until we have an interlude of time to ourselves."

"If you say so." Lucy did not appear in the least offended. "Later, in the nursery, we'll have a fire and you'll tell the whole gruesome story and scare my hair off!"

At that moment came the chug of a machine from somewhere down the drive. James and Marjorie appeared on the landing, assuming it to be their friends, Mr. and Mrs. Sivam. We all rushed outside to see what could be coming.

The servants hurried behind us to restore their greeting formation.

"Aah," breathed Hector.

"A horseless carriage!" squealed Lucy.

It came up the drive with its motor humming like an enormous insect, flashing yellow wheels, its passengers enveloped in furs. The driver appeared to struggle with the steering, or perhaps the rubber rims on the tires did not meet well with the frosted surface of the road. The vehicle skidded when coming to a stop, causing the row of servants to jump back like a flock of frightened chickens.

"It is a model of the electric variety," said Hector. "Very popular for city driving, and no need for a hand crank to start the engine."

"Let's watch from inside," said Lucy. "It's too cold out here."

Within a minute we were perched on a window seat in the breakfast room, happily nestled on damask cushions instead of shivering on the doorstep like the frostbitten servants.

A footman tugged uselessly on the handle of the door beside Mrs. Sivam. Her husband hurried around from the driver's side to show how it was done. He assisted his wife in stepping down. They both wore fur coats nearly to their ankles and a bearskin rug was tossed across the back of the seat.

"The vehicle is entirely open to the wind and snow!" said Hector. "They must dress like bears to survive the journey." He shuddered.

"And they've been visiting the tropics!" I said. "England must feel like an Arctic wasteland."

"He has an excellent mustache!" said Hector.

"She looks like the Snow Queen," I said. "Her hair is like . . ." *Spun gold? A cloud in the dawn sky? Lemon meringues?*

James introduced Marjorie to his old friend, and Marjorie introduced her school chum to James. Everyone seemed very jolly. Marjorie and Mrs. Sivam, arm in arm, paused to meet Mrs. Frost, the housekeeper, and Pressman, the butler.

"The Sivams didn't bring their servants either," said Lucy, "because of traveling. They need to borrow also."

"There is a trouble with the motorcar." Hector pointed. Mr. Pressman and the footmen were all shaking their heads in response to a question from James.

"I expect it's just that none of the servants knows how to drive," I said. "The owner will have to park it himself."

Mr. Sivam retrieved an ornate wooden box from the front seat and handed it carefully to James. He climbed in behind the wheel, steered the car backward in an elegant turn, and then drove out of our sight around the side of the manor. James stepped through a drift of deepening snow, carrying Mr. Sivam's box with both hands.

"What do you suppose is in that box?" I said.

"Let's find out!" Lucy hopped off the window seat and we did likewise.

When we came into the Great Hall, my sister was leading Mrs. Sivam up the stairs. Lucy beetled over to James before he could disappear. He showed her the box but held it out of reach of her curious fingers.

"She's very bold," I murmured.

"Indeed," said Hector.

"I've put you in the Juliet suite," came Marjorie's voice from the landing, as she explained to Mrs. Sivam. "You have connecting rooms with a little balcony that overlooks the conservatory."

Lucy bounded back to join us. James strode away toward his study, the box tucked under his elbow.

"Uncle James says that if we're lucky, Mr. Sivam will tell us the spooky family legend about the contents of that box . . . something so precious that it has been hidden away in a bank vault for many long years. And now . . . it's here at Owl Park!"

CHAPTER 2

A BREACH OF MANNERS

A SPOOKY FAMILY LEGEND? A precious something inside a vault for eighteen years?

But Lucy was not one to pause or ponder. She corralled us for a tour of the house.

"We'll start with the best bits," she said, "because we won't have time to see the whole place now. I know everything because I've been here hundreds of times, visiting Grandmamma."

I had a quick rush of gratitude that Dowager Lady Greyson was not *my* grandmother. So stiff and forbidding! Grannie Jane was nearly perfect, being quite observant about other people and often willing to answer questions.

Lucy led us speedily along a passage painted forest green and lined with portraits of many pudding-faced ancestors. "You can look at them later," she said. "They've been here for a hundred years and will likely stay another hundred. This door is the lavatory, in case you need to know that. See?" She opened it to show us a sink and a toilet in a room painted the color of a sunset. "Grandmamma might die if she knew I'd shown you a toilet."

She explained that some of the rooms had been updated with electrical wiring, but others still were lit with gas lamps. James was all for modernizing, but Grandmamma . . . was not so eager.

"This"—Lucy tapped on a set of double doors but didn't stop—"is the drawing room. You can see the ordinary rooms tomorrow. The drawing room, the music room, the Avon Room, the conservatory, all those and thirty more." We went a few steps farther. "This"—she tapped on a tall, narrow door that began at waist height—"is the drawing room wood cupboard." It was painted the same dark green as the wall, only a small knob making it visible.

"What, please, is a wood cupboard?" Hector asked.

Lucy paused her march and opened the door to show us rows of neatly stacked logs. "The servants fill the cupboard from out here in the passage," she explained, "so they don't disturb the family and guests. There's a door on the other side, next to the fireplace, so Uncle James—or whoever—can add wood to the fire when we need it. Do you not have them where you come from?"

"Not in any house I know," said Hector, "but is most ingenious."

"Let's go to the kitchen," said Lucy, "and see if we can swipe a biscuit. This way!"

Lucy thundered ahead of us around a corner, chattering long past when we could distinguish her words.

I glanced at Hector.

"She *is* a bit much, isn't she?" I whispered.

He lifted one eyebrow and then the other, making me laugh.

"She's only ten," I said.

"And I am pleased," he said, "to think of biscuits."

Lucy's head popped back around the corner. "Are you coming?"

Yes, we were coming.

"This," said Lucy, "is the kitchen!" She opened the baize door that separated the main house—the Upstairs—from the domain of the servants—the Downstairs—though it was really only four stairs in this case. The kitchen was on the ground floor, not in a basement the way it often is in a town house. The room we came into was the actual kitchen, with a big fire, and the ovens, the sinks and worktables. Stepping from the quiet passage to the buzzing world within was like arriving at a village fete. Girls in caps and aprons chopped vegetables and stirred soup; a footman polished cutlery; another footman, very blond, came whistling in from the courtyard with a block of ice wrapped in a towel; a boy a bit younger, and certainly skinnier than we were, sat on a stool near the fire rubbing the toe of a man's boot to a high sheen. The cook, Mrs. Hornby, had a row of featherless dead birds on the table in front of her, while a scullery maid frantically plucked another.

The servants' hall, where they ate their meals, was a second room that mirrored the kitchen, with windows the length of the dividing wall, so that anyone sitting at the table in the hall could see what was happening in the kitchen.

"There's the pantry over there," said Lucy, "where some of the food is stored. And the butler's pantry there . . ." She pointed. "Where Mr. Pressman has his headquarters and locks up things that no one's meant to touch. Scullery's in there, bakehouse is out in the courtyard, same as ice and wood and coal. Mrs. Frost's sitting room is that one. She and Mr. Pressman are the head servants, like king and queen of Downstairs."

"Well, I'm queen of the kitchen," said Cook, "and I'm telling you that no one is welcome to hang about gawking. We're making your dinner and we'll thank you to move along."

"Have you got any biscuits, *dear* Mrs. Hornby?" said Lucy.

"There's squashed flies in the jar, Miss Lucy," said Mrs. Hornby. "And that's all before your supper. Now get along out of my hair."

"Better than nothing, I suppose." Lucy pouted but I could see it was all for show. She reached for the porcelain cookie jar with eager hands.

"Squashed flies?" Hector murmured, looking miserable. "An English specialty?"

"A delicacy," I whispered. "Much more difficult to catch than ants."

Lucy removed the lid and offered the open jar to Hector. He waved his hand with a polite "Non, merci," before Lucy and I laughed.

"They're having you on," called the boot-polishing boy. "It's not real flies in there, only currants. Go on! Try one!"

Hector bravely nibbled at a corner. Then he bowed to Mrs. Hornby. "My first squashed fly!" he said. "A memorable occasion."

A clock chimed the quarter hour in sharp notes. The cook pulled a handkerchief from her apron pocket to wipe the perspiration from her face.

"Nearly time for the dressing bell," she said.

Lucy tugged me toward the stairs. Hector caught my hand and off we galloped, through the green baize door, along a passage and then another passage until Lucy took us into a dim room. Tall windows were draped with graceful swaths of a pale lavender silk that seemed to reflect the snow outside.

"This is the morning room," said Lucy. "The fire's not lit because it's not morning. Only Aunt Marjorie ever comes in here, to write her letters or to give servants their orders. Grandmamma does letters in her bedroom now that she's so old. This room is very pretty when the sun is shining."

"Let's come back in the morning," I said, with a shiver.

"Wait!" said Lucy. Her voice dropped to a dramatic whisper. "*This* is where the real tour begins."

She hurried across the carpet to an ornate cabinet standing against the wall. On the upper shelves, behind a paned glass door, were rows of teapots. None was the ordinary sort that a person might find in a kitchen. No Brown Bettys here. They were shaped like cats and temples, elfin heads and beehives. A matching pair of elephants with raised trunks that worked as spouts. The glazes were Japanese red and glimmering gold, ancient green and cobalt blue.

"These are beautiful," I said. "May we come back when there is light and heat? To look properly?"

"We're not here for the silly old teapots," said Lucy. With a flourish, she turned the handle on one of the lower drawers.

The entire cabinet seemed suddenly to sigh. It swung away from the wall, a thick, oversized door, so quietly and gently that the teapots barely trembled.

"Ohh!"

A secret passage!

We gaped at the entrance to a tunnel, as black and uninviting as a coal chute. *Like the throat of an ogre. Like the opening to a cave that promised a colony of bats . . .*

"May we go in?" said Hector.

"That's why we're here!" Lucy grinned as if she'd built it herself. "There's a torch . . . just . . . here." She retrieved it from a ledge and pressed the button on its side. "The battery's quite low, but it will get us there and back."

"Where is *there*?" said Hector. "If I may ask?"

"Just follow me," said Lucy. "It's narrow, but you don't need to bend over. Even Uncle James can nearly stand up. He's the one who showed me this, on my tenth birthday. No one else knows, Uncle James says, now that his father's dead, not even Grandmamma. Not even my mother, because it was meant to be for boys only." Worry flashed across her face. "I hope he doesn't regret showing me, now that I have a baby brother."

"You'll be the one to show Robert," I assured her.

"But not for ten more years," Lucy said.

She stepped blithely into the passage, the torch beam fluttering like the flight of a lightning bug. I followed, expecting cobwebs to hit my face. Hector came behind, both of us shuffling in the near dark.

"Pull the cabinet shut, will you, Hector?" said Lucy. "We can't have a maid coming in and finding it!"

"Ugh, Lucy!" I said. "It's shining right into my eyes."

"Sorry!" The light swooped down.

Hector ran his hand along the edge of the door, groping for something to hold onto without smashing his fingers.

"It's higher than you'd expect," said Lucy. "Shaped like the handle of a suitcase."

"I have it now." We were plunged into night with a wheezing thud. The weak shaft of light from Lucy's torch made a circle the size of an orange on the floor.

"Don't be bothered if the light goes out," said Lucy. "I know the way. Keep one hand on the wall and stay close. It's not far, but we need to be *very* quiet. If we can hear them, you know they can hear us."

"They?" I said.

"You'll see," said Lucy. "Now *ssh*, and follow me."

We inched forward. I rather wished I could hold one of her plaits for guidance. Instead, I told a story in my head, making us as brave as brave.

Only the long-lost sarcophagus of an Egyptian pharaoh, studded with gems and gleaming with gold, could make this fearsome venture worth the risk. A noise ahead sent a shudder through the small, courageous company of explorers. What might be moving in such a place as this? A colony of ravening bats? Or ghosts, perhaps? The phantom remains of travelers who had come before, lost and starved to death in the perilous underground maze—

"I'm going to turn off the light," Lucy whispered, "to save what little is left."

Click. I blinked several times but could see nothing. I reached out a finger to touch the folds of Lucy's dress in front of me. Her voice sounded hollow when it came out of the dark.

"There's a corner just ahead, and then—*oof*—watch it, right turn here."

We'd inched around the sharp bend when Lucy paused again, her words hushed. "The passage has spy-holes into two different rooms. We'll stop at the first, where the study is, because the men are always there before the dressing bell rings. Absolute silence, right?"

I should not have been surprised at the word *spy*. The purpose of a passage is to lead a person somewhere. And the purpose of a *secret* passage is that no one knows you're there. Lucy squeezed herself aside to let me have the first go. She nudged my face into alignment before a narrow slot where I had quite a good view of one slice of James's study.

James stood behind his desk, laughing as he poured amber liquid from a decanter into three glasses on a tray.

I was so close that I could hear the ice clinking as it shifted. No wonder Lucy had warned us to be quiet! James handed a drink to Mr. Sivam, who sat in front of the desk on an upright chair. Mr. Sivam passed it along to another man whose back was to me and then accepted a glass for himself. The other man was old, I saw, because what little hair he had was gray and tufty, poking out around drooping ears.

"A toast!" James lifted his glass. "To new friends and old."

"To renewed family honor," said Mr. Sivam, raising his glass in return.

"Hear, hear!" agreed the other man, slurping his drink.

"Dr. Musselman," murmured Lucy, into my ear. "Grandmamma's physician. So dull!"

"You were saying, Lakshay?" said James. "Your intentions for . . ." He tapped the carved box that sat beside the ice bucket on his desk.

Mr. Sivam sighed. "My wife and I differ on this matter, but I feel duty bound . . . to correct a historic wrong, I suppose, by returning the treasure to its original home."

Lucy poked me. "*Treasure!*" she whispered. "Give Hector a turn."

Reluctantly, I traded places. Luckily, the voices were still audible even when not watching. I pressed my ear to the wall, not wanting to miss a single word.

"*Honor* is a personal matter," said James. "We each of us knows what feels right, but it can be difficult to uphold when others declare us mistaken."

"Yes, yes," said the doctor. "Whole wars are fought to avenge honor. I could tell you tales that would make your blood run cold."

"Perhaps not now, Dr. Musselman," said James, quickly. "Would you like to keep your treasure secure inside my safe, Lakshay?"

"A safe is the first place a thief would look," muttered Dr. Musselman.

"I thank you for understanding, gentlemen," said Mr. Sivam. "The notion of a curse is absurd, but I am compelled to return what does not belong to me. Until then, I shall keep it near me at all times, and guard it with my very life!"

"Hear, hear!" said the doctor.

A sudden echoing *bong* made us jump like rabbits after a gunshot. We clamped hands over our mouths to stifle the giggles and scurried back along the darkened passage.

"That was the dressing bell!" cried Lucy, as we emerged. "We have thirty minutes, and half of them will be spent climbing the stairs!" She maneuvered shut the cabinet to hide the secret passage and then rushed to the door.

"Come on!" she cried, and was gone.

"It is not calm, an English visit," said Hector. "Here is much activity."

"And mystery!" I said.

"Does he mention there is a curse?" Hector's voice deepened dramatically as he quoted Mr. Sivam. "'I shall guard it—'"

"'With my very life!'" I finished.

"What can he be hiding?" said Hector.

"We are *honor bound* to find out," I said. "But first we must dress for dinner."

CHAPTER 3

A TALE OF WOE

WE ARRIVED, PANTING, at our rooms on the third floor of Main House, without being seen or scolded for our dishevelment and dirt-smudged hands. Poor Hector was most dismayed at the ruffling of his hair and the grimy state of his sailor collar.

As neither Lucy nor I had a nursemaid in attendance, an under-parlormaid had been assigned to assist with our dressing and undressing. Hector was not considered old enough to have a valet, but he was well accustomed to looking after his own grooming. One luxury was that Stephen, the boot boy, would polish our shoes each night. We had only to leave them in the hallway outside our doors before going to bed, and they would appear as shiny as brand-new by morning.

"A veritable magic trick!" said Hector.

We were met by a thin girl with a turned-up nose and white-blonde hair. Pale eyelashes made her blue eyes look as round as buttons. Her name was Dot, she said. She was fourteen and had come into service last summer.

"My brother is one of the footmen," she confided. "Lord Greyson's been ever so good, hiring Frederick after his spot of trouble, and then me soon after. There's four more littler than us at home, so we're happy as anything, working here."

What had Frederick been in trouble about, I wondered? It would be too rude to ask.

"What was Frederick's spot of trouble?" said Lucy.

Dot flushed and told us. He'd fallen in with the wrong sort of lads and they'd nicked things from the village shops. But it was all behind him now, Dot swore. He was an excellent member of the household, Mr. Pressman had said only last week.

Lucy and I were to sleep together in the big nursery, and Hector was next door in a little room to himself.

"You won't find it spooky?" Dot wondered. "Being up here all alone?"

"We love it!" Lucy flung wide her arms.

"Truly, Dot," I said. "It's like having our own domain!"

"Only until tomorrow," said Dot. "When the actors come. They'll be staying in the servants' wing, across the landing, top floor of East House."

"Actors?" I said.

"Yes, miss. That lady who come today with her foreign husband, it's a troupe of actors she knows somehow."

"Mrs. Sivam," I said. "And Mr. Sivam."

"Yes, miss." Color warmed Dot's cheeks. "So, young Lady Greyson—"

"My sister," I said.

"Yes, miss." Her cheeks got pinker. "We calls her the young Lady Greyson so she don't get mixed up with the old one, his lordship's mother. M'lady, your sister, hired them to come make tableaux, special for the holiday."

Lucy clapped her hands and bobbed up and down on her toes. Part of me wanted to squeal like a child too, but most of me was grown-up enough to say, "Was this meant to be a surprise, Dot?"

"I s'pose it mighta been, miss. But I only told so's you'd be ready for the invasion of your . . . *domain*, come morning. That's how I started, right? Telling you there'd be more guests on this floor tomorrow." Dot stepped into the corridor and pointed across the landing to another suite of rooms. "The two men actors will have what used to be the schoolroom when there were little'uns here, that's what I was told. And there's a . . . a lady actor too, though I don't see as how she can be called a lady. She'll be in the extra maid's room down at the end," said Dot. "But old Lady Greyson, she thinks—"

BONG!

The dinner bell! And we hadn't begun to change our clothes!

"No!" cried Lucy. "We haven't even washed! Grandmamma will be livid. Come on, Dot, lickety-split!" She turned around so that the maid could unhook the fastenings all down her back. My dress had front buttons, and my fingers flew. I could not shame Marjorie on our very first evening!

A quiet tap at the door. "I am ready," said Hector.

"Well, we're not!" I called. "Give us one minute!"

Lucy rolled her eyes. "One minute? Can you tidy those curls in one minute?"

I dipped a flannel into the basin and cleaned my face and hands. At least Dot had brought us warm water. The cloth came away grimed with tunnel dust. My new dress, made especially for this week, was an over-the-head sort, with only one button under the collar at the back. Lucy did up mine while Dot fussed with Lucy's. I helped undo her plaits and we hurriedly brushed while counting to fifty.

"The other fifty strokes will have to wait until bedtime." Lucy hurled her brush onto the bed.

"If our heads haven't been chopped off by our grandmothers," I said. "Making tidy hair unnecessary."

"I believe," Hector called through the door, "that promptness is required?"

"We're *coming*!" growled Lucy.

Dot tied our hair with matching ribbons and pushed us through the door. Hector dashed down the stairs in front of us.

"I am always punctual!" he cried.

Not this time. We were the last to arrive, scurrying through the drawing room door like worried mice.

The room glittered, with candles and firelight and the twinkle of several chandeliers, as inviting a party as any could be. But all those critical eyes upon our tardy arrival, and all those frowning mouths! I wished for nothing more than a thick blanket to put over my head. But Lucy had clearly weathered this before. She went directly to her grandmother and curtsied, apologizing for all of us, claiming that we'd got turned about in the maze of corridors.

Marjorie's exquisite appearance made her quite unfamiliar. Her dress was a midnight blue chiffon, with tiny silver beads sewn to look like flowers on the bodice. Her hair was swept elegantly up and held with a silver comb. And her cheeks were rouged! I had never seen her do that before. She seemed more like a duchess than my sister, tall and gracious, with a gleaming rope of pearls around her throat. James, handsome in his evening coat, had a hand beneath his wife's elbow, gazing at her as if he couldn't believe his good luck.

We were taken on a round of introductions, though we'd met nearly everyone already—or eavesdropped upon their confidential business!

Here was our first close-up look at Mr. and Mrs. Sivam. They had come to rest at Owl Park after a long sea voyage from Ceylon. Mrs. Sivam was slim and wore a coral dress with fluttering wisps of silk at the neckline and all down the sleeves. Rather like a ship at full sail. Her pale skin was faintly freckled, from sailing on the ocean for weeks and weeks, I supposed. Her pale hair coiled at the nape of her neck, showing off an elegant choker made of a million black seed pearls. She mixed us up, Lucy and me, and then apologized with giggles, for how could we be mistaken for each other?

Her husband was the first native Ceylonese I'd ever met, but spoke perfect English, as he had lived in London since finishing his time at Oxford with James. He had a shapely mustache but no side whiskers, making him more handsome to my eyes. He gravely shook our hands and then smiled so broadly that I said, "Pleased to meet you, sir," before I'd even thought about being shy.

Next was Dr. Musselman, who was at least fifty years old but not yet bent or in need of a cane. The trim of his beard was a little lopsided and the hairs spilling from his ears quite impressive. He was tickled pink when Hector bowed. He bowed right back, chuckling, so Hector bowed again, as did the doctor. It might have gone on all evening, but Marjorie saw that James's mother was waiting, and she moved us along.

The serving of the meal was both refined and laborious—far beyond any ritual we had at home. How had Marjorie learned such graceful manners? And such apparent ease with the fuss of servants and etiquette? Thank goodness I was not expected to say a word, for I could think of nothing to offer. Hector and I were thankfully at James's end of the table. Lucy was beside her grandmother at the other end, chewing on her lip to avoid chattering. The Dowager Lady Greyson was a firm believer in children being permitted at table only on condition of silence. Seen but not heard. Danger lay in meeting Hector's eye, in case we should guffaw. Yet I gleaned essential comfort from knowing he was there, directly across the table, sharing my suffering.

We made our way through prawns in savory jelly, fish consommé, pigeons in wine sauce, a red currant sorbet, lamb cutlets and roasted hare for the main course, cauliflower and broccoli, and finally dessert. We listened with polite respect to Dr. Musselman's recollections of his time attending a viscount who was thrown from a horse, to old Lady Greyson's series of complaints about various sauces, and to James's effort to remember a story concerning a dog named Bouncer given as a gift to the Duke and Duchess of Cornwall on a visit to Newfoundland, near Canada.

Things looked up when Marjorie asked Mrs. Sivam to tell something of the sea voyage from Ceylon.

"Neither of us was seasick," said Mrs. Sivam. "The sky and the waves seemed endless, but not in a worrying way." She looked upward as if seeing the sky above her now. "There is nothing like it, is there, Lakshay?"

"The ocean is incomprehensible to those who have never been upon it," agreed Mr. Sivam. "Truly a marvel."

Old Lady Greyson cleared her throat as if to object, but Grannie Jane spoke quickly.

"Were you visiting family in Ceylon?" she said.

"It was to see my father on his deathbed that we went," said Mr. Sivam.

A flutter of condolence went around the table. Marjorie's eyes met mine in recognition of a shared sorrow.

"He asked especially that we come to Ceylon before he died," said Mr. Sivam. "He charged me with a task that I now must perform, to right a grievous wrong."

"Goodness," said Grannie Jane. "The stuff of novels."

Mr. Sivam's smile flashed with mischief. "A Gothic novel, perhaps, Mrs. Morton. The tale contains treachery and fatal errors, as well as a curse. As the poet Lord Byron said, 'Truth is always strange, stranger than fiction.'"

"Lakshay's story might seem unbelievable to some," said his wife, "but we heard it from a dying man's lips."

"My father bequeathed to me a treasure," said Mr. Sivam. "It has lain for many years in a vault at Lloyds Bank in London, put there by my father to protect his family, when he could not imagine an alternate action. Although I knew of it before we traveled to Ceylon this time, it was not until my father's final hours that I heard the entire tale."

"So mysterious," said Marjorie.

"Lakshay, darling," said Mrs. Sivam. "Do tell them! Is anyone nervous of hearing a scary story?"

Lucy's grandmother made a noise that sounded like a spitting rooster—if roosters spit—but James was quick to say, "That sounds intriguing, don't you think, Mother? I know Lucy's not afraid, are you, missy?"

"Not one bit," said Lucy. "We're not afraid of anything, are we, Grandmamma?"

Lady Greyson managed a brittle smile, and we turned to Mr. Sivam.

"The treasure we are harboring," he said, "is an emerald."

Hector and I looked at each other and waggled our eyebrows.

"A large emerald," said Mrs. Sivam.

"A large and very old emerald," said her husband, "that is reputed to carry a deadly curse. I will tell you as much as I know, but there are missing pieces and shadowy episodes that even my father did not know, except by hearsay."

He sipped from his glass of glimmering dark red wine.

A footman leaned forward to pour a refill, but was waved away. The footman must be Dot's brother, Frederick, for he shared her white-blond hair and round blue eyes.

"I will mention some of the history so that you will understand the burden I have inherited. The jewel is first mentioned in the diary of a Danish explorer, a scholar of Hindi texts, who visited Ceylon late in the 1700s. He was most particularly interested in the—"

"Sweetheart!" said his wife, laughing a little. "We don't need a history lesson! Just tell the parts that matter!"

"To me, the history is significant," said Mr. Sivam. "It is the conflicts and sorrows of the past that tell us what matters in the present. Though I realize it is the rumor of a *curse* that will thrill my younger listeners." He winked at Lucy.

"I apologize for rushing you," said Mrs. Sivam.

"Where did the explorer see the jewel?" said Lucy. "Surely it wasn't sitting on his breakfast tray."

"Mr. Bjornssen visited an ancient temple," said Mr. Sivam, "near a village that housed a monastery. There is a spring in the cloistered garden that is said to be the source of healing waters, and many statues overlook this place of sanctuary."

"It sounds beautiful," said Marjorie. "Have you been there?"

"Not yet," said Mr. Sivam. "But I am returning to Ceylon early in the new year and will carry the gemstone back to the garden where it belongs . . ." He broke off to smile at his wife, whose hair shone gold in the candlelight. He lowered his voice to a ghostly whisper. "Now . . . I will tell the tale . . . but I begin with a warning that the jewel is stained with a century of misfortune for those who have sought to possess it. Misfortune . . . and bloodshed."

CHAPTER 4

A FAMILY CURSE

WE'D ALL BECOME so quiet that when Lucy drank from her water glass with a gurgly slurp, several faces turned her way.

"Emeralds are believed to bring good fortune," said Mr. Sivam. "In this holy garden stands a statue of Aditi, the goddess of infinity, of freedom and the sky. Travelers to the monastery ask Aditi to free them from their sorrows. Echoes of her blessings are believed to resonate forever. For this reason, the magnificent stone on her temple was called the Echo Emerald.

"One deplorable day, over one hundred years ago, a carpenter was brought into the garden to mend the railing of a bridge that crosses a burbling stream. He had been there before, both to work and to pray. He performed this new task diligently, but it took three days of meticulous labor. Each day he carried away a bag of sawdust, in part to leave no disarray in the temple garden, and also because his wife kept chickens. The woodmeal was used to pack eggs for market. The guards of the sanctuary were accustomed to seeing this carpenter with his bag and thought nothing of it."

"He stole the jewel!" cried Lucy.

Mr. Sivam nodded. "Was it his idea? Or was he hired to do the job by someone else? The story is different, depending on who tells it. There was a notorious scandal surrounding the theft. The Echo Emerald disappeared for many years. The carpenter himself died very soon after the bridge was fixed, from an infection of the bloodstream contracted through a small cut to his thumb. This we know. He was the first to fall victim . . . to the curse."

Gasps and sighs buzzed about the room. We'd been hooked like fat fish and could not wait to hear more.

"Oh, for Heaven's sake!" Old Lady Greyson put down her spoon with such force that it seemed the table shook. "Must we listen to such nonsense during Christmas week?"

Her bite was so sharp that a silence fell. After a moment of staring at my blancmange, I dared to look up.

"Mother." James's voice was quiet, his lips tight. Marjorie's cheeks flamed, as did Mrs. Sivam's. Lucy was bouncing in her chair, eyes round, eagerly watching her grandmother for what might happen next. Hector met my flitting scrutiny with his own.

"Mother," said James again. "Mr. Sivam is our guest."

"I do not care to have my other guests upset," said Lady Greyson, icily. She gestured toward the doctor and Grannie Jane.

"Be content," said Grannie Jane. "I am not in the least upset. I am intrigued to hear more!"

"Hear, hear!" said Dr. Musselman.

But Mr. Sivam had risen and now made a small bow. "I apologize, Lady Greyson, if I have offended you." He nodded to Lucy and Hector and to me. "It is merely a story. I thought the children would enjoy it."

"Thank you, Lakshay. I believe the children are having a marvelous time." James gave his mother a stern glare. "Please sit."

Lady Greyson waved for her cane to be brought by a footman. "I suppose I am tired," she said. "I shall retire and let you all carry on."

Marjorie sprang to her feet to assist, and Grannie Jane offered to go along with her ladyship. I knew Grannie was thinking it would be rude not to, though she would far rather stay and hear the story of cursed gems and family horrors.

Mr. Sivam made a great show of lowering his voice, so that we all leaned toward him. I barely noticed as the dessert plates were removed and an array of cheeses offered.

41

"I have not, as yet, had any luck in tracking its complete path. Eventually, though, it came into the possession of a man named Aadhan, a partner in business with my thatha, my grandfather, Timeer Sivam. Where he got it, my father could not tell me. It had certainly caused trouble wherever it had been, for it now lay in a box accompanied by a letter with this warning . . ." Mr. Sivam paused to cast his warm, dark eyes directly into those of every listener. My hands were tucked firmly under my thighs to stop myself from bouncing off the chair in anticipation.

"What does the letter say?" Lucy whispered.

Mr. Sivam pretended to be reading an invisible letter in a fearsome voice. "'Whosoever takes this stone shall call down wrath and anguish upon his own head and the heads of all kin who follow' . . ."

Ping! Frederick, the footman, had dropped a cake knife to the floor. Each of us jumped as if pricked with a pin, and all laughed in relief, including Mr. Sivam.

"A sign I have succeeded in telling a good story!" he said. "Do not be frightened off, young man!"

But Frederick blushed poppy red and retired from the room, bearing away the offending utensil.

"Do not stop there!" I pleaded.

"Aadhan's business with my thatha failed and the blame fell on Aadhan's shoulders. He wished to make amends by selling the emerald to recover from debt but

42

would not tell my grandfather how he came upon such a prize. Mistrust between them grew and bad feelings were not resolved before Aadhan drowned himself."

Another gasp went around the table. Mr. Sivam had warned us but we still were horrified.

"Lucky thing Grandmamma has gone to bed," said Lucy.

Mr. Sivam hurried on with the tale. Aadhan's widow, Divia, was distraught and impoverished. No greater calamity could befall a woman than to have her husband die in such a shameful manner. Timeer Sivam was driven by remorse to extend a helping hand. It was shocking news to Divia that Aadhan had owned a jewel so precious that it might have changed their fortunes. She accepted Timeer's offer to buy the emerald, though it seemed he paid far less than its value.

"Oh no!" said Lucy. "He should have been fair. Did the curse get him too?"

Mr. Sivam nodded solemnly. "My thatha became ill with a terrible cancer. By the time he died, my father was ten or eleven years old and heard the story as I have told it to you. He inherited the emerald when he came of age at eighteen and vowed to remove it far away from anyone he loved, though it took him a great long time before he could travel such a distance. Why did he not simply carry the emerald back to the temple? I suppose he feared punishment."

Instead, Mr. Sivam's father had left the family behind to sail to England, taking the treasure with him. He feared a shipwreck throughout the stormy voyage, alarmed that everyone on board would be struck down by the gem's curse. But he arrived safely in London and left the emerald in a bank vault with a letter of explanation. He returned home with a lighter heart.

"And now I shall right the wrongs of my forefathers," said Mr. Sivam, "and put this nonsense to rest at last. I will return the Echo Emerald to its place in the garden of Aditi, where it will abide in peace."

After dinner, Marjorie walked us up the stairs and helped to get our dresses off and our hair brushed out. Hector did for himself, but he was used to that. We were all so tired that barely a word was spoken. Marjorie checked that Dot had put warming pans between our sheets to take away the chill. Lucy was in the bigger bed, in the center of the room, the one she always had when visiting Owl Park. But I was perfectly content with the narrow cot under the window, with a headboard that formed a shelf for books. Surely I would have sweet dreams with all those stories above my head?

And yet I awoke with a jolt, the black windowpanes glinting above me like devilish eyes. A moment passed before I remembered where this window was, my heart hammering as if I'd suffered a nightmare. I saw a dim flash as Lucy tossed aside her coverlet and then I did the same. It had been no dream that had frightened me awake, but an insistent shrieking from somewhere below us in the house.

CHAPTER 5

AN UPSET HOUSEHOLD

WITHIN MOMENTS WE had on our robes and slippers and found Hector in the hallway tying the cord to his own quilted bed jacket. It was much broader in the shoulders than his body required, and I suspected it was a loan from the vicar in Torquay.

Another shriek sped us down to the second floor, at the front of the house.

"Juliet suite," said Lucy, nearly breathless as we ran. "Where the Sivams are staying."

Rounding a final corner, we found ourselves in the midst of a gathering of servants, all wearing nightclothes. Pressman, the butler, had an ear to one of the doors, unnecessarily, as the wailing within was audible to all of us. As we arrived from one direction, James and Marjorie arrived from the other. The noise stopped abruptly and the door flew open. Pressman hopped backward amidst a chorus of gasps from the maids. Mrs. Frost, the housekeeper, shushed them with a glare and flapped her hand to shoo them back a few paces.

But who would not be alarmed at the sight of Mrs. Sivam, her face blotched and hair wild? Her husband appeared at her shoulder, his worried eyes meeting those of his host.

"We apologize for the disturbance, my friends," said Mr. Sivam. "My wife has had a fright." He glanced toward the cluster of servants still hovering in the passage. "It seems we've had an intruder." His grip tightened around the woman now trembling under his arm. "I wonder . . ."

"May I be of assistance?" Mr. Pressman threw back his shoulders and stood as rigidly straight as if he were in his formal butler garb instead of a woolly tartan dressing gown.

"Make a quick circuit of the doors, will you, Pressman?" said James.

The butler nodded and strode away in his slippers.

"Kitty is shivering." Marjorie placed a calming hand on Mrs. Sivam's shoulder. "Mrs. Frost, will you provide a cup of sweet tea?"

The housekeeper sent one of the maids to make tea, and then barked at the others to go along too. Poor luck,

I thought. Roused and fussed in the middle of the night and not allowed to watch! It could happen to us at any moment, as children were never welcome at moments of high drama. I signaled Hector and Lucy with a finger to my lips and we kept still in the shadows.

Kitty refused to go back inside the suite, so it was Marjorie who fetched a blanket. Mr. Sivam and James had a hurried whispered exchange, but we were not close enough to hear. Mr. Sivam held his precious box, and shook his head when James offered to take it.

Kitty Sivam, warmly wrapped and calmer, began to tell what had frightened her so.

She'd been startled awake, by a bump, perhaps? As if someone had collided with the washstand in the dark. She could see from her bed that the door connecting her room to that of her husband was half ajar. Lakshay's window was firmly shut. Her own window was open, overlooking the glass-paned roof of the conservatory, presently covered in snow. No intruder could have entered that way. She was not certain that she had locked her door to the passage. Why would she, in so friendly a household?

What she saw, peering into the dark, was a figure frozen to the spot by her sudden gasp. He seemed broad and tall, but perhaps the shadows had exaggerated his size. He waited, in silence. Kitty pulled the bedclothes over her head and did not see which way he went. She heard a scuffling and felt a draft, though from where she could not say. She mustered her courage and went to the connecting door. Her husband's bureau had been plundered. She began to scream, waking him and everyone else.

She came to the end of her tale with a ragged little sob.

"Ssh," said Mr. Sivam. "It's all over." He guided his wife, protesting only faintly now, back into their suite.

Mr. Pressman returned along the passage.

"Windows and doors are secure, my lord. All the servants are accounted for. I have footmen circling the grounds with torches, to see if we can flush the scoundrel."

"Thank you, Pressman," James said. "I presume they'll be alert to footprints in the snow? And not disturbing anything unexpected with their own boots?"

"Indeed, my lord, though the snow is falling thickly."

James sighed. "What time is it?" he said.

"Ten minutes past four, my lord."

"I think we might all try for another hour of sleep, don't you? Best to avoid waking my mother. Perhaps a visit from the constabulary in the morning?"

"My lord."

Hector tapped my elbow. Lucy and I followed him around the corner where we paused to whisper.

"If a thief is outside, he is gone by now," said Hector.

"And his footprints already covered with fresh snow," I said.

"Uncle James should call the police," said Lucy, "and summon dogs to chase the man down."

"I believe this would be of no use," said Hector. "Logic tells me that whoever is wishing to steal the jewel . . ."

I caught his meaning at once. "He is very probably still inside the house!"

DECEMBER 24, 1902
WEDNESDAY

CHAPTER 6

A COMPANY OF ACTORS

WE NEVER DID GO back to sleep and we were famished by half past six. Lucy felt brave enough by then to scurry down to the kitchen to ask for cocoa. Poor Dot brought up a tray the size of a sled, with a pot of cocoa, ramekins of coddled eggs and a stack of hot crumpets under a tea cloth.

"If you want anything more," she said, "you'll have to go down to the breakfast room."

Hector sniffed a small bowl of preserves. "Blackberry, Miss Dot?"

Dot blushed. "You don't call me miss, Master Hector. I'm under-parlormaid, so just Dot. But yes, that's one of Cook's special jams, that is."

"This is a *majestic* breakfast, Dot, thank you," I said.

We tucked in. It was one of the best meals of my life, sitting by the fire wrapped in a blanket with snow whirling outside.

"*And*!" said Lucy. "No adults!"

"And," said Hector, "an attempted burglary to consider."

"And, it's Christmas Eve!" I added. "With a company of actors coming to deliver tableaux to our very own drawing room."

"I expect they'll use the ballroom, actually," Lucy said. "I didn't take you in there yesterday, but it's much bigger and grander than the drawing room."

"The *ball* room?" said Hector.

"The dancing sort of ball, not the sort to kick about with a dog," said Lucy.

"Ah, oui, le bal," said Hector. He took an enormous bite of crumpet and quickly mopped a trickle of butter from his chin.

The arrival of the actors was somewhat delayed because many of the country lanes were near impassable with the fallen snow. Lucy's grandmother, according to Lucy, did not intend to be overly gracious to those she called "vagabonds." They would not be greeted by a line of respectful servants outside the front doors, and they would have their meals in the kitchen.

Mr. Sivam had offered to show James the underworkings of his motorcar, so the welcoming committee for the company of actors was only Marjorie, Mrs. Sivam, Hector, Lucy and me. Calling it a *company* was a bit misleading. There were only three, and their appearance was disappointing, to say it plainly. The two men and a woman were so ordinary-looking that one might expect to see them selling fish in a market or collecting tickets on a train. No dash or bluster, no glamor or sparkle. Their clothing showed no ornament or whimsy, though I was cheered to see that the older actor wore a small gold ring in his ear.

"Mr. Mooney," said Mrs. Sivam, coming forward with a hand outstretched to the man who seemed to be the leader. It was through his acquaintance with the Sivams that this little troupe had come to Owl Park. Mr. Mooney had removed his hat when he entered the house, showing off dark hair rather longer than was usual for a man, and a fine pointed beard as well. Quite Shakespearean and not so drab, after all.

"As lovely as ever, dear Mrs. Sivam," said Mr. Mooney, bowing over her hand and kissing it, making her blush. His greeting to Marjorie was more sedate, before introducing his fellow actors, Mr. Corker, who wore the earring, and the woman, Miss Day.

"It is enough baggage to supply a circus," said Hector.

The actors and two reluctant footmen stood amidst an impressive heap of packing cases, large wicker baskets and brassbound trunks. Costumes! Scenery! Hats and boots and jewelry! And it all must be dispersed in little more than an hour, before old Lady Greyson passed through the Great Hall on her way to luncheon at one o'clock.

"I did not realize there'd be quite so much apparatus!" said Marjorie. "We might have arranged a different entryway. Take everything to the ballroom," she instructed the footmen. "And please remove the packing cases to the coach house when essentials have been retrieved."

"Before you disperse!" Mr. Mooney waved his hat in the air, commanding our attention. He put out a hand to stop the footmen who were lifting a table. "Let it be known throughout the household that we are eager to share the stage with anyone who wishes to participate in our entertainment this evening, from upstairs and down. From the lady of the house to the scullery maid."

The footmen glanced at one another and grinned. Tradition said that Christmas Eve was a night of topsy-turvy, where the servants dressed in their finest clothes and the family poured the drinks and passed refreshments.

"We have particular need of young people willing to assume important roles in our tableaux. May I depend upon your goodness?" He made a deep, graceful bow before Lucy, causing her to burst into happy giggles.

"Yes!" she said. "I've always dreamt I might . . ."

"Marvelous. Will you come as well, young man?"

Hector nodded, very keen.

"And you, miss?"

I hoped my head shake was not impolite, but I simply could not appear upon a stage. Whenever I tried to say aloud one of my poems, for instance, my mouth turned as dry as sand on a desert plain.

"Who will I play?" said Lucy.

Mr. Mooney tapped the side of his nose and whispered, loudly enough for everyone to hear. "That, my dear, will be revealed out of earshot of the curious onlookers. Rehearsals will begin directly we've shifted our caravan of belongings."

Lucy giggled again, and picked up a basket holding several pairs of knee-high boots with gold buckles.

"Isn't he the *most* handsome?" she whispered to me.

Quite close by, the lady actor sighed. I looked her way and she flushed at being heard. I tried a small smile and she sent me a bigger one back.

"He can't help himself," she said, quietly. "Sebastian Mooney feels compelled to charm every lady in the room, whether she's twelve or ninety-two. It gets a bit boring for the rest of us."

She wasn't flashy the way I'd expected, though her high cheekbones were tinted with a tinge of rouge over tawny skin. Her hair was dark auburn, her eyes light brown and merry. What sort of woman became an actress and traveled about in the company of men? She knew I was studying her and smiled again.

"I am Annabelle Day," she said. "Are you certain you won't join us?"

I bit my lip and shook my head no. "I'd rather watch," I said.

Mr. Corker piled a stack of tricorn hats upon his head, leaving his hands free to carry an oddly shaped leather case.

"We're always grateful for one or two who are faint of heart," he said. "We do like an audience, however small."

"I am renowned for my skill at applause," I said, tickled to make him smile.

"Never an undervalued talent in our profession," he said. "If nobody claps, there's not much point in showing off, is there?"

I agreed that there was not. "I shall clap until my palms sting," I promised. "I'm curious about your fancy case. What fits in there?"

It was long and narrow and only about three inches deep, firmly buckled in several places.

"Sebastian?" called Miss Day. "We've had a request to inspect your precious armory."

"Aha!" said Mr. Mooney. "Nothing could delight me more!"

He took the long case from Mr. Corker and stepped carefully over a roll of bright fabric to put the case down on the marble floor. He unbuckled the clasps, with a circle of admirers watching closely. When the lid came up, there was an excited *Oooh!* all around. Inside lay a pair of gleaming swords and a matching pair of daggers, each with a crafted bronze handle and a very sharp-looking blade. Lucy reached out to touch, but he put up a hand to stop her, removing a sword from its nest of velvet.

"*Arghh*, me hearties!" He swung the weapon above his head, doing a trick with his wrist so that the point remained balanced upward for a few moments, even as he flung his other arm into the air with a flourish. He looked straight at me and winked.

"Who will be the first pretty maiden to walk the plank?" He brought the sword down with a rapid swish and jabbed the air toward Hector. "And who will be the first traitor to get run through with my trusty blade?"

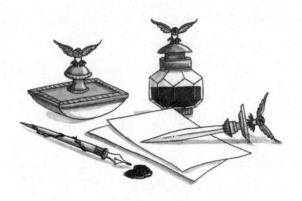

CHAPTER 7

A SISTER'S STRUGGLE

WHEN MY FRIENDS joined the rehearsal, I went to sit with the young Lady Greyson during her hour of household management, delayed today because of the actors' arrival. I approached the morning room tasting two distinct flavors of anticipation. One, I would have nearly a whole hour to visit with my sister! And two . . . I was obliged to visit with my sister for nearly a whole hour . . .

Marjorie had gone to boarding school when I was still a child and then married James soon after graduating. I suppose I'd told her little girl secrets before she'd gone away, but we'd had no recent practice sharing thoughts and dreams. Would we find a way to be easy together? She was a married woman with a manor house full of servants to command. I suspected that in her eyes I was still a child.

She was at her desk when I came in, her elegant script unrolling across a page of creamy paper. I sat near her in a chair upholstered in dusky pink velvet. Not a place to spill one's cocoa. Marjorie asked at once, how was Tony? Well, Tony was getting a bit stout. Our maid, Sally, liked to feed him buttered toast.

"He likely needs to fatten up for winter," said Marjorie. "Like a bear. And our neighbors next door at the EverMore villa? What do you hear of them?"

"It has been a quiet few weeks," I said, since I'd discovered Irma Eversham's corpse on the floor of the Mermaid Dance Room. "Our dancing lessons have been suspended until the new year."

"I had a note from Rose, full of sadness and confusion," said Marjorie, "but we know how that feels, do we not?"

Yes, we did.

"And how do you think Mummy is faring? It is so hard to discern from her letters."

"Mostly well since your wedding," I said. "Despite the upset of our murdered neighbor. But recently, she has been very low indeed. Perhaps because of the gray winter sky."

"And you, Aggie? Is Groveland terribly quiet and lonely with just the three of you?"

How to explain the tremble from my ankles to my scalp when I passed the door of Papa's study and knew he was not there to wink at me? How to describe the ache in my throat when I turned the pages of his dictionary or stood in his dressing room with my face pressed to the sleeve of his velvet smoking jacket? How to relate the moment, many times in a week, while we ate our supper when Mummy, Grannie and I each found one another's eyes resting on Papa's empty chair?

"Well, yes," I said. "Very quiet."

Marjorie sighed and scooped me under her arm and had me stand close as she finished her letter—which was to let Mummy know that we'd arrived safely, and to ask for a recipe for sorrel soup that Marjorie wished to share with her cook.

"Possibly the worst burden of being Lady Greyson," said Marjorie, "among many, I confess, is the planning of meals. I would so prefer to curl up in a chair and eat cheese on toast than worry all day about whether to serve Swiss chard or broccoli with the veal."

"What are the other burdens?" I said. "You still love James, I hope?"

"I love him more than ever," said Marjorie, "for being so patient with my inept efforts to be the new Lady Greyson. Sadly, his mother is not so rich in patience." She sighed heavily as she folded the letter and put it into an envelope, adding it to a stack of three or four others waiting for seals. She took out a new page and wrote the date across the top, while I imagined the wrinkly lips of

Dowager Lady Greyson pursing in disapproval, and shuddered in empathy.

"At the very least, you have a lovely desk set," I said, admiring the row of matching implements for writing.

Marjorie laughed. "It was a gift from James's mother," she said. "One of her kinder gestures, when we were married. It comes from a collection begun by James's father. He was a great collector of odd things."

"I noticed the teapots." I eyed the cabinet that opened into the secret passage.

"Yes," said Marjorie. "The horned owl teapot on the top shelf was his first acquisition. And see?" She passed me her paper knife with its ivory handle carved to show an owl in flight. The inkwell had one too, as did the smaller knife for trimming pen nibs and the rocking ink blotter.

"For Owl Park," I said. "How sweet."

"The set in the library has owl heads embossed on silver handles," Marjorie said. "But mine is made for a lady's hands, and it suits me very well." She glanced at the bookshelf beside the fire. "Now, if only there were time to read all these books," she said, "or even one of them. The greatest loss of married life seems to be that I haven't read a novel in months."

"I suppose when you've learned how to be the lady of the manor," I said, "you'll have time to read a book."

"Where is my little sister?" said Marjorie. "She has become rather wise and grown-up."

"Not quite all grown, I hope, if that means no time for reading! I will always choose murder with Sherlock Holmes over tea and corsets with anyone else."

"Well, I'm very happy to have you keep me company while your friends are rehearsing," she said.

"I would rather have measles than perform in a play," I said, "but I do love going to watch them!"

"What an odd day, don't you think?"

"Starting with Mrs. Sivam screaming us all out of our beds in the middle of the night?" I said. "As odd as a day can be!"

"She was just as good at piercing shrieks when we were at school," said Marjorie. "Kitty Cartland's special trick. Cartland was her name before she married Mr. Sivam. She made the same noise whether it was a spider in the washbasin or an intruder in the greenhouse."

"Did you have many of those?" I said. "Intruders, I mean."

Marjorie laughed. "Just the one. Though no one saw him except for Kitty, her scream being so effective in scaring him off. The headmistress guessed he'd been lost after too much ale at the village pub and came into the greenhouse to find shelter on a mound of burlap scraps. Kitty was collecting lilies, to decorate the chapel on Sunday morning, and got frightened to bits."

I loved Marjorie's stories about school. During her holidays, I'd beg to hear about the time she and her friends had purloined a pot of jam and shared it in the dark of the dormitory, or how, on the stroke of eleven, they'd all dropped their pencils during maths.

"Was Kitty one of your close chums?" I said.

"No, no," said Marjorie. "She was older. We overlapped by only a year. She was in the sixth form when I got there in the fourth. Poor girl was called Oinks at school, even by us younger girls, for being so piggy about eating more than her share."

"She's not piggy in the least bit!" I said. "That was very mean-spirited of you!"

"I shouldn't have told you," said Marjorie. "So unfair to expose youthful flaws when one has grown up to have such pretty dresses and silky hair and not a hint of roundness."

"Her husband is ever so nice," I said. "Almost as kind as James."

"James and Lakshay were great pals at Oxford," said Marjorie. "I have the sense that James befriended Lakshay when he first arrived from Ceylon, a lonely boy far from home, though James wouldn't put it like that. He tells about seeing Lakshay carrying a table on his shoulders up the stairs to his rooms, and how he enticed him to join the rowing team."

"How did Kitty come to marry him?" I asked.

"I do not know their love story," said Marjorie. "James has been so busy with Owl Park since his father died, he hasn't had time for friends and fell out of touch with Lakshay. They met again recently and found they still liked each other. That's when I learned that Lakshay had married Kitty. So, we thought to invite them for Christmas."

"Is it usual for an Englishwoman to marry a man from Ceylon?"

"I do not imagine it is common, but it does happen occasionally," said Marjorie. "They seem to be at ease, which is really all that counts, is it not?"

"Like you and James," I said, and was rewarded with a smile. "He will feel gratified to return the Echo Emerald to the goddess Aditi, will he not?"

"A gentleman is coming here the day after Christmas to appraise the gem so it can be insured for travel. Mr. Sivam's dream will come true very soon."

"He's awfully far from home," I said. "Even if he lives here now. Like Hector."

"Just like Hector," said Marjorie. "Or like me, at Owl Park. I feel like a toad dropped into the middle of a frog pond—and we all know that toads can't swim!"

A knock at the door. "Come in, Mrs. Hornby," Marjorie called out. And then to me, "This will be Cook, I'm afraid, about today's meals."

I quickly vacated the chair next to my sister's desk where Mrs. Hornby was accustomed to sitting each morning. Marjorie had a list of things to discuss with the cook about her current guests, beginning with thanks for taking the trouble to make nut rissoles for Mr. Sivam's vegetarian diet. What would she provide this evening? Grannie Jane could not tolerate tomatoes. What did Mrs. Hornby think about this or that and this?

I listened politely for a few moments before wandering—ever so casually—to the cabinet that hid the entrance to the secret passage. I noted the handle on the second drawer down that Lucy had turned yesterday. I daren't touch it in case it sprang suddenly to life. I imagined Mrs. Hornby clutching her bosom in shock if part of the furniture began to move!

"I make a lovely rum cake, if you'd like that, your ladyship," said Mrs. Hornby. "No one is a teetotaler that I've been informed about."

"That will do very nicely, Mrs. Hornby, thank you."

When the cook eventually made her way out, Marjorie sagged in her chair.

"Whatever menu I choose, James's mother has a reason to complain. I never seem to get things right!"

"What if you asked for her advice?" I said. "She must have been the young Lady Greyson herself at one time?"

"Oh, Aggie," said Marjorie. "My greatest fear is being revealed as the imposter that I am. Asking for help would be like shouting out loud all the things I do not know. My only comfort is that I do not see how things can get any worse!"

CHAPTER 8

AN EVENING ENTERTAINMENT

HECTOR AND LUCY WERE infuriatingly secretive about what they'd been doing all day. I found Hector limping up and down the hallway with a silly smile on his face, occasionally pausing to raise a fist in the air. Lucy used the poker from the nursery fireplace to practice what she seemed to think were the moves of a dashing swordsman. Lucy frightened Dot nearly out of her wits by lunging with her weapon just as the maid opened the door to say that the volunteer actors were wanted in the ballroom to be costumed.

"I could bring you a cup of tea, Miss Agatha," said Dot, once the others had slipped away and down the stairs. "Only, it'd have to be right now. It's Christmas Eve, you see. We've already laid out the supper for after the play, because we servants are at liberty tonight. We watch the entertainment just as you do, and get handed drinks by her ladyship and the rest of you lot. My brother, Fred, and another of the footmen have roles in the pantomime."

"It's not really a pantomime," I said. "You might be disappointed if that's what you're expecting." I explained that a tableau was more like a living photograph or painting, with everyone in costumes and makeup, frozen in the most dramatic moment of the book. It was usually a book, or a famous painting, or something from the Bible.

"The actors don't move or speak to each other. And they won't be acting silly or singing naughty songs."

"Whatever it is," said Dot, "it'll be better than washing out socks."

Grannie Jane and I passed the last hour of the afternoon threading popped corn to make garlands to decorate the numerous statues and busts that inhabited the rooms of Owl Park. Marjorie eventually led us to the ballroom, where we sat with Dr. Musselman and tried not to twitch with excitement.

A curtain of plush maroon velvet hung in deep folds in front of a platform at one end of the room. On the evening of a real ball, the orchestra would play on this little stage, just two feet above the dance floor. Tonight, there'd be as many people on the stage as sitting in chairs, even counting the dozen servants who'd come to watch. James was backstage, becoming an actor, but Marjorie made a fine show of escorting Mrs. Frost and Mrs. Hornby to seats in the front row. Soft notes from a piano tinkled out from behind the curtain. Once we'd all found seats, we rustled and murmured for a few minutes until the lights dimmed and the gentle music stopped.

I loved this minute in a theater, when the lights went down on the audience and came back up inside a play. The curtains were drawn back to show three people encircling an impressive goose, trussed and roasted upon a platter. Mr. Mooney was dressed in a caped overcoat and tweed hat. He held aloft a magnificent jewel, the size of a plum and glowing blue in the stage lights. He examined it through an oversized magnifying glass. The other actor, Mr. Corker, wearing a stiff brown suit, gaped into the innards of the goose as if there might be more treasure to discover. I barely recognized Annabelle Day as the plump, astonished housekeeper. Padding and makeup increased her girth and age remarkably.

I leaned over to whisper directly into Marjorie's ear. "Sherlock Holmes and Dr. Watson in 'The Adventure of the Blue Carbuncle'! The story by Mr. Arthur Conan Doyle! I mean, *Sir* Arthur, now."

Marjorie had sent me the book and I'd read it aloud to Papa during the weeks of his illness. The gemstone in the story is stolen from a countess and turns up in the gullet of a Christmas goose. Mr. Holmes makes clever deductions by simply examining a man's hat.

"That's why I selected it from their list of tableaux," said Marjorie. "For *you*! Now, *ssh*."

The curtains slid together after a bit, the piano music started up, and the audience began again to breathe.

"I'd faint dead away," said Mrs. Hornby loudly, from the front row, "if such a stone turned up inside any bird I cooked! That bird weren't washed proper before it went into the oven." Everyone laughed. And then the lights dipped, signaling the second tableau.

Another Christmas feast, a crowded table this time, again surrounding a roasted goose. The same goose, I could tell, made of painted plaster with a garland of cranberries draped across its breast. Mr. Mooney, who moments ago had been Sherlock Holmes, was now dressed in a wrinkled nightshirt with a striped nightcap on his head, gazing in at a merry dining room through a window in the scenery and beaming with pride. Miss Annabelle Day was the mother of the household, a silver ladle in her hand, ready to serve from a tureen. Mr. Corker played her husband. Their family was shabby of costume, each watching the unexpected gift of a roasted bird with hungry anticipation. I spotted Lucy in a cap and patched pinafore, Frederick the footman with a pretend piece of pie, and Dot holding the pose of a ghostly sprite.

"*A Christmas Carol*!" I said. "By Charles Dickens!"

Marjorie squeezed my arm and then began to clap.

"Look at Hector!" I said. "He's Tiny Tim!"

He wore a huge checked cap, a rough linen shirt and a gleeful grin. "God bless us, every one!" he cried. His crutch, waving in the air, came close to knocking off the head of his stage-Papa, Mr. Corker. As promised, my hands were warm from clapping so hard.

"One more," said Marjorie, when the curtain had closed.

"Another book?" I said.

"You'll see."

We had a longer wait this time, but the audience cheered when the curtain parted. A painted backdrop showed the rolling waves of a bonny blue sea. We were aboard a pirate ship in a rare moment of merriment. Five grimacing pirates were dressed alike in rough muslin shirts, wide orange trousers, and dark curling wigs beneath battered hats or kerchiefs. One of them was a bit taller—Frederick, the footman; one a bit shorter—Mr. Roger Corker; and one small and slim—Miss Annabelle Day. Mr. Sivam and James were like twins, almost, except for their coloring. All of them wore high buckled boots and had hands and faces smeared with coal smut and pot rust to make them appear sea-roughened and sunburnt. Mr. Mooney was dressed in a frock coat with gold epaulets. He had a peg leg and a tattered parrot pinned to one shoulder.

"Dastardly rogues!" Dr. Musselman began to clap his hands with great enthusiasm.

"Three cheers for Long John Silver!" called out Kitty Sivam. For that's who Mr. Mooney portrayed.

"*I'm* meant to be the hero!" cried Lucy, stepping out of her character to hurl an unfriendly glare at Mrs. Sivam. "*I'm* Jim Hawkins!"

"And so you are, darling," said Kitty. "But I thought the villain might need some encouragement before you trounced him."

Lucy froze into position again, but did not quite erase the look of pique on her face. Long John Silver laughed a mighty pirate laugh. He swung a cardboard cutlass over their heads, keeping the real sword and dagger safely attached to his belt.

The curtain closed and the entertainment was done, an excellent night in the theater.

And a party still to follow!

CHAPTER 9

A JOLLY SUPPER

LUCY WANTED TO PLAY the piano in the drawing room during the supper buffet after the tableaux, but James told her no.

"He says I am too heavy-handed," she complained. "That I may play for guests only when I have refined my touch."

Miss Annabelle Day took her place on the piano bench instead. The vivid makeup of a pirate had been wiped from her face, though she still wore the white shirt with a low front that displayed considerable bosom. Previously hidden by a ragged black wig, her auburn hair was pulled into a high knot that emphasized the scoop of her neckline.

She shuffled the sheets of music and made a selection, smiling up at Mr. Corker, who set a glass of champagne next to her. He was still in full pirate garb, except for the sword, which he'd jammed into the coal scuttle by the fire. James had stayed in costume too. His face makeup, like Mr. Corker's, was streaked and sweaty.

Annabelle's fingers moved gently across the keys for a few bars and then she began to sing, softly. A hush fell as we listened for a while, before chatter began again.

Hector wore his ragged Tiny Tim jacket and breeches, reluctant to put aside his moment of triumph. Lucy kept her hair tucked under a cap to look like brave Jim Hawkins for an hour longer. She held two cakes, urging Hector to choose one. They now were colleagues of a sort, who had shared an afternoon apart from me. I tried not to itch in my new Christmas dress.

"It is *unnerving*, James, to look at you," came old Lady Greyson's unhappy voice. "I do wish you'd wash your face and put your proper clothes back on."

"I'm showing my Christmas spirit, Mother. All in fun, you know. The servants are having a splendid time, seeing us behave a bit foolishly."

"Foolish does not become you," she grumbled. "Nor does it suit the drawing room, to be invaded by a platoon of pirates."

"How is your toothache, Mother?" said James.

"Dr. Musselman put in a drop of chloroform earlier, but I'm afraid it has quite worn off."

"I will see if he can supply another dose. Perhaps you'd like to retire to the comfort of your own room? Evelyn can take you up and get you settled. But mind you don't keep her long. Tonight is for your lady's maid to enjoy as well."

Lady Greyson sighed loudly. James caught me watching and winked.

"Here's Aggie to keep you company while I find Evelyn."

I would have far preferred to be sent on the Evelyn-seeking errand, but never could have said so. I assisted Lady Greyson into a chair and waited for her to get comfortable, dreading the moment when I must speak. What to say, what to say? Where was Grannie Jane in my time of need? Across the room, conversing with a pirate, whose back was to me. Mr. Corker or Mr. Sivam? I couldn't tell which because the costumes were all the same. Not James, I hoped, as he should be bringing Evelyn to rescue me.

"Do you like the music?" I said.

"Fortunately, I am hard of hearing," said Lady Greyson, "and am not compelled to listen." She closed her eyes and tipped her face upward, as if an invisible thread joined the end of her nose to a point among the plaster roses on the ceiling. I thought she might have fallen instantly asleep, but then, "The ballroom has much better acoustics for listening to music," she said. "I danced there on my wedding night and on many a night after."

"Oh!" I was startled by the sweetness of her recollection. "Did James's father like to dance?"

"He was the best partner I ever knew," she said. "Any woman he danced with became the belle of the ball." Her eyes were still closed and this time I think she floated away.

Evelyn arrived to escort Lady Greyson, just as my grandmother appeared beside me.

"I should very much like to see whether the pirates might perform an encore while wielding their cutlasses," said Grannie Jane, in a low voice. "But James tells me that for decency's sake, I must retire with my hostess." She followed Lady Greyson toward East House.

And there I was, free to roam the party!

Mr. Mooney, like the other actors, was still in his Long John Silver garb, but now had two legs and two boots instead of the peg he'd had strapped on during the *Treasure Island* tableau. He had replaced Mr. Corker next to Annabelle on the piano bench, and whispered into her ear. She began at once to play a different tune, one that he played with her, commanding more attention from the room—especially when the pianists finished with a finger-flying flourish. Lots of jolly applause after that.

"Mrs. Sivam," said Mr. Mooney. "Would you care to sing? I remember that you had a voice like an—"

"Do not say an angel," said Mrs. Sivam, laughing. "Four years have passed since I sang for an audience. I'm an old married woman now. Only my husband hears me sing." She slipped from the room before the invitation could come again.

Mr. Mooney and Miss Day commenced another song, a little noisier this time. Marjorie's worried look and James's lifted eyebrow told me that it was not the sort of song usually heard in the drawing room of Owl Park. James leaned in to say something and Miss Day's next offering was a gentle nocturne by Chopin. My dance teacher at home had arranged this very music to accompany a performance of girls swaying like trees. Marjorie looked much relieved as she circulated, servant for the evening, with fresh champagne and plates of mushroom caps stuffed with crab meat. I ate four.

Mrs. Sivam was back, holding her husband's cherished wooden box above her head.

"Ladies and gentlemen," she said. "I want to thank you for your patience with the ruckus early this morning. You deserve to know the reason behind it."

"Kitty!"

"My husband may be a bit miffed," she said, with a sly smile at Mr. Sivam, "but I'd like to give you all a glimpse of our remarkable treasure."

Mr. Sivam reached for her arm, but she laughed as if they were playing a chasing game and twirled away. He pulled back his hand as if scalded and put it into the pocket of his jacket. She was teasing him, but it seemed to take some effort for his smile to appear.

Kitty opened the box and took out a small bag made of pale green silk. She passed the box to the nearest person, Mr. Mooney, so that her own hands might be free. We all drew closer, as if the bag held a powerful magnet rather than a gemstone.

"I would ask you again," said Lakshay Sivam, "not to—"

Kitty rolled the Echo Emerald out of its nest and held it above her head, green and glinting, the size of a peach stone. She turned it this way and that, catching light from every lamp and candle in the room. I was not the only one to gasp at the shining glory of a single stone.

"You've had your fun, Kitty," said Mr. Sivam, quietly. "Time to put it safely away." He held out his hand, waiting for her to drop the emerald on his palm.

"How can such a beautiful thing carry a curse?" said Kitty, still holding it high. A murmur rustled through the room, like a breeze that promised rain. I saw Marjorie look imploringly at James.

"Thank you, Mrs. Sivam," said James, "for a glimpse of your astonishing jewel. Now, please, I beg you . . ." He was using a jolly voice, but he meant to aid Mr. Sivam's wishes. "I *beg* you to withdraw temptation from our sight and lock up the Echo Emerald for the safety of us all."

The company laughed nervously, while Kitty obediently replaced the gem into the silk bag, pulled tight the drawstring and gave it to her husband. Mr. Sivam closed the box lid and bowed to the assembled company before taking his treasure upstairs. More champagne was poured, and Miss Day began to play a soothing song on the piano. James invited Marjorie to dance, and Mr. Mooney offered his hand to Kitty Sivam.

The day had started before the sun came up and now it was very late on Christmas Eve. Hector and I must have climbed all those stairs to the nursery, but how? I tried not to think greedily about my stocking from Father Christmas or the packages that might be waiting, or about the heaps of taffy and truffles to be eaten. Indeed, I had no time to think of anything, for I was asleep before I'd closed my eyes.

DECEMBER 25, CHRISTMAS DAY, 1902
THURSDAY

CHAPTER 10

A TREASURE HUNT

DOT MANEUVERED THE breakfast tray through the nursery door and placed it carefully on the table without so much as a bun rolling off.

"Happy Christmas." She bobbed her head. "Master Hector is waiting ever so patiently, and you're still lying in your beds!"

"Happy Christmas, Dot!"

We pulled on dressing gowns and gave Hector the task of pouring our cocoa. We merrily peeled boiled eggs, spread butter on warm buns and sipped the steaming chocolate. Lucy scalded her tongue by gulping instead of sipping. I blew gently on mine, ruffling the milky skin across its surface.

Hector lifted a linen napkin to pat the corners of his mouth, and Lucy let out a little squeak.

"Look!" She reached for the small roll of red paper tied with a gilt ribbon tucked discreetly under a plate.

Dot stopped her from snatching it up. "Lady Marjorie asked me to remind you, Miss Lucy, that the guest should open the first clue."

"There are two guests," said Lucy. "Not fair to choose between them."

"Clue to what?" I said.

"The *treasure* hunt, silly!" Lucy looked back and forth between Hector and me. "You truly don't know? On Christmas morning we always have a hunt at Owl Park to find our stockings full of presents."

She reached for the pretty packet.

"Him what's not family." Dot tilted her head toward Hector. "Him's the guest," she said.

Lucy sighed and nudged the clue toward Hector.

"Go on then."

Hector's mouth was full of bun. He finished chewing, wiped the butter from his fingers and untied the ribbon on the miniature scroll.

"Who makes the treasure hunt?" I asked.

"Uncle James, and now Aunt Marjorie too, I should think. What does it say?"

Hector unfurled the paper and read aloud.

I sit with many cousins
Near a cooking fire.
If you call me clean,
I could name you a liar!

Hector said, "A cooking fire suggests—"

"The kitchen!" said Lucy, hopping up from the table.

"But the breakfast!" said Hector. "I am wishing to enjoy a second bun."

"Bring it with you," said Lucy, scooping one up for herself. "Where are my slippers?"

Infected by her eagerness, we were quickly ready.

"Back stairs!" cried Lucy, leading us to the narrow steps normally used only by the women servants. There were *two* servants' staircases in the main house, she said. Women used the wooden ones and men used the marble, because marble could withstand the bumps of hauling people's luggage up and down.

"Come on!"

"Hector?"

He was behind us, still on the landing.

"It is unpleasant to consider," he said, "what is *not* clean in a kitchen."

The kitchen rooms were abuzz, even so early on Christmas morning. It seemed that twenty people had urgent tasks. Peeling turnips, plucking geese, chopping celery and dried apples, stirring oxtail soup, shelling walnuts, polishing spoons, scrubbing pots for further duty . . .

I supposed Cook knew about the treasure hunt tradition. She was very patient with us poking about her kitchen looking for clues. The servants bustled around us, politely pretending we weren't obstacles while they prepared for the big day ahead.

"Near the cooking fire," said Hector.

We stood in a row, staring at an enormous side of lamb, roasting evenly as Stephen turned a handle on the spit. The aroma! The crackling fat!

"Many dirty cousins," I said. My eyes and Hector's landed on the coal scuttle at the same instant. Lucy dove to dig through it, blacking her hands, until she pulled out the next clue. She wiped her fingers on her dressing gown, leaving sooty smears down the front.

In a giant volume,
More than one letter C
Will be on the page
Where you want to be!

"Giant volume?" said Lucy.

"Dictionary!" I said.

"Library," said Hector.

And we were off.

We passed James, who was wearing a bright red cardigan.

"Good morning, Lord Greyson," said Hector.

"Merry Christmas, James!" I called.

"We're following the second clue already!" Lucy boasted.

"Well done," said James. "I expect you'll be dragging your socks into breakfast before I've finished my second cup of coffee." He gave us a cheery wave and disappeared into the breakfast room.

Lucy was first into the dark, chilly library, because she was always first, it seemed. The drawn curtains showed a sliver of morning between them. One lamp burned on a small table beside a tall-backed chair. The library was rarely used before noon, so the fire was not yet lit. I followed Lucy, with Hector on my heels. Quite actually on my heels, for his toe caught my slipper and pulled it partway off. I stumbled, knocking Lucy forward. She gasped and fell—or, possibly, she fell and *then* gasped.

"It's wet," she said. "Something has spilled."

Hector moved to the window and drew open one of the heavy damask drapes. Lucy held up her hands, eyes as round as pennies. Her palms were covered in blood.

CHAPTER 11

A Pool of Blood

LUCY'S MOUTH FELL open and stayed that way.

"Ooh la la," murmured Hector.

The slash of light now pouring through the window illuminated a body lying facedown on the floor. A man wearing the loose white shirt, rough jerkin, and dark orange britches of a pirate. Bulges of bare skin showed through holes in his striped socks. More impressive was the dagger standing straight up from the middle of his back, its bronze handle gleaming faintly. A prickle started in the same place on my own back, creeping up to my neck and ears.

"Who is it?" Lucy whispered. His face was covered by a matted wig, and his hat sat crookedly, so we could not see at once who had met this dreadful end. I thought of

Irma Eversham under the piano in the Mermaid Dance Room, of her blue face and floppy feet.

"So many similar pirates," said Hector. "Which one is it?"

"Not James, thank goodness," I said. James was calmly eating toast in the breakfast room, wearing his cheery cardigan.

"The footman?" said Hector. "The actor?"

"Mr. Sivam is a different color," said Lucy.

"I hope it's not Frederick," I said. "Think of poor Dot."

"Frederick is skinnier, don't you think?" said Lucy.

"Mr. Corker, then," said Hector. "The logical deduction."

"The carpet is soggy," said Lucy. She was now vigorously rubbing the blood off her hands, adding scarlet streaks to the coal dust on the front of her robe.

"As well as our slippers," I said.

Lucy made an odd little jump, as if she could escape her own toes.

"I don't suppose there's a chance he might still be alive?" I said.

Hector crouched and poked a finger through the curls of the wig, to touch the man's neck.

"Not a bit warm," he said. "He is most certainly dead."

"He's pretty whiffy," Lucy whispered. And it was true. Mingled awful smells that I didn't recognize, and one that I did, an alcoholic drink.

"Why do you suppose his pockets are pulled out?" I said.

Lucy made a noise that might be a whimper. "I wish my mother were here," she said.

I was ever so grateful that my mother was not. She would be dismayed beyond words.

"We should call for Uncle James," said Lucy.

"Wait," I said. "Wait just one little minute, please." I wanted desperately to think, to carefully look at the scene before us.

"Grandmamma will be ever so troubled," Lucy said. "Must it be me to tell her?"

"James will," I said. I thought of my own grandmother. She would be decidedly enthralled by the arrival of a corpse.

"The police will come," said Hector. "I should not have touched the drapery. Even the Dowager Lady Greyson cannot stop the police when a body bleeds in the library."

The police! Most certainly they'd be here. The room would be swarmed in no time!

"This is our only chance," I said, "to be in here alone." I gazed at the body, at the bloodstain, and then, in wider and wider circles, at everything else in sight, trying to memorize exactly what sat where. When I'd found the deceased Irma Eversham in October, Inspector Locke said that I was an excellent witness. I wished to honor my reputation.

The dictionary that had brought us here stood open, upon a pedestal. Next to it was a globe of the world on a cast-iron stand with pale azure oceans and sand-colored continents. Bookcases lined the walls, showing hundreds of leather spines in orderly rows. A green-shaded lamp on a little table illuminated the silver rim of a magnifying glass. A desk of polished wood near the window had a stack of writing paper and a tray of implements—the ones with silver owls that Marjorie had mentioned. Further off was a pair of armchairs with another small table between them. The lamp there was unlit, but a cut-crystal glass holding amber liquid glimmered faintly. A pair of high buckled boots lay nearby.

Aside from the boots and the dead body, nothing was apparently amiss. The library was calm and tidy, awaiting only a reader. Except that Lucy seemed to be huffing noisy breaths beside me, each one huffier than the one before. Her cheeks were pale, her mouth open.

"Lucy?" I said.

She squeezed shut her eyes and began to scream. A long, admirable scream.

My eyes met Hector's. "That should do it," I said.

"Most emphatically," said Hector.

The noise stopped when Lucy paused for breath. "Sorry," she gulped. "It just came over me."

Footsteps thudded in the passage, like heartbeats in the hush of the pirate's tomb. The housekeeper, Mrs. Frost, threw open the door, her cheeks mottled red.

Archer, head parlormaid, was a step behind. She took one look and set to screaming herself.

Mrs. Frost smacked Archer's face with a swift slap. "Pull yourself together. Find Dr. Musselman. Tell him to come at once."

Archer slouched away, holding a hand to her face.

Pressman appeared just as James strode through a second door on the far side of the room. The butler clasped a poker borrowed from the kitchen fire. James was equipped with an enormous pistol, though it looked old and blackened.

"There is no one to shoot," I said. "He's already dead."

Marjorie came a moment later, and froze in the doorway, aghast. Her gaze flew from the corpse to me, to James and back to the body on the floor. Pressman pulled open more draperies until Hector spoke up.

"Perhaps not to disarrange the room?" he said.

"Quite right," said James. "Don't touch anything else, Pressman. Though the light helps."

"So much blood," said Marjorie.

"So much blood," I repeated. Now that the scarlet marsh upon the carpet was brightly illuminated, I felt a bit of a *whoosh*, as if someone had blown very hard against the inside of my face.

"I can't promise we'll get that stain out, my lady," said Mrs. Frost, frowning.

"But who is it?" said Marjorie.

James put aside his weapon and stepped gingerly along the fringe of the carpet.

"It's hard to see," I said. "Because of the wig."

James leaned closer. "I suppose we'd best wait for the doctor, but if there's any chance . . ."

"Hector touched him," said Lucy.

"He is dead," said Hector.

"Marjorie, darling?" said James. "Do you feel up to placing a telephone call to the police?"

"Certainly," she said. "I'll go at once." She looked at me. "Perhaps you should come too. Mummy would be vexed to think I'd left you in the company of a—"

"I'll look after the children," said James. "The call is urgent."

Thank goodness Marjorie did not argue but hurried away, nearly colliding with Mr. Mooney as he came in.

"What's this?" The actor's eyes bulged at the grim sight while two footmen tried to peer over his shoulder. "Is that one of our daggers?"

"Please may we stay, James?" I said. "It's not my first dead body."

He put an arm about my shoulder. "You do realize that's not a normal thing for a young lady to claim? And what about you, Lucy?" he said. "Are you quite recovered after your alarming scream?"

Lucy nodded vigorously, and it seemed our presence would be allowed a while longer.

"Let me through!" came the doctor's voice, more harshly than we'd heard it the day before. "Medic's here."

Mr. Mooney and Mrs. Frost moved over to let Dr. Musselman shuffle in. He wore an old wine-colored dressing gown, tightly knotted about his round tummy. Archer must have called him from his bed, for his sparse hair stuck up like blades of grass and his spectacles sat crookedly on his blobby nose. He clutched his black bag, taking in the scene with a single look.

"I'll be jiggered," he said. He put the bag aside—no use now!—and leaned over the body, careful not to step where blood was darkening the pattern on the carpet. His fingers went to the man's wrist and then fumbled under the wig to his neck. I suspect I was not alone in holding my breath while we watched. A small shake of the head confirmed that he hadn't felt a pulse, though we'd already known that he would not.

Dr. Musselman leaned farther over, gently lifting the pirate's curls, as if parting a curtain. The light caught a ring of gold in his earlobe. Oh, poor man. Every one of us sighed when the face was revealed. Mr. Roger Corker.

The doctor creakily straightened, and patted the spot on his chest where usually he would find his watch in its pocket, except that he was in pajamas and robe.

"Does anyone know the time?" he said, looking about.

James pulled out his watch and told him, "Eight forty-nine, old chap."

Marjorie came back in just then, shaking her head. "The line is down," she murmured. "Too much snow."

Dr. Musselman cleared his throat, rubbed his mustache and spoke in a low, even tone. "A male person is pronounced dead at eight forty-nine, Christmas morning, 1902, apparently by violent means."

Apparently? Whatever else might a dagger in the back indicate?

The doctor took a giant step backward, off the carpet and away from the corpse. Now, officially, a corpse.

"Mrs. Frost, I would like a cup of coffee," he said, in his normal voice.

"At once, sir." As she turned one way, her departure was blocked by Mr. Mooney, the other, she nearly tripped on the doctor's bag. She tucked it under the dictionary lectern before bustling away. One moment later, Kitty Sivam appeared in the doorway, gold hair streaming down her back. She, too, wore a dressing gown instead of proper clothes, though no one cared, of course. Her eyes widened in ghastly fright when she saw what lay on the floor.

"Is it Lakshay?" Kitty Sivam inched toward the body and let out a cry. "Stabbed in the *back*?"

Marjorie put a hand out to prevent her guest from going any closer.

"No, dear," said Marjorie. "It's poor Mr. Corker. You must stay clear. The doctor . . ." Her voice trailed off as Kitty took in a ragged gulp of air and began to shudder in my sister's arms.

The door at the other side of the library opened with a bang. Mr. Sivam strode in.

"Lakshay!" cried Kitty. "Where were you?" She stepped toward him, her arms lifting and then dropping in a slow flap. She'd meant to embrace him, I saw, but stopped herself. Her husband had gone rigid, gaping at Mr. Corker.

"Noo . . ." Mr. Sivam's anguish in one little word. He fell to his knees and covered his face with his hands.

And now the actress, Annabelle, appeared at the door. She stared at the men on the carpet, one so still with a dagger in his back, the other moaning in dismay. A hand crept up to cover her mouth, wide in distress. Her gaze jumped from the corpse to the faces of those watching her, from Mr. Mooney to James and Mrs. Sivam, to us children and the old doctor. Then, in a sudden terrible moment, her eyes rolled back—they truly did! I saw them!—and she slumped to the floor in a melting swoon.

CHAPTER 12

AN ALARMING SITUATION

DR. MUSSELMAN GRUNTED as he knelt beside the actress, wincing when his knees met floor instead of carpet. I was examining the bloodstain pooled around the head of the corpse, only a few feet away. How much blood did a human hold?

A red tide rushed from its vessel, soaking into the deep pile and splashing the floor beyond. Splashes soon turned to puddles and puddles joined to become a flood. Minutes later, the library was ankle-deep in blood, books on the lower shelves in peril, as the scarlet torrent swelled like an angry river after a rainstorm . . .

"Where's my bag?" said the doctor, holding Annabelle's wrist and looking awkwardly about. "My bag? My bag?"

"There." I pointed to where the housekeeper had placed it.

Mr. Mooney picked it up. "What shall I look for?" he asked, already searching the contents. There came a clinking of glass as he looked through bottles and vials.

"Smelling salts," said Dr. Musselman.

"Shouldn't we get her off the floor?" said Marjorie.

"Can't see anything in here," said Mr. Mooney. He held out the bag to Marjorie, his cuff catching on the buckle for a moment. "Maybe you'll do better."

Marjorie took the bag but was looking at James. "Can we lift her onto the divan?"

"Not in here," murmured Hector.

"Too many people in here," I whispered to James. "It's a crime scene."

James shot me a look and nodded abruptly. He clapped his hands to command attention. "We need to clear the room," he said, putting on his Lord Greyson voice. "Will everyone please step outside."

Dr. Musselman pulled himself to his feet. "Peace and quiet is all the girl needs," he said. "Carry her up to wherever she's sleeping. She'll be right as rain when the shock wears off. No doubt this fellow can do it." He indicated Mr. Mooney.

"Certainly," said the actor. "I've had plenty of practice on stage." He scooped Annabelle into his arms before anyone had time to object, and carried her out the door. Lucy followed, watching her new hero play a hero.

Kitty, at her husband's shoulder, urged him to rise, but turned her face away from the sight of Mr. Corker.

I shuffled ever so slowly, wanting James to think that I was obeying his command to leave, but not wishing to miss a moment of the drama. Hector waited politely behind me, keen to hear everything too. Marjorie, on the threshold, soothed those gathered in the passage, while beckoning to Hector and me.

"Mrs. Sivam?" said James. "I understand your relief at the safety of your husband, but would you please be so kind as to accompany Miss Annabelle. It does not seem quite right that a man is taking her to her room without . . ."

Kitty Sivam was alert at once and stepped toward the door. Naturally it was unthinkable that the actress be placed upon her bed without another woman present.

"I will send a maid along," said James, "to assist."

"You needn't do that, Lord Greyson," said Mrs. Sivam. "I'll sit by her as she rests. If you are quite recovered, Lakshay?"

Mr. Sivam was on his feet again, had smoothed his hair and adjusted his jacket, which was cut differently to our English ones, longer and with curious silk toggles instead of buttons.

"Terribly sorry to add to your troubles, James. This heinous murder is not the only crime at Owl Park this day." Mr. Sivam looked at his wife, as if afraid to say the words. "The Echo Emerald is no longer in its box. I fear this time it has indeed been stolen."

"No!" cried Marjorie, at the door.

"No, no!" cried Kitty.

James looked from his friend's sorrowful face to the body on the floor and back to Mr. Sivam. His cheeks paled as he saw how the calamity had doubled in size. But he rose to the occasion—as a lord must—and began to issue orders.

"Mrs. Sivam, if you please, attend to the patient. Aggie, Hector, it is time to leave this room. Pressman, please wait."

We scurried out, but stayed by the door near Marjorie to hear the rest.

"Lakshay . . ." James paused. "I shall ride out for the police directly, as the telephone line is down. Will you—"

"This man's death is upon my head," said Mr. Sivam, in a shaking voice. "Some cruel prank to suggest that the curse of the Echo Emerald is real?"

"Lakshay," said James. "We are all in shock." He extended a hand. "You know that the jewel is merely a jewel."

"An immensely valuable jewel," said Mr. Sivam. "One that should have remained my secret and not become part of a story told for thrills."

"You are not responsible for a man lying murdered on my library carpet," said James. "Go to your room, old chap, and we'll have tea sent up."

"Where is Kitty?"

His wife was assisting Miss Day, James explained, and would join him before too long. Mr. Sivam moved slowly from the room as if under a spell.

A spell? Or a curse?

"Pressman," said James. "You'll man the front door. No one is to leave or enter until my return. No one."

Lucy wriggled back into the room. "Mr. Mooney carried her all the way to the top of the house," she reported. "She's staying in the servants' passage. He didn't even pause for breath."

James sighed and continued his instructions. "Put footmen anywhere you need to, Pressman. We've got to secure this place until we know what's what. Have my horse saddled, will you?"

"But James," I said. "What if he's already gone? Wouldn't *you* be gone if you'd stolen an emerald and murdered a man?"

"If he's gone, he's gone," said James. "If he's here, then here he stays."

"Lucy," said my sister. "Take the others and . . ." She looked as if her brain cells had entirely stopped moving. "I don't know what you might do . . . Just do it elsewhere."

103

"Children," said James. "You must obey all orders without question. Do you understand?"

Yes, yes, of course, we agreed.

James cupped Marjorie's face with his palms. "I think it's best if I ride for the police myself," he told her.

"Yes, darling, go at once," she said. "You'll be faster in the snow than anyone else."

"I'm afraid the running of the house is yours for now. I will go up to tell my mother the dreadful news before I ride out. Pray that she is upset enough to remain inside East House. I'm so sorry to leave you with all of this, but . . ."

"Of course."

James leaned down to kiss Marjorie's cheek. Then he locked the library door and handed her the key.

"Do not fail to lock the other door," he reminded her. "No one may enter until the police arrive."

Only poor Mr. Corker remained within, cooling on the carpet.

"Right, then, Pressman. Onward." James strode away with the butler following.

"I wonder how Grandmamma will like waking up to such news on Christmas," said Lucy.

"Goodness," said Marjorie. "It's Christmas." She looked down, seeming surprised to find Dr. Musselman's medical bag in her hands. "Lucy, will you please keep your grandmother company once she's had the news from

James? I'll have a tray brought up with breakfast. Cinnamon buns. And bacon."

Lucy blew out a huff of breath but agreed to follow orders. "I'll find you later!" she said to Hector and me. "Don't let anything else happen until I get back."

"That child would do anything for a cinnamon bun!" murmured Marjorie. She knelt in the passage, pulling one vial after another out of the doctor's bag, squinting at the labels. "He doesn't seem to know his alphabet," she complained. "They're all—silver nitrate, catgut ligatures, laudanum, Aspirin, peppermint oil . . . You see? All out of order. Ah! Here it is!" She held one up. "Aggie, be a dear, will you? Run and give these smelling salts to Kitty in case the poor actress still needs to be revived."

I took the little bottle, just like the one I'd seen a hundred times in Grannie Jane's knitting basket at home. The label read Jeever's Lavender Pocket Salts and, in tiny letters: Refuse Worthless Imitations.

"Hector, come with me. If we're not permitted to watch over a dead body, we may as well see a living one reawakened from a swoon!"

CHAPTER 13

A HEAP OF CONFUSION

I HELD ON TIGHTLY to the bottle of lavender salts, my single aim for the moment being to revive the ailing Miss Day. Hector and I raced up the gracious stairway to the open mezzanine that overlooked the Great Hall we'd just come from. The stairs stopped here, and we were already lost. Under Lucy's leadership, we had mostly used the servants' back stairs and wily ways through corridors that did not seem to adjoin this elegant gallery.

"What now?" I said.

"We want the East House," said Hector. "Across the landing from where we are staying, yes? One of these doors must lead us there."

"Which way is east?" I cried. "Are you carrying a compass?"

Hector leaned on the ornate railing and gazed at the leaded panes above the enormous front door below us. Pale morning light shone through, no doubt made brighter by the snow reflecting it, casting gentle shadows upon one wall.

"Voilà!" said Hector. "The sun, as always, is the best compass. It rises in the east and tells us now, from the direction of the shadows, which way to go." He marched confidently to his chosen door at one end of the mezzanine, watched by the stone statue of a maiden holding a basket full of flowers.

We arrived in familiar territory only a few minutes later: the back stairs to the upper levels. Swinging around the final corner, *thwack*! I crashed headlong into a man! Hector ran smack into me, and for a moment, we made a jammed-up bundle of limbs.

"Whoa, there!" Mr. Mooney put his hands on my shoulders to steady me. Hector reeled against the wall.

"We've got the—" I showed him the bottle rather than finishing the sentence, as breath was difficult to find just then.

The actor pointed down the passage. "Third door," he said. "Be quick."

Kitty Sivam responded to our knock with a face of consternation. She took the bottle of salts and said her thanks, but closed the door quickly, without us having a chance to see anything beyond a glimpse of the actress lying on the bed with half-closed eyes.

"Well, that was disappointing," I said, and Hector agreed.

When we made our way down to the Great Hall, Lucy was waiting, manipulating one arm of a suit of armor forward and backward in a creaking salute.

"Finally!" she said. "Grandmamma didn't want my company. She is *beside* herself, so vexed with the murderer for upending Christmas. Aunt Marjorie says we're to have our Christmas luncheon early, in the kitchen with the servants before the guests eat upstairs. And we'll have the actors too, though I suppose they mightn't be too jolly. Aunt Marjorie doesn't want children anywhere about when the police arrive. Strictly forbids us to be underfoot, is what she said."

"Did you see Grannie Jane?" I said. "I'd like to go up—"

"Archer was just going in to help your grandmother dress, so you needn't go up now. She waved at me, and said to tell you she'll find you. Grandmamma is snarling about the police and her poor maid, Evelyn, has to listen. Pity us all when she comes down."

The servants' hall had been done up gaily, with red bunting looped above the doors and bits of evergreen tied with bows to the back of every chair.

"It's a nuisance," said Mrs. Hornby, when Lucy cooed about how pretty it looked. "But it raises up the spirits and that's something. It'll all be gone by tomorrow."

A kitchen maid edged past with a tureen full of something that smelled rich and delicious, moving it from stove top to warming oven. She tried to bob a curtsy but her load made her off-balance.

"Don't fret about us being Upstairs," said Lucy, a bit grandly, I thought. "We'll all muck in to help, since it's not a proper Christmas."

"'Not a proper Christmas,' she says!" cried Cook. "With a pirate lying dead in the library from what I hears." But she told Dot to show us where to find the cutlery and told us how she liked the table laid. And she gave us paper crowns to give around and a butterscotch wrapped in foil for beside each place.

"I can't find my gentleman." Frederick came in with a tea tray. "I took this up in case he needed a cuppa, but he's not there. Every drawer in the room is turned upside down."

"Whatever next?" said Mrs. Frost. "I hope you tidied?"

"I did not," said Frederick. "What if it was the robber and not Mr. Sivam who made the mess? The police might be interested."

"You'll get up there straightaway after you've eaten," said Mrs. Frost. "I'm not having the Tiverton constabulary thinking we don't keep things neat at Owl Park."

And then a scullery girl named Effie nicked her finger on a knife and got Cook worried about blood in the creamed onions.

"They're not meant to be pink!" she scolded.

Mr. Sebastian Mooney appeared with a smile and a wave to all. Hector and I traded a look. Wasn't he a bit cheerful for a man whose friend was lying dead upstairs? And didn't the cheeks of every maid in the servants' hall turn as pink as berry cake at the sight of him?

Not Cook's, though. "Humph," she muttered. "Well, come in, Mr. Mooney. Word came down we'd have the actors joining us. Oh! Miss Day, up and about so soon? Feeling better?"

For someone who spent every waking hour in the kitchen, Cook seemed well informed as to any whisper of activity in all of Owl Park. Miss Day had followed Mr. Mooney through the baize door, looking a bit peaky but bright-eyed and upright, considering she'd been stricken on a bed only half an hour ago.

"I'm *much* better, thank you, Cook," she said. "A bit of your marvelous food will restore me in no time. Oh, look!" She put on her gilt paper crown, and so did most of the rest of us.

"You'll eat more than a bit, Miss Day, I hope," said Cook. "You're as thin as a book, you are."

Miss Day flushed and protested. I supposed that Cook liked to see people grow round from eating her food, not lolling about looking wan and slim.

"I feel well enough," said Miss Day. "We've just been wondering whether the police will let us head out."

"We've got another engagement," said Mr. Mooney. "Next Wednesday, New Year's Eve."

"We'd have to replace Roger, if we keep the booking," said Miss Day. "It's dreadful to think of."

"The new hire will need to rehearse," said Mr. Mooney. "We're hoping for someone Roger's size, so the costumes fit."

There was an awful silence.

"That sounds a bit heartless," said Miss Day. "But we need every shilling . . . No one hires actors *after* the holidays, so this is our last chance to make a little money. Weeks and weeks ahead of bread and soup for supper."

The baize door had been opening and shutting, over and over again, as servants moved in and out. They couldn't sit all together for meals, especially today, because the people upstairs needed tending to. But this time, the person coming in made Mrs. Frost get quickly to her feet. The other servants jumped up to show respect as well. Even Miss Day and Mr. Mooney, who weren't servants.

"Goodness," said Kitty Sivam. "You're having a party."

"No, no, madam, not really," said Mrs. Frost.

Our paper crowns said otherwise, as did the table's splendid feast. Mrs. Sivam must wonder how we could celebrate while a corpse lay upstairs and a priceless gem had been stolen from her husband's bedchamber.

"How can I help, madam?" said Mrs. Frost. "Is there something you wanted?" Upstairs guests did not often come to the kitchen, her voice said. It was possibly even wrong, her being here. But the entire day was wrong, we all knew that. A corpse in the library was wrong.

Mrs. Sivam told everyone to please sit. Her voice trembled when she spoke.

"I can't find my husband," she said. Was she angry? Or fighting tears? "After all the upset . . . that poor actor, and the Echo Emerald missing . . . I haven't seen Lakshay since he left the library. I thought . . ." She looked back and forth between the footmen, Frederick and John. "I thought one of you might have seen him?"

"I'm the one who's assigned as his valet," said Frederick, "only I was just up there to see if he needed anything, and he weren't in his room. I've been worried where he might be."

Mrs. Frost led her to a chair. "You sit for a minute, madam. Would you like some lunch? Or a cup of tea?"

Kitty shook her head, no tea, thank you, and she wouldn't sit. But then she sat.

"I heard something," said Stephen, "in the library, where you found the dead man."

"Stephen," said Mrs. Frost, sharply. "This is not the time for one of your ghost stories."

"It weren't a ghost," said Stephen. "Ghosts do moaning and chain-rattling. But I never heard a ghost saying 'dunderhead' as loud as a minister talking, even being midnight. That, alongside having the wrong boots in odd places, it were a very peculiar night."

"What do you mean by 'wrong boots'?" I asked him.

But Mrs. Sivam had begun to shiver and Mr. Mooney half-stood, as if he might be required to assist another fainting woman.

"Ignore the boy, Mrs. Sivam, if you will," said Mrs. Frost.

"Not to mention, a *murder!*" said Stephen, with a touch of glee in his voice.

Mrs. Frost raised a finger to warn him, and turned back to Mrs. Sivam.

"Are you certain you won't have tea?"

"No, no thank you." Mrs. Sivam looked pale and sick. She stared at Miss Day. "You've recovered quickly," she said. Her eyes traveled to the shiny crown jauntily tilted on Miss Day's auburn curls.

"Tip-top," said Miss Day. "Thank you for watching over me."

"And you?" said Mrs. Sivam to Mr. Mooney. "How are you feeling, about . . . Mr. . . ."

Mr. Mooney did not meet her inquiring eyes. "Heartbroken," he said simply.

Well, I knew what that felt like.

A bell chimed, and then again.

"That's you, Frederick," said Mrs. Frost, nodding up at the box fixed to the wall at the bottom of the stairwell. One circle on the display had turned green, indicating the need for a footman at the front door of the Great Hall.

"On my way." Frederick pushed back his chair. He left his emptied plate on the table and reached for his jacket from its hook. The bell chimed again before he'd clicked the lever to show he'd heard.

"We've got all the modern touches here," said Cook, flapping her hand at the bell box. "Ee-leck-tro-fried, that's what I calls it. They rings a bell up there to tell who's wanted, and off they go."

Suddenly a crackle sounded from somewhere near the steps.

"Must be important if Mr. Pressman is using the speaking tube," said Mrs. Frost.

The butler's voice boomed. "His lordship is back. The police are making their way up the drive, on snowshoes. They will arrive shortly. Footmen up front please, and a groom to the stables. Put snowshoes and poles in the box room. Stand by for further instructions. I repeat, the police are here."

The men pushed their plates aside and jumped to their feet. The maids gave them a quick look-over to make certain nothing was out of place.

Mrs. Sivam stood, seeming bewildered amidst the hubbub.

"Only the beginning," sighed Mrs. Frost. "Police means snow and muck from their boots melting all over the floor. More buckets. More scrubbing. And *men* every which way!" Her fingers flew up to pat her hair and met the paper crown instead. "Wouldn't that be a fine way to meet a detective?" She slid it off her head and onto the table.

"Look sharp," she told the remaining staff. "We'll all be wanted, one way or another." She clipped her way up the stairs while the maids cleared the table and got on with their tasks.

"Thank you for a delicious lunch." Annabelle, too, took off her paper crown and laid it on the table. "Having police come makes it horribly real," she said. "Roger has been murdered."

"I'll speak with the detective in charge," said Mr. Mooney. "Find out when he thinks we might move along."

"We'll likely have to cancel Inverness," said Annabelle.

"I should think so!" said Mrs. Sivam, turning to rebuke before she went through the baize door. "One man killed and another missing, as well as a priceless emerald? None of us will be going anywhere."

"No one cares about us, just for the moment," I whispered to Hector and Lucy. "Let's go back to the secret passage while we've got the chance. We can watch the police examine the body!"

CHAPTER 14

AN EAVESDROPPING INTERLUDE

THE MORNING ROOM was thankfully empty. Poor Marjorie would be occupied by far more than letter-writing today. Lucy had the cabinet open in a flash, and the torch switched on.

"The library is the second spy-hole, a few feet beyond the study," she said. "Hector, you go first. I'll tap your shoulder when we're in the right spot. I'll turn off the torch. Remember, no talking!"

The passage wasn't scary this time. Hector had just got into position when a sudden flash of light filled the narrow viewing slot.

"What was that?" whispered Lucy.

"Photograph," Hector whispered back.

"Who's in there?" I said, soft as a mosquito.

"Three policemen," said Hector, "and Lord Greyson."

We heard a knock and the library door opening.

"Ah, there you are, Doctor," said James. "How is Mother?"

"Not happy," said Dr. Musselman. "Can't find the chloroform drops I use to moisten the cotton packing in her tooth. I've had to rub on clove oil instead. The taste is . . . not pleasant."

"Oh, dear," said James. "Well, the patient here in the library is past complaining. This is Detective Inspector Willard, and his sergeants, Fellowes and Shaw. Shaw is taking photographs of the scene, before Mr. Corker's body is moved."

We heard murmurs as they presumably shook hands, while James finished the introductions. "Gentlemen, this is Dr. Musselman. He is a family guest and a private physician. He confirmed the death at eight forty-nine this morning."

"Damn cold in here," said the doctor.

"I asked for the fire to remain unlit," said James. "Best to preserve the chill until the bod—until the *deceased* is taken elsewhere. We can't have servants trucking in and out."

"An excellent decision," said Inspector Willard.

There came another bright flash. Hector pulled back from the spy-hole and blinked a couple of times before resuming his post. I was *longing* to see what he could see!

"Two more angles, Sergeant Shaw," said the inspector, "and then we'll turn him over."

"Do you wish to sit, Inspector?" said James.

"I prefer to stand, my lord. It helps me commit the room to memory."

Another burst of light, then quiet, broken only by an occasional muffled word. Hector made room for me to take his place. I could see the head and torso of poor Mr. Corker on the floor. The sergeant named Shaw was setting up a tripod to hold steady his box camera. The other sergeant and Dr. Musselman were not in my sightline just then. James leaned on the lectern that held the dictionary. Inspector Willard stood in the center of the room, rotating slowly, muttering to himself the whole time.

"Bookshelf. Reading chair, squashed pillow. Glass of . . ." He went over and bent at the waist to sniff. "Rum, I'd say." Then, "Fire tongs, oil painting in gold frame. Very fine landscape, by the way," he said. "Is that an original by Edwin Landseer?"

"Yes, it is," said James. "You've a good eye."

"Dictionary," continued the inspector. "Open to what page, my lord?"

"The *M* section," said James. "*Maudlin* on the upper left. *Meticulous* on the lower right."

"*Maudlin*," repeated Inspector Willard as he turned. "Occasional table. Lamp. Writing desk. Sterling-handled accessory set: two pens, a blotter, a seal, a paper knife, a page-turner, an inkstand. *Meticulous.* Queen Anne chair with tufted cushion . . ."

And so on. A bit dull. No wonder Hector had shifted.

But then, *pop!* Another flash, and, "I'm done, sir," said Sergeant Shaw.

Willard perked up, the moment he'd been waiting for. "I'd like to have that blade out, don't you think, Doctor? Before any shifting? Can we do that?"

"Certainly," said Dr. Musselman. "Certainly." He shuffled into view and, with a helping hand from James, got to his knees next to Mr. Corker.

"Do you know," he said. "I've been a country doctor for thirty-three years. I've delivered more than three hundred babies. I've amputated two legs—from two different men, mind. I've sewn back a few fingers and seen my share of death. But I have never removed a dagger from the body of a pirate."

Goodness! I thought. Three *hundred* babies! More than! And *two* legs!

James patted Dr. Musselman's shoulder. "There is no one I would rather trust," he said.

The doctor leaned in to look closely at the weapon.

"*Harumm,*" he said, though it was more of a growl.

"What is it?" asked the inspector.

"Not enough blood, I'd say." The doctor gently prodded the pirate jerkin around the wound.

"But it seems like a tremendous amount of blood," said James. "Practically a pond full."

"Not in the right place," said the doctor. He reached for the handle of the dagger, and paused. "I don't suppose you've latched on yet to this notion of fingerprints on things, Inspector? Do I need to mind what I'm touching?"

The Inspector sighed. "I'm very keen for the Tiverton constabulary to catch up with London on that matter," he said, "but for now, we've not got the proper kit for analyzing what we cannot see. It's an expensive enterprise, and we'll all need training. Not there yet. Go ahead, take hold of the handle."

The dagger came out, with a faint slurp. I swallowed hard.

"Looks to be the real thing," said the inspector. "Not a stage prop."

"It belongs to the actors, though," said James. "Mr. Mooney showed us during rehearsal for the tableaux. He and Mr. Corker like to wear the real weapons, makes them feel more the part."

"Does it now?" said the inspector.

"We'd best look for other wounds," said Dr. Musselman. "I don't see how this one can be the cause of death."

Inspector Willard crouched at Mr. Corker's top end and slid his hands beneath the shoulders. "Fellowes," he said. "Look sharp. Umm, sorry, bad choice of words."

There was a shuffling while Fellowes presumably got into position by the corpse's feet.

"Ready?" said the inspector. "We turn him to the left—*my* left, mind! Your right! In three . . . two . . . one!"

"Oof," said someone, but I couldn't see who.

More grunts, and they got him over. The hat and wig dislodged, revealing the yellowy, waxen face of Mr. Corker, his eyes rolled back—*Heavenward?*—and his jaw agape. A wound was evident on one side of his neck, blackened and crusty, but freshly seeping now that the body had been turned. The small gold ring glinted in his earlobe.

"God's teeth," said James. He put a hand over his face.

"Like flipping a park bench," said Sergeant Fellowes. "That stiff."

Dr. Musselman cleared his throat. "Full rigor mortis," he said.

Lucy gave me a nudge but I ignored her.

Was the open mouth a result of rigor mortis? Or was the man expressing alarm at the violent end coming his way?

"This explains the blood," said Dr. Musselman, leaning in to look at the neck wound. "Too small an incision for the dagger, though. Whatever the weapon, it must have punctured the artery."

"*Two* weapons, Doctor?" said the inspector. "Just my luck. Can you narrow the time of death?"

"A broad guess would say between eleven o'clock last

night and two this morning. The temperature may have affected the process."

"Let me *see!*" hissed Lucy.

"And you'll confirm my opinion that this is not a self-inflicted injury, Dr. Musselman?" said the inspector.

"I will indeed, Inspector. Indeed, I will."

"The best close shot you can manage, Shaw, up close to that entry point."

"Yes, sir," said the sergeant.

"It's MY turn!" Lucy had forgotten about utter silence.

James snapped his head around and glared—it seemed—directly into my eyes. He could not *really* see me, the slit being so narrow and across the room from where he stood, but he certainly knew that someone was watching. I shrank back, holding a finger to my lips and another to Lucy's in case she did not understand the danger. We dared not breathe.

The inspector kept on talking. "I apologize in advance for the inconvenience, my lord, but we'll need to interview everyone in the house."

"I will arrange for a room," said James. His voice was closer to us now.

"With a table and chairs," said Inspector Willard. "And preferably a fire."

"Have we finished in here, Inspector?" said James. "We can have the carpet cleaned, once the man is moved?"

"We'll get him out today," said Inspector Willard, "and you'll have your library back . . . though I'd discourage common use, in case I need another look. We'll have a man keep watch if we can spare one. Blast this snow."

"May I suggest," said James, from what seemed now to be *right next to us* on the other side of the wall, "that you speak first with the children who found the body? Accounting for some of those bloody footprints, I'm afraid. They are waiting nearby in the morning room, if you—"

Hector jumped. Lucy squeaked. I did both. We fumbled and bumped and squeaked again. We ran as best we could in the dark and narrow passage, trying to be stealthy but not succeeding well in that endeavor. We tumbled into the morning room, closed the cabinet door and heard it click into place. The relief of escape tickled my chest and I began to laugh, more so when I saw the smear of grime across Hector's nose and chin. He pointed at my face, laughing also, showing that I had the same marks from pressing up against the spy-hole.

"Quick!" Lucy pulled a doily from the arm of a chair. "Wipe it off! They'll be here any moment. Ooh, I wish Uncle James hadn't heard us!"

Us? I thought, but did not say. I *had* been a bit greedy about my turn. I rubbed my nose and passed the lacy cloth to Hector.

"He is most calm and clever, your uncle James."

Hector dabbed at his chin. "He gives to us a warning but does not alert the police detective."

A tap at the door made us all jump. Frederick, the footman. We began to laugh again.

"His lordship requests that you join Mrs. Morton in the Avon Room," said Frederick. "At once. To attend the police."

"Well, that's good news," I said. Grannie Jane was the ideal companion when facing a detective inspector. She'd been quite stern with the imposing Inspector Locke after the murder in Torquay.

"Tell him we're coming," said Lucy.

"I am to escort you," said Frederick, gazing blandly at one of the curtain rods.

"Mr. Frederick," said Hector. "May I ask, have you found your gentleman, Mr. Sivam?"

Frederick glanced over his shoulder to confirm that we were alone before speaking like a normal person instead of a footman. "He's not been seen by no one," he said, "since when he come to the library where the body was, telling Lord Greyson about the missing jewel," he said. "I'm getting curious why he's run away!"

We filed out of the morning room in front of Frederick, along the passage, around a corner and down another corridor. In truth I was not paying attention to where we were because the image of Mr. Corker's blood-encrusted wound had settled before my eyes and was becoming more grotesque with every step.

The man's artery had been pierced; life extinguished in a few breaths. Though his spirit had fled in terror, his body remained in the darkened room, an invitation to more earthly visitors. It was the body—the torn tissue, the blood, the residue of fear—that became a beacon for a near-invisible population of carpet mites and flies, gnats struggling to survive the winter, and maggots already breeding within the corporeal remains . . .

"Aggie!" Hector's hand prevented me from stumbling. We were at the top of three wide steps that led into a room I hadn't seen before. One whole wall inside was a painted mural of a riverbank, with willow trees and sunlight blinking through silvery leaves.

"How lovely!" Spring had suddenly arrived in the fluttering reeds and dappled water, despite the snow whirling against the real-life windowpanes.

"That's the River Avon." Lucy plunked herself down on a sofa. "That's why this is called the Avon Room. Frederick, where is Mrs. Morton?"

"Madam is coming now." He held open the door.

"Thank you," said Grannie Jane. She had her knitting bag tucked under one arm, creamy white wool peeking out. Under the high ceiling and next to upright Frederick, she seemed to have shrunk overnight. I carefully wrapped my arms around her. A bubble of warmth swelled in my chest and threatened to leak through my eyes in the form of tears.

"Hello, Grannie," I said, and then laughed a little. "Merry Christmas."

She kissed me and patted Hector's shoulder. Lucy stood and received a pat as well. "My dears, my dears," she said. "'Merry' does not seem quite the right word."

"Will you sit, madame?" said Hector.

"I will," she said. "Houses of this size are such a nuisance to one's legs." She sat on one of the upright chairs, keeping her knitting bag on her lap.

"I am here now," she said to Frederick. "You may go."

She waited until the door had closed behind him. "Now then." She turned her attention to us. "You've had a morning unlike any other, if what my maid was chattering about is true."

"If she told you we found a dead body, Grannie, then her chatter is as true as the sky."

"Goodness, Agatha, you'll get a reputation if this keeps up."

We three sat in a row, perched on the edge of the sofa. Grannie extracted her knitting project from the bag, adjusted the stitches to her satisfaction, and began to work the needles.

"Well?" she said.

"Well, what?" I said.

"You must be vivid and specific in your descriptions, my dears, as I have not had the pleasure of seeing the crime scene for myself."

CHAPTER 15

A FULL REPORT

AS WE DID NOT know how long it would be until Detective Inspector Willard arrived, our first telling of the tale to Grannie Jane may have been a bit rushed, but we did our best to please her.

"It began with the treasure hunt," I said. "James and Marjorie devised a hunt for us to find our stockings from Father Christmas."

"We never did get them," said Lucy. "Which is not fair, as we're certainly deserving. It was not our fault we tripped over a body while in pursuit."

"The library is gloomy," explained Hector. "We cannot see."

"Only one lamp was on," I said, "on the little table, where the magnifier lay."

Grannie's gaze shifted to each of us in turn as we added to the story, rather as if she were watching a game of shuttlecock. Her ability to knit without looking at her hands was one of her great skills, in my opinion. We explained how Lucy had screamed and how everyone came running. No one knew, at first, who it was on the floor, because he was dressed as a pirate, and there'd been five of those, though Annabelle hardly counted, being so womanly.

"Mrs. Sivam thought it was her husband until he appeared, alive and well," I said. "Though he was quite distraught to see the corpse."

"The body is wearing no boots," said Hector.

"His boots were beside the chair," said Lucy.

"His socks needed a good darning," I said. "Bumps of bare skin were poking through."

"His pockets, they are . . . what you say, turn outside?" said Hector.

"Turned out," I said. "As if someone were searching for something."

"And what might an actor wearing a pirate costume be carrying in his pocket?" said Grannie Jane.

"The Echo Emerald!" said Lucy.

"Oh, Grannie!" I said. "Have you not heard that the jewel is gone as well?"

She gave us the satisfaction of a hefty gasp. "This I did not know," she said. "A murder *and* a robbery! How engrossing. But such an odd cast of characters. The connections are baffling." She held up her knitting to inspect her progress. It seemed to be the back of a very small sweater, creamy white like nougat. "Do go on."

"A murder, a robbery and, possibly, a disappearance," I said. "Kitty Sivam has been looking for her husband all morning, but he is nowhere to be found. Frederick is acting as Mr. Sivam's valet, and he hasn't seen him either."

"Now that is interesting." Grannie Jane started a new row.

"I think Mr. Sivam is the killer," said Lucy. "He found Mr. Corker stealing his gem and stabbed him. And then ran away."

Hector walked over to the windows. The draperies were pulled back to reveal the snowy woods of Owl Park.

"Why does he kill a man and flee through a blizzard," he said. "Simply to reclaim his own property? Why does he not speak to his host? It is not logical."

"An intelligent observation," said Grannie. I grinned at Hector and he pretended to look modest.

The door opened and Frederick came in with another footman, each carrying a chair.

"Begging your pardon, ma'am," Frederick said to Grannie Jane. "We've been asked to set up a headquarters for the police. We'll be right back with a table."

"Tell me, young man," said my grandmother. "Have you been informed as to the removal of Mr. Corker?"

"No, ma'am," said Frederick. He and the other footman shared a sideways glance.

"Is there some mystery?" Grannie's voice sharpened.

The second footman flushed, a smile slipping onto and then quickly off his face.

Frederick tried again. "Her ladyship, the dowager, has requested that the bod—the deceased gentleman be out of her library before dinnertime, it being Christmas and all."

Grannie Jane nodded. "A natural wish, I would say."

"Yes, ma'am. Only the police haven't given the say-so yet, and there's no medics or anyone to move him, like."

"Ah."

"So, John and me, we're doing the chairs and table first, and then it'll be us who've got to, er, shift the gent."

"You have conveyed the situation splendidly. Thank you, Frederick."

"You're Dot's brother," said Lucy. "And one of the pirates."

"Yes, miss," said Frederick.

"May I inquire . . . ?" said Hector. "Where is the place to which Mr. Corker will be, er, shifted?"

The footmen again exchanged question and answer in a brief look.

"He'll be in the stables for now. Out of the house, but not too far. Cold enough to keep him from . . ." Frederick paused, with a glance at Lucy and me.

"Yes, you have supplied enough information," said Grannie Jane. "We appreciate your candor. You'd best get on with your tasks."

"Yes, ma'am." And they were gone.

"Fancy having 'move dead body' on one's list of tasks," I said.

Hector made a croaking sound, which turned out to be how he smothered a laugh.

"I am reminded," said Grannie Jane, "of a maid in the church hall, long ago when I sang in the choir. Hattie Granger spoke in a whining tone of voice, poor girl, some blockage in her nose. She was accused of stealing money from the alms box. But they found her washing dishes in the church pantry well after the time she might have gone home. The pieces did not quite fit. If she were the thief, why hadn't she disappeared while she had the chance. Do you see?"

"Perfectly, madame," said Hector.

I was still a step behind in thinking this through.

"I believe you have a most logical mind, Mrs. Morton," said Hector, "even if it is occasionally disguised as story-telling. This gives me hope for Aggie. She has the tendency to *imagine* things, without always inserting the logic."

"Do you mean," I said, "that if Mr. Corker stole the Echo Emerald, it seems odd that he took off his boots and lingered in the library?"

Grannie Jane, nodding, patted me fondly on the arm. "Why was he in the library at all?" she said.

"He was drinking," said Lucy. "There's a cabinet full of bottles in there, next to the globe of the world."

"Do you remember what Stephen said at lunch?" I asked. "Stephen is the boot boy," I told Grannie, as it was unlikely that she'd had reason to meet him.

"And what did Stephen say?"

"He said, 'The wrong boots in odd places,'" said Hector.

"And *dunderhead*!" said Lucy. "Someone shouted 'dunderhead' when he went past the library."

"When did he go past the library?" said Grannie Jane.

"Late," I said. "When he collected people's boots for cleaning, so the party was over and everyone was in bed. I suppose we can ask him precisely when. The person wasn't calling Stephen a dunderhead. No one knew Stephen was there. And he did not go into the room to see who was shouting," I added. "Naturally."

"What did he mean by the wrong boots?" Grannie asked Hector.

"We do not know, madame."

Grannie Jane thought for a moment, before making an

intriguing point. "Unless Mr. Corker was rehearsing his part in an upcoming play that features the line 'dunderhead!' it seems almost certain that he was not alone in the library."

"Is it imagination," I asked, "or a logical deduction? To say that the murderer was with him?"

CHAPTER 16

A Young Inspector

THE DOOR FLEW OPEN with such force that it thudded into the wall. First came a stout, red-faced sergeant, one we'd heard through the spy-hole, straining to turn over the corpse. Behind him was Inspector Willard, a tall man, even a bit gangly, as his bony wrists hung extra inches below his jacket cuffs.

"Good afternoon, Mrs. Morton," said the inspector. "And children. Sergeant Fellowes here will be taking notes while we talk, and he himself will not say a word." It sounded like a warning, as if Sergeant Fellowes had been naughty and was being told to remain in his corner. His red face got redder as he opened his notebook.

We were asked to sit across from the inspector. His eyes were brown and his hair quite black, except for a shock of white like a feather near the front. Aside from that oddity, he seemed to be near James in age, which is twenty-four.

"I will begin by informing you that the actor Mr. Roger Corker died last night at about midnight from an assault on his person in the shape of a knife wound to his neck."

He paused and looked at us. Too late, I realized he'd expected a gasp of surprise. We who had found the body should know only about a dagger in the back.

"To his *neck*?" I said.

The inspector nodded, seeming a bit miffed that his news had not caused more excitement. "The blade," he continued, "severed an artery and caused the victim rapid and catastrophic loss of blood."

"Really, Inspector, is this necessary?" said Grannie Jane.

"Better to hear the whole truth from me than uninformed gossip from every which way," he said.

Grannie agreed that this was likely so, though I happened to know that she was very fond of gossip from any source at all—as long as "one sifts it as carefully as cake flour," she liked to say.

"To proceed," said the inspector. "You three have been ruled out as suspects. None of you is tall enough to have done the deed, considering the angle of entry. If Mr. Corker had been stabbed in the heart, instead of the neck, you would still be on the list," he said. "Within easy reach for any of you."

"Sir," protested Grannie Jane.

"You, Mrs. Morton, are tall enough to have performed the reprehensible deed, but are perhaps lacking the strength. He was, however, somewhat intoxicated, going by the reek of rum coming from the body, so you might have managed."

"There was a stink of spirits," I said. "We noticed that."

"What else did you notice, Miss Morton?"

"I stepped in the blood," said Lucy.

"Yes, you did," he said. "As did Miss Morton, according to our study of the floor. We will need your slippers to confirm which marks are yours, and which may belong to the killer."

We both nodded. I'd put mine in the empty bathtub on the top floor. They were likely stiff and dry by now, just like Mr. Corker.

Sergeant Fellowes scratched away at his notes. Had he washed his hands since flipping the body of the deceased, or only wiped them on his dark trousers?

"We noted evidence that the victim—or someone else—had spent time in the room during the minutes—or likely longer—leading up to the murder," said Inspector Willard. "A chair pillow appeared crushed, as if sat upon. A glass on a table had—"

"Ah, yes," said Hector, interrupting. "The magnifying glass!"

The inspector's expression did not change but he looked at Hector with a new light in his eyes. "I was not referring to a magnifying glass," he said. "What we found was a drinking glass with a slosh of rum in the bottom, on a table next to the fireplace, where someone had removed his boots and enjoyed a drink."

Hector's chin dropped to his chest.

"But please," said the inspector. "Tell me where you saw the magnifier. I am most interested."

I remembered Inspector Willard's careful survey of the library, his monotone inventory of the scene. I closed my eyes, summoning my own view from the secret passage. The upper half of Mr. Corker on the floor, part of a window with green velvet drapery, the dictionary stand with the huge book open, the small table aglow from the reading lamp . . . and *no magnifying glass*.

I turned abruptly to Hector and shook my head. During our visit this morning to the library, the magnifying glass had most certainly been present. But when we were spying from the secret passage, it was nowhere to be seen!

"It was gone," I said.

"I notice this also," said Hector, voice low and worried.

"First you see it and then you do not?" said Inspector Willard.

We dared not say. What we had seen, or rather *not* seen, had been *not* seen from a hidey-hole behind the wall. We had sworn an oath to Lucy—and through Lucy to James—that we would not tell of the secret passage. We could not admit that we had *spied* on the police during their private examination of a crime scene! Hector and I looked at Lucy. Would she confess our transgression to the inspector? But no, she had missed her turn! She did not know what we had noticed. An object *not* sitting on a table wasn't something a person could eavesdrop on.

The silence was becoming more awkward with every passing moment.

"The magnifying glass," said Lucy, "belongs on the desk with the silver pens and penknife, all those things with matching owl-y handles. It sits in a box made especially for it and lined with satin so it won't get scratched."

"Oh," I said. "That's nice."

That's *nice*? My mind was scrabbling to think of how to change the subject. Inspector Willard and Grannie Jane both were watching me. My cheeks got warmer by the second.

"What I want to know," said Lucy, "is whether the pirate dagger is the one that belonged to Mr. Corker's costume? And why was he stabbed in the back if he'd already been killed in the neck?"

"Lucy," I said.

"What makes you presume the cut to his neck was made before the other?" said the inspector. "Are you an infant genius in the matter of criminally induced blood flow?"

Lucy saw her mistake, and flushed. "He was on his tummy," she muttered. She glanced at me but then stared at the floor in what I assumed was deserved misery.

"Why do I have the feeling that I have missed a bar of music?" said Inspector Willard.

Hector sneezed. A trumpeting sort of sneeze. And then again, *Aaa-choo!*

"Goodness," said Grannie. "The boy is quite unwell. If that is all for now, Inspector? I believe we need to make a lemon-ginger toddy for young Hector."

"I am certain he will survive a few more minutes, Mrs. Morton," said Inspector Willard. "I'd like to—"

A sharp rap and the door opened. Sergeant Shaw poked his head around, though of course we weren't meant to know his name.

"Pardon the intrusion, Detective Inspector. Mr. Sivam does indeed seem to have left the premises. The box that held this famous emerald is empty. There is also some dispute about moving the deceased. Her ladyship wishes it gone, but the footmen are inexperienced with the stretcher—"

I giggled. "So, there it *remains*," I said.

Grannie Jane clucked her tongue at me, though I knew that secretly she appreciated a good pun.

"Her ladyship," said Sergeant Shaw, "is, er, not delighted."

Lucy huffed out a laugh. "Grandmamma! 'Not delighted'!"

"Thank you, Sergeant," said Inspector Willard. He turned back to us. "My attention is momentarily required elsewhere, but I believe we have more to discuss. I shall be calling upon you again."

He stood and nodded curtly to Grannie Jane. Sergeant Fellowes pulled his superior's chair out of the way.

"Appearances would indicate that Mr. Sivam has perpetrated a misguided form of personal justice," said Inspector Willard. "If he caught this fellow in the act of attempting to steal a valuable jewel, he may have felt justified in fighting for it."

He turned a stony gaze to each of us in turn. The skin around my eyes tingled, as if he were casting a spell by staring into them with such intent. "I have learned, however, to mistrust appearances," he said. "Anyone watching right now would mistakenly see three *innocent-looking* children. But you are not deceiving me."

CHAPTER 17

A PATCHY INVENTORY

MARJORIE ARRIVED AS Grannie Jane was shepherding us out of the Avon Room. Her face was flushed, her hair losing its pins. "Goodness, but battles are raging whichever way I turn today," she said. "I don't know whether it will be James's mother or the Tiverton constabulary who will finish in triumph. Nor whom to cheer on, if I'm truthful."

"Have you eaten, my dear?" said Grannie Jane.

"Not one bite," said Marjorie. "There is a bountiful Christmas luncheon on the dining room table that I was forced to abandon at the arrival of the police. And now they wish to interview every person in Owl Park! When a few constables can be pulled from their seasonal festivities, there will be what they casually call a *search of the premises*! I wonder if they realize the *size* of the premises?

James is attempting to calm his mother and get her out of the way so that he may assist inquiries as best he can. Two servants have given notice and two of the Christmas hires have announced they will leave as soon as the police allow. Kitty is pacing the hallways like a nervous lioness, distraught about where her husband might have gone. One of the footmen is frantic, thinking Mr. Sivam's disappearance is somehow his responsibility. Where do you suppose he is? James is so concerned!"

Marjorie began to flick her hands in agitation, but her rattled flow of worries did not cease. "Dr. Musselman is encouraging the transferal of—of—Mr. Corker to the privacy of the stables . . . while the actors are hauling pieces of scenery from the ballroom to the coach house and trying not to think about their murdered friend. Murder, in my house! It all makes me . . . I don't . . . I don't know . . ."

And that's when my sister burst into tears like a six-year-old and threw herself into Grannie Jane's open arms.

"There, there," murmured Grannie, stroking Marjorie's hair and letting her weep. Lucy and Hector edged away down the passage, pretending to look at the paintings. I slipped my hand into Marjorie's, which seemed very small comfort to extend.

The crying quickly calmed, and Grannie asked what might anyone do to help.

"No one should be doing anything," said Marjorie. "It's Christmas!"

Not Christmas for servants or policemen, I did not say. Or for Mr. Corker.

"However." Marjorie gave herself a little shake and stepped out of Grannie Jane's embrace. "If not I, then who?" She used a dainty handkerchief to blot her face and wipe her nose.

"Good girl," said Grannie. "Chin up. Face the world. We shall do whatever we can. Am I correct, Agatha?"

"Always," I said.

"You are both so dear," said Marjorie. "I will assign you awful tasks, and we will get through this day."

"Whatever you devise," I said, "it could hardly be as awful as moving a dead body."

"On any other day, I would offer a cheeky reply," said my sister, "but today I haven't a flicker of mischief in me."

"Hector and Lucy will help too," I said. "Won't you?" I called to them.

"We are at your service, madame," said Hector, beaming at her.

"Lucy, your grandmother—"

"Again?" protested Lucy. "There is nothing left to talk about!"

"Then play cards," said Marjorie firmly. "Off you go."

"Aggie, you and Hector run along to the ballroom to

see whether Mr. Mooney and Miss Day can use your assistance. It seems dreadful that they arrived with three and are leaving as two. I will arrange for footmen to help with the heavy lifting when the time comes to load their wagon, but I suppose their departure may now be delayed . . . which will send James's mother into a tizzy! Perhaps you can help sort or pack the troupe's belongings? So that at the very least their presence is not so insistent?"

"It will be our pleasure." Hector bowed his bow, and we turned toward the ballroom, so lucky not to be Lucy just then!

Miss Day sat on the floor amidst heaps of costumes. Tattered white pirate shirts in one pile, burnt orange pantaloons in another, ragged jackets, billowing aprons, battered hats, black suits and gowns, boots and shoes of all styles and sizes, paupers' vestments, fine ladies' dresses, leather masks and feathered boas.

On a table was a collection of props, some familiar and some from other scenes in the repertoire. Tankards and crockery and foods made of plaster, featured in the various feasts. A couple of clocks, bouquets made of paper roses and lilies, the oversized magnifying glass and pipe of Sherlock Holmes, oars and pirate weaponry, and the splendid goose that had appeared on both Mr. Holmes's and the Cratchits' Christmas tables.

Miss Day was matching gloves and counting as she put the pairs into a box, all the fingers carefully stacked, one upon the next. Hector watched with happy approval.

"Oh, hello," she said. "Nine, ten, eleven . . ."

"My sister wondered whether you might like help with packing your things," I said.

"That is kind of you, but—"

"Especially," I said, "as you are recovering from a swoon, not to mention shock, and no doubt full of sorrow."

"We are able to count," said Hector, and the actress obliged us with half a smile.

"We do an inventory every time we pack up," she said, "so that we know if we've misplaced something or need to repair it because of a stain or a tear. It's a simple task, but it does take time. I'm particular about how things are folded."

Hector vigorously nodded his head. "We are birds of a feather, I believe you English say. I, also, am most happy with careful folding."

"Doesn't Mr. Mooney help?" I said.

Miss Day sighed. "Inventory was never his favorite activity. And today he's very shaken. He will show his face eventually. Usually, it's Roger and me." Her voice cracked

147

a little when she said his name, and tears filled her eyes. "I know he had his faults," she whispered. "But he was a good and loyal friend."

"It's very sad." I tried to think of any single phrase said to me after Papa died. *He is in a better place. Our Heavenly Father has called him home. Prayers will ease the loss.* None of these were true, or useful, so I turned my mind to more practical matters.

"We'll help you get the counting done. Then you'll be ready when the police say that you may leave."

"Loading the caravan will be the hardest bit," she said. "Roger always did more than his share because Sebastian is a lazy old sod."

"I believe," said Hector, "there are several footmen waiting to assist with such an endeavor."

Miss Day wiped her eyes and smiled at him. "Funny how I've played a servant on stage a hundred times and never had one of my own. It does not occur to me to ask for help." She patted the tidy stack of gloves she'd already counted. "I've lost my place."

"Is there a list, Miss Day?" said Hector. "We count the piles and call out the numbers for you to record, yes?"

"Only if you'll call me Annabelle," she said, "now that we're sitting around on the floor together. Is that agreed?"

Hector was not truly sitting on the floor, because he had placed a pirate flag between his bottom and the marble, but we agreed with Annabelle's terms. We soon were tallying the piles and announcing totals so that she could make notes on her chart.

"Four aprons."

"Eight pair of hose."

"One deerstalker hat. One child's crutch."

"Five white shirts," I said, "if you can call this white." The fabric was so old and worn it looked closer to gray in color.

"Five?" said Annabelle. "Not six?"

"Five," I said.

"Item missing," she said, adding *pirate shirt* to her list of things to look for.

"Mr. Corker is wearing one," I said, not liking to remind her.

"I've taken account of that on my list," said Annabelle. "His whole costume will need to be replaced, but there should be one more shirt."

Hector handed a tidily folded stack of pirate breeches to Annabelle. "The pants, they are a bit shabby."

"They haven't been cleaned in a while," she admitted. "They get splashed with makeup or cider or mud until we're terribly grubby. Then we give them a good scrubbing or make new ones."

"Six pair of pirate boots," said Hector, "but also there is a pair held by the police, I assume?"

"The police returned the pair from the library," said Annabelle, "as they were not . . ." She swallowed. "Not *on* the body. That's the pair tied together with string. Boots were rounded up from all over the house—his lordship's, the footman's, your guest's and ours. So, six pair altogether, including mine."

We carried on sorting and stacking and counting and folding, slowly clearing piles from the floor. It was the dull and methodical sort of chore that made a person want to hum, except that we were thinking about a corpse. A few tears escaped Annabelle's eyes from time to time, but we pretended not to see.

Mr. Mooney burst through the door, out of breath, cheeks flushed and hair tousled. Seeing us, he stopped short and began to applaud. "I've come a-running," he said, "not wanting to let you down, Annabelle. And here you've hired two able-bodied sailors to perform my duties."

"Where have you come a-running from?" asked Annabelle, not quite hiding her exasperation.

"I bumped into young Lady Greyson and Mrs. Sivam," said Mr. Mooney, "looking for her missing husband. She is very upset. Understandably."

"We are all upset." Annabelle pushed a loose curl off her forehead. "Where does she suppose he has gone? Taken his precious jewel and run for the hills? If he killed Roger, good riddance."

"Is that what you think?" said Mr. Mooney. "I suppose a disappearance does point to guilt, though I favor the scoundrel footman as thief and bandit."

"That seems a bit far-fetched," said Annabelle. "And I wish you wouldn't treat Roger's murder as a joke."

"Lady Greyson and Mrs. Sivam were sharing concern about the state of Mr. Sivam's room," said Mr. Mooney. "Ransacked, they said. Mrs. Sivam blames the footman, which made me think of it."

"Did Mr. Sivam leave his wife a note?" I asked.

"She did not mention a note," said Mr. Mooney. "Ours was a brief conversation."

"Not so brief that we've been counting and folding for an hour without you," said Annabelle. "You didn't offer her an acting job, I hope, if she has been abandoned?"

"Don't be a silly goose," said Mr. Mooney. "We have room for only one leading lady and that is you, my dear Annie."

We were interrupted by the sudden and noisy arrival of Detective Inspector Willard with Sergeant Shaw. Boot soles clattered the length of the marble ballroom floor, making the officers' approach more ominous. Annabelle stood and smoothed down her skirt. Hector and I hopped to our feet as well.

"Good afternoon." The inspector introduced himself to Annabelle and Mr. Mooney. "I am here with a number of questions," he said, "beginning with the matter of weapons."

He gestured to Sergeant Shaw, who ceremoniously opened a brown paper parcel to reveal a bronze-handled dagger, most recently seen standing upright between the shoulders of Mr. Roger Corker on the library carpet.

All four of us took a small step backward. The blade was stained with a dull, dark film of dried blood.

"Oh," said Annabelle.

"I understand you fainted this morning, Miss Day," said the inspector. "Are you feeling shaky now?"

"No, sir, I'm fine. Though it is not a pleasant sight."

"Surely, however, a familiar one?" he asked. "Does this weapon not belong to the theatrical troupe? You have seen it many times before?"

"It is one of ours," Mr. Mooney confirmed. He looked about at the piles and boxes we'd been arranging this afternoon, until he spotted the long, leather case and opened it. Two swords and a dagger, tucked beneath velvet bands, one loop dangling empty.

"These do not appear to be stage weapons," said Inspector Willard, touching his finger to the tip of a sword. "Far too sharp for playacting."

I had the feeling that Annabelle and Mr. Mooney were purposely not looking at each other, that they had already exchanged words on this very topic.

"It is safe to wear such a weapon in a tableau," said Mr. Mooney, "because all the players are stationary. The real blades are never used for performing combat."

"Why do you have them?" said Inspector Willard. "If they are never used for what they are?"

Mr. Mooney smiled. "They were my father's," he said. "And now my talismans of good fortune."

"Not this time," muttered the sergeant, catching a sharp look from his superior.

"When was the last time you saw this dagger, Mr. Mooney?" asked the inspector. "Prior to the scene of the crime?"

"Roger and I each wore one for the *Treasure Island* tableau on Christmas Eve," said Mr. Mooney. "I returned mine . . ." He tapped the open case. "After the performance and before the party, at the same time that I removed my peg leg."

"A most clever device," said Hector.

"I invented it myself!" Mr. Mooney's eyes were bright with pride. "My leg gets strapped up under the frock coat, and the knee rests on a sturdy peg that is built to fit me precisely. I can show you, later, how it works."

Inspector Willard seemed to notice for the first time that Hector and I were part of the small circle standing next to the weapon.

"I think it would be best," he said, "if the children were to leave us for the remainder of this interview."

Hector blanched. I knew he was thinking that if he hadn't commented on the peg leg, we might have been ignored. I was thinking the same thing. But I did not hold it against him, as Long John Silver's costume had been worthy of comment.

"Sir," I said. "Inspector Willard, sir. Please allow us to continue helping to stow the props and costumes. We'll remove ourselves to . . ." I waved toward the packing cases. "Over there. Please, sir? Old Lady Greyson has been most adamant about having the ballroom cleared."

He considered. As occasionally happens, it was to our benefit that children are not considered highly. He shooed us away with a wave.

"I am so sorry," whispered Hector.

"Shh," I whispered back.

We went to stand next to the crate full of boots, and banged them gently so the police could not imagine we were listening. But we were.

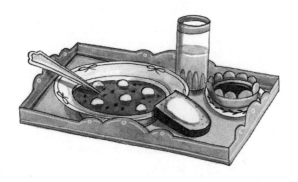

CHAPTER 18

A CLOSING ARGUMENT

"It may surprise you to learn," said Inspector Willard, "that the dagger inside that brown paper was not the murder weapon."

Mr. Mooney and Annabelle, without the advantage of having seen the true wound from the spy-hole when the body was flipped, both gasped and clutched each other's hands.

"He died from something other than a knife in his back?" said Annabelle. "But how . . . ?"

"What killed him?" said Mr. Mooney.

"We do not yet know the full story," said the inspector. "But to help us get there, I'd like to hear exactly what you did last night after the party in the drawing room."

Annabelle spoke up at once. "Sebastian and I had our

meeting," she said. "We always chat after every performance. What went well? What could we do better next time? That sort of thing."

"Mr. Corker did not participate?"

"Not last night," said Annabelle. "He didn't always."

"And where was this?" the inspector asked.

"We, uh . . . sat on the stairs, up there, near our rooms." But Annabelle's pause had been just long enough to make the rest sound like nonsense.

Mr. Mooney rested a hand on Annabelle's shoulder. "It's all right, Annie," he said. "There's no harm in me telling the good inspector the truth."

"There's a great deal of harm in telling me anything otherwise," said Inspector Willard. "Shall we sit?"

Sergeant Shaw trotted back and forth, collecting chairs from different places in the room. Ballroom chairs, with padded seats and yellow ribbons trailing from their spindled backs.

Hector busied himself counting the same stack of gloves that had been counted three times already, while I leaned deep into the bin full of boots. I found that two of them had balls of newspaper stuffed into their toes.

"Annabelle's," I whispered.

"I went into the library," said Mr. Mooney. "His lordship had invited us earlier to prevail ourselves of the liquors he kept there in a cabinet. As I was still enlivened by the success of the evening, I thought to pour myself a brandy."

"You were alone?" asked the inspector.

"I came into the room alone," said Mr. Mooney, "but found that Roger was there before me. He'd had the same thought as I had and was making some progress with the rum bottle."

"Do you mean to say that he was tipsy?"

"Sozzled," said Mr. Mooney.

Annabelle sighed, a long, sad sound. I picked up a pirate boot and rubbed the shiny buckle.

"What happened next?" asked Inspector Willard.

"I am grieved to say that we argued," said Mr. Mooney. "He was not supposed to drink in the homes we visited. He knew that. He was too likely to become unpleasantly drunk. And that's what happened on Christmas Eve. I admonished him. He became belligerent with me, called me names. I left the library and went to my room. That is the end of the story. I'd give anything . . . to have had a different parting."

The inspector was quiet. He tugged on the swatch of white hair over his brow, as if that might help him think.

"What time did you leave the library, Mr. Mooney?"

"I'd guess it was about half past eleven?" As if to confirm his guess, he pulled the watch from his pocket to see the time.

"And where were you at that time, Miss Day?" asked Inspector Willard.

"I'd gone to bed," she said. "And I'm not usually a liar, Inspector. Just that Roger being drunk . . . well, I didn't like to let the rumors fly."

"Drunk and *murdered*, Miss Day," said Inspector Willard. "With Mr. Mooney being possibly a final witness."

Annabelle bowed her head.

"Did either of you see anyone else up and about?"

Annabelle shook her head no.

"There was a servant coming down the stairs as I went up," said Mr. Mooney. "The footman who joined us for the tableau, young Frederick. He'd changed back into livery, but that sunny blond hair of his is unmistakable."

Inspector Willard rose abruptly. "I'd like you to recreate the paths you took last night," he said. "Sergeant Shaw will follow and take notes."

They filed out of the ballroom without a glance our way. I dropped a boot back into the crate.

"We didn't really learn anything new," I said, "except that Frederick was running about rather late in the evening. Why do you suppose Annabelle tried to lie about what they were doing last night?"

"She makes an alibi," said Hector. "For Mr. Mooney? Or for herself? Mr. Mooney, he is fighting with his friend for the last time."

The door creaked open again and Dot appeared.

"Miss?" She scuffled her way across the marble floor.

"Hallo, Dot. Why, what's the matter?"

Her eyes and nose were pink, her hair escaping every which way from under her cap.

"Oh, miss," she said. "It's me brother. First he was fretting over the foreign gent gone missing, wondering if he'd been dressing a murderer . . . but then the police come to the kitchen and got terrible pointy with their questions, asking has Fred gone back to his thieving ways, does he own a knife, was he a burglary partner with the dead man, and all manner of cruel suggestions that'd break our mother's heart."

No wonder that Mr. Mooney saying he'd seen Frederick had pricked the inspector's interest. But how would the footman have become so quickly intimate with Mr. Corker that they plotted a crime together? And even if Frederick had assisted in the jewel theft, did that mean he'd suddenly become a killer?

"Fred is the softest-hearted boy I ever knew!" Dot was crying. "He rescued kittens from a sack when the grocer tried to drown them last summer. He never forgets Mama's birthday, and he—"

Hector awkwardly patted Dot's shoulder.

"The truth is still hidden," he said, "like the shy bird in a bramble bush. But do not upset yourself. The truth, she will be coaxed into the light."

"Frederick has nothing to fear if he is innocent," I began, but that word *if* prompted a whimper from Dot. "He *will* be proven innocent," I amended (for what else could I say?). "Though I expect it will take the police a day or two to speak with everyone, and then to make their deductions."

We clucked and soothed a little more, until Dot said, "I'm forgetting! The reason I was sent to find you flew right out of my head! Your grandmother says to tell you that enough is enough, miss. You and Master Hector are to go to the nursery. I'll have your supper upstairs on a tray nearly before you get there."

Twilight had deepened to winter darkness when we entered the Great Hall. Flames danced in the fireplace and the chandelier far above our heads reflected splinters of light from the candles burning on the festive tree.

A bell chimed at the front door. More police? Mr. Pressman crossed the tiles to open it. His back obscured our view, so we could only hear the visitor without seeing him.

"Good evening," said a hearty voice. "I am Blake Cramshot from the *Tiverton Bugle*. I have a few questions about the tragic event that disturbed your Christmas morning."

Mr. Pressman raised his hands, palms up. "I cannot help you, Mr. Cramshot. His lordship prefers that we decline to make any comment on the matter."

"You don't think his lordship would want to set the record straight? It's rumors what'll get in the paper if we don't have direct word."

"Good night to you, Mr. Cramshot." Mr. Pressman closed the door with a firm click and lifted a key from the chain at his waist to lock it as well.

Upstairs, Lucy was in her nightdress, grumbling that we had never finished the hunt for our stockings or opened a single package. Dot had delivered the supper tray and gone away, leaving Grannie Jane—despite the many stairs!—to oversee our cozy supper. Chicken soup with tiny dumplings, salted butter smeared on warm bread and a blackberry jam tart. With the fire leaping and snow hurling itself against the windows, we ate our feast and were just a wee bit merry. The day had not been the Christmas we'd expected, but truly? Aside from the wretched end for poor Mr. Corker, Hector and I confessed to each other that we were content, even *invigorated*, by the unfolding events.

"I do not regret," said Grannie Jane, "that my penchant for curiosity has been passed along to you, my pet. Though some consider it unseemly when expressed in the extreme. But really, is there anything more fascinating than the misdeeds of others?"

"Nothing at all," I agreed. "Every day becomes a day at the theater."

"Act One is done!" Hector stood to go to his own room. "When we awake, another act begins."

Grannie and I stayed beside the fire as Lucy crawled beneath her quilt. She was asleep in minutes. But my head buzzed with characters and conversations, motives and questions. Were all the players now onstage? Could Dot's brother be a villain? Had Mr. Sivam fought to protect his country's heritage? Or would the second act reveal an unknown killer hiding in the wings? Were the clues required to solve the crime already noted, or might some unexpected detail come to light? Which moments were the ones that mattered and which could be disregarded?

"Agatha," said Grannie Jane. "I have been thinking about your mother."

I hurriedly scratched my forehead so that Grannie would not see me flush. Mummy had not entered my thoughts all this Christmas Day!

"I shall write to her at once," I promised. "Now, before I sleep."

"It seems to me," said Grannie, "that were she to know the full truth of what has occurred here today, it would cause great worry."

Mummy would be frantic. *As fussed as a sick cat, as fretful as a hungry baby, as unsettled as a moth in a windstorm.*

"I would like to suggest a small deceit." Grannie Jane had lowered her voice to a near-whisper.

"Yes!" I caught her meaning at once. "But Marjorie must be also in accord."

"We have already discussed the matter and are agreed," she said. "How I worry for your sister, bearing the burden of a murder in one's library while being scrutinized through narrowed eyes by her mother-in-law. Good night, pet."

She toddled off toward East House, braver than any of us, I thought, having to spend the night in a suite next to that of old Lady Greyson.

Christmas night, 1902

Dear Mummy,

Did you know that Owl Park has a tradition of hiding the Christmas morning socks? James and Marjorie wrote clever clues for a treasure hunt first thing this morning.

And what surprises awaited us!

There has been so much snow that we haven't been outside, but we are not bothered. Marjorie hired a small company of actors to entertain on Christmas Eve. Hector and Lucy played parts and I watched. The house is enormous with many unexpected things to see, including a cupboard full of teapots—in the morning room!—and other secrets besides.

Marjorie is a little nervous about feeding so many guests, but her menu choices have been delicious. No one is going hungry, despite the blizzard preventing some deliveries.

I do not think I shall ever forget this day.

Please rub Tony's ears for me and know that I am sending you kisses.

My very best love,

Aggie

DECEMBER 26, 1902
FRIDAY

TIVERTON BUGLE

DECEMBER 26, 1902
by Blake Cramshot
Early Edition

Police were dragged from their Christmas suppers yesterday to attend the scene of a heinous crime at the manor house in Owl Park, one mile from the village of Tiverton in Devon. An unidentified male was found dead in the home of Lord and Lady Greyson several hours after his demise. The case will be handled by Detective Inspector Thaddeus Willard, newly appointed to the Tiverton constabulary under some protest, as certain local men of standing consider him to be an outsider and too young for this position of responsibility. A murder at our most prominent address will be a test of his abilities that many expect him to fail. Lord Greyson's family and servants are nearly united in avoiding questions from the press. If police meet the same resistance, a solution to this barbaric act will not be soon forthcoming. The family have only themselves to blame if the situation is not quickly resolved. A few details have slipped out from the close-lipped household: The deceased was part of a theatrical troupe that performed for the Christmas Eve party. According to a member of the staff, the crime involved bloodshed. A bucket of vinegar and a pound of salt were used to clean the carpet. It is hoped that D.I. Willard will soon make a statement to satisfy the natural curiosity of a village that is now forever tainted by this violent act.

CHAPTER 19

A GOOD MANY QUESTIONS

WE HEARD QUITE A ruckus as we came down for breakfast on the morning of Boxing Day. The sort of ruckus caused by heavy boots pretending to be discreet but not managing very well. Hector and I watched from the mezzanine, while Lucy marched boldly down the stairs to get some answers.

How many officers had come? she asked. Four, said one of the constables (so young his mustache was barely fluff above his lip). *Only four!?* scoffed Lucy. *Did they not think a murder at Owl Park was worthy of more than four constables?* The Tiverton constabulary had only six constables, and two of them must remain at the station house to direct the hunt for the runaway guest. *What hunt?* Looking in the wood, checking inns and coaches along the

169

carriageway, and combing through trains. *What were the constables going to do here at Owl Park, exactly?* The house was to be searched. *It would take a long time with only four.* And for that reason, miss had best run back to her nanny and let them get on with it. No, they would not be requiring her guidance.

"Detective Inspector Willard!" The imperious voice of Lucy's grandmother rang through the Great Hall.

Lucy scampered up the stairs. "What is *she* doing up and about?" she muttered to us. "It's not even half past eight."

"I simply will not have it," said the Dowager Lady Greyson.

Lucy tugged my sleeve and I tugged Hector's. We slid quietly away and did not hear what Lady Greyson would not have, though it was bound to be something the police considered an urgent matter to accomplish.

In the breakfast room we were informed as to what none of us could have, on account of the snow preventing deliveries. There were no kidneys or sausages, but we were welcome to bacon or smoked kippers from Owl Park's own smokehouse.

Grannie Jane was alone at the table, poking at a dish of porridge with little interest.

"Do you miss your newspaper, Grannie?" I said.

"How astute of you to notice, my pet. The local

news"—she nudged a copy of the *Tiverton Bugle*, only four pages thick—"does not satisfy. I feel quite cut off from the world."

She asked the footman—it was Norman—to bring buttered toast. And then, "Did my granddaughter, Lady Greyson, mention that the *Torquay Voice* is delivered each day?"

"Yes, Mrs. Morton," said Norman. "She likes to keep up with the news from home. But it arrives later in the day. We have the *Voice* from Christmas Eve, if you'd like it, ma'am."

Grannie Jane waved him away. That issue was useless, having been printed before the murder.

Norman returned to his place by the sideboard, where Lucy was sprinkling cinnamon sugar over a bowl of stewed pears.

"Norman?" asked Lucy. "Do you think Frederick stole the jewel?"

"I do not think that, Miss Lucy," said Norman, rather stiffly. "As I share a room with him, I prefer not to consider him a thief or a murderer."

"Hmm," said Lucy. "To that I say, sweet dreams."

"You may take this away," said Grannie Jane, nudging the *Tiverton Bugle* toward the footman. "This fellow has filled his article on the murder with puffs of thin air, no substance whatsoever."

"If no one will speak to the reporters," I said, "how can they find substantial news to write about?"

"One of the conundrums of the modern age," said Grannie.

"*Co-nun*—what is this word?" said Hector.

"*Conundrum*," said Grannie Jane. "A difficult or puzzling matter to resolve. In this case, we do not like to have people interfering with our privacy, and yet we prefer our newspapers to tell us the truth."

"Beg pardon for interrupting, madam," said Norman, refilling her coffee cup. "But if it's news you want, there's a pack of fellas around the kitchen door won't leave us alone. They were at the front door before the sun was up, but Mr. Pressman threatened them off with a horsewhip. Imagine if her ladyship had come downstairs to find that! Now we've got reporters camping in the kitchen courtyard like a band of tinkers."

He offered the coffee pot to the rest of us and we said no thank you.

"Have you any cocoa?" said Lucy.

Yes, he'd fetch it.

"My goodness, but reporters move quickly," said Grannie Jane. "Like flies to the jam pot."

"They have to be quick," I said. "First, they hear that something has happened and hurry along to where the news is. They interview people and gather whatever facts they're given. And then they write the whole story, hundreds of words, with a few made-up bits, so that you may enjoy it over breakfast."

Grannie Jane gave me a lengthy look over the top of her reading spectacles. "I believe your infelicitous choice to speak with the reporter in Torquay has put you in favor of these men being allowed to perform their jobs."

"They must be terribly cold, that's all," I said. "Standing about on the flagstones hoping for crumbs of news like seagulls on the wharf."

Grannie Jane was not to be diverted. "Agatha, may we agree on a particular kindness to your sister? We mustn't add to her troubles by mingling with or encouraging members of the press. Are we in harmony on this?"

"We are," I said. "And Hector is too, are you not?"

"In fact, I am," said Hector, pleasantly ignoring my speaking for him.

Lucy chewed her pears and said nothing at all, giving us a rare moment of silence.

Breakfast done, we three wandered into the conservatory, which we'd only seen through its glass doors during our house tour on the first day. We stepped into a summer garden, warm and humid with an abundance of blossoms and greenery. Above our heads, the domed ceiling was also glass, letting us glimpse a sky mottled with snow-filled clouds.

"Si belle," said Hector.

"Like an enchanted castle," I said. "It smells delicious."

Lucy threw her arms wide. "I love it in here," she said. "But the only place to sit are those awful iron benches." She made a circuit of the perimeter, sniffing every flower she came to.

Hector whispered, "I am thinking very much in the night. My brain cell friction is overly agitated."

"Mine too," I said. "Did you come up with anything clever?"

"I have many questions and not, as yet, the logical answers. Most important is the location of Mr. Lakshay Sivam—and the reason for his departure. Also, where is the cursed Echo Emerald? With its owner? Or in someone else's pocket?"

"Do you suppose," I said, "that Mr. Corker is the latest victim of the evil curse upon the stone? When Kitty pulled the jewel from its case on Christmas Eve, its gleaming allure overcame his common sense and forced him to perform a bold and wicked act of thievery—"

Hector shot me a look of grave disappointment. When it came to sleuthing, he did not like my imagination getting in the way of perfectly good logic.

"What are you two whispering about?" said Lucy, done with her blossom-sniffing.

"The murder, of course," I said.

"I dreamt about it," said Lucy. "I woke up screaming."

"You did not," I said. "I was sleeping in the same room."

"It *felt* as though I woke up screaming," said Lucy. "I can't believe I stepped in his blood, up to my ankles almost. And then Mr. Sivam, the wicked murderer, was kneeling at the side of his victim with an evil leer across his face!"

"Lucy," I said. "We don't know that Mr. Sivam is the murderer. You're making things up."

Hector laughed. "It is most amusing," he said, "to hear Miss Aggie Morton accuse someone else of the odious crime of telling fictions."

I scowled at him. "I tell stories, not lies."

"And even policemen must have theories," he agreed.

"What if . . ." I began. "What if Mr. Sivam was followed from the bank vault after he collected the emerald? The robber drove a second motorcar, all the way to Owl Park. He crept into the house during the festivities, disguised as a servant especially hired for the holidays . . . He watched the tableaux right there in the room with the rest of us! And afterward, with so many pirates running around—"

"He became confused!" cried Lucy. "And killed the wrong man!"

"Mr. Sivam saw the body in the library, and fell to his knees," I said. "Devastated that his emerald had caused such bloodshed, but also filled with dread. He took the gem and ran for his life."

"Do you not think," said Hector, "that someone would have noticed a stranger in the room? A stranger with a motorcar?"

He was right, of course.

"But still," I said. "Just because Mr. Sivam is missing doesn't mean that he's the killer."

"This is true," said Hector.

"Also, the real weapon has not been identified," I said. "We would have heard some sort of fuss if the police knew what actually killed him."

"All the kitchen knives are where they should be," said Lucy. "I heard Mrs. Hornby say so to Aunt Marjorie. We needn't worry that the murder weapon is now being used to chop onions."

"We can look for the weapon," I said, "and keep an eye open for the magnifying glass. And we must ask Stephen what he meant when he said the boots were wrong. Weren't all the pirate boots the same for everyone? Also, there's a pirate shirt missing."

Where was my notebook when I needed it? We should be writing down all our clues and questions.

"Oh!" A tiny idea had just popped into my head. A bit of spatter, one might say, from a bigger idea.

Hector waited. Lucy said, "Oh? What's *oh*? Why did you say *oh* that way?"

"It's morbid," I said. "But, the pirate shirt . . . I suppose it may have been swept up by a maid and be sitting in a laundry hamper right this moment. Or mistaken for someone's regular shirt and put away in a wardrobe. But . . . What if—as I suspect that stabbing is not a tidy task—what if Mr. Corker's shirt was not the only one covered in blood!"

Hector's eyes lit up like those of a cat in lantern light, *like beacons in a storm, like fireflies on a summer night.*

"Aha!" he said. "A logical breakthrough! If the murderer *is also a pirate* . . . this will allow us to logically consider the six pirates who perform *Treasure Island* on Christmas Eve."

"Five, really," I said, "because I don't like to include James."

"Lord Greyson is not a likely killer," agreed Hector. "But he should remain on the list until we can dismiss him *logically*."

"Uncle James?" cried Lucy. "No!"

"Already we know the shirt of Mr. Corker is covered in blood," said Hector. "Leaving us four shirts to consider, with the outside possibility of a fifth, belonging to your uncle James."

I ticked off on my fingers. "Miss Annabelle Day, Mr. Sebastian Mooney, Mr. Lakshay Sivam and Frederick the footman."

"Blood on the missing shirt is a guess only," Hector said. "But a good one. And these names become suspects as the outcome of this guess."

"A deduction," I said, "with further discussion required."

I was graced with Hector's beautiful smile.

"But first," I said, "since we were so hurried yesterday . . . and didn't even know who he was at first . . ." I dropped my voice to a whisper, though we were alone in the conservatory. "I think we should have another look at the corpse."

CHAPTER 20

A PACK OF NEWSHOUNDS

WE BUNDLED UP WITH hats and mittens, but a sharp wind blew careless gusts of snow into our faces as soon as we stepped from the shelter of the warm kitchen. Just outside, the service courtyard was a village of industry. The coalhouse, the bakehouse, the woodshed, the stable, the smithy, the coach house, the laundry, the icehouse—all the essentials for running Owl Park were nestled within a few steps of the back door. Servants traipsed back and forth through the snow, carrying logs or bricks of ice or loaves of bread.

Two men, not wearing livery and clearly not servants, were hunched and smoking cigarettes beside the door to the bakehouse.

"Reporters," said Hector.

They nodded to us, puffing streams of smoke into the frosty air.

"Oi," called one. "Anything you can tell us about the murder? Did you see anything?"

With a friend on each side, I was not shy. "No," I called back. "We're children."

Lucy giggled, and dragged us toward the stable.

"Whoa, there," said the constable standing guard. "Where do you think you're going?"

"I want to introduce my friends to Buttermilk," said Lucy. "She's the pony in stall number seven. I always ride her when I'm visiting my uncle James."

"Not right now you're not," said the constable. "No one's to go in here today. There's a dead body inside. No place for little girls."

"Really?" Lucy feigned surprise.

"Aye," said the constable. "And you'll leave him be. My gran told me that the ghost of a murdered man is fearsome vengeful." He stamped his boots in the snow.

My own toes were noticing the cold, so I stamped too.

"Have you heard anything?" I said. "Phantom howling, for instance?"

"I did hear some moaning," the constable whispered, "but the actor fellow told me it was only the wind." He nodded up at the roof and shivered. "There's holes up there, where the wind goes through."

Lucy led us to the next building along, the roomiest one in the yard and nearest the gate to the drive. "Coach house," she said.

James and Marjorie have a small carriage, one that needs only two horses, so there is plenty of space leftover in the coach house. Here is where Mr. Sivam had parked his motorcar and the actors their caravan.

"When a coach drives up, it goes through the big doors on the other side," Lucy explained in a whisper. "But you'll see, there's an archway that lets you pass into the stable from the coach house. James keeps six horses, plus Buttermilk, but there are ten stalls, so he could have more." She pulled on the door handle, but there stood Mr. Mooney blocking our way.

"Hullo," he said. Behind him were painted flats leaning against the side of the Sivams' motorcar, Mr. Holmes's dining room and the rolling waves of *Treasure Island*. A stack of packing cases stood between us and the actors' caravan.

"Things are a bit tight in here," said Mr. Mooney. "What can I do for you?"

"We were going to say hello to Buttermilk," said Lucy. "Next door. She's a pony."

Mr. Mooney glanced over our heads at the constable guarding the entrance to the stable. "Ah, well. I can't help you there, missy. We've all got our orders. Leave old Roger to rest in peace."

"I suppose," said Lucy. She shrugged at us.

"Oh, well," I said. "We can try again later. Oh, look, there's Stephen."

The boy was running from the bakehouse to the kitchen, a large loaf of bread tucked under each arm. He slipped this way and that on snowy ridges made by foot traffic in the courtyard. "Inspector's making a statement," he shouted to us. "Follow the reporters 'round front!"

Three or four men stumbled out of the bakehouse, along with a wonderful smell of hot bread. Grumbling about wind, they buttoned bulky coats and pulled caps low over their eyes and ears. The smokers ground their cigarettes into the snow and joined the others.

"Let's go," I said. "We want to hear this!" We trotted out of the courtyard and along the drive, the long way around to the front door.

Mr. Pressman held open the door, allowing Inspector Willard and his two sergeants to pass onto the top step. The inspector held a piece of paper with both hands to prevent it from flapping in the wind.

"During the night of the twenty-fourth December," he read, "a guest of Lord and Lady Greyson met an untimely end on the premises of Owl Park. The body was discovered at approximately half past eight on Christmas morning, and the police were summoned to the scene. The deceased is not related to his lordship. All efforts are being made to secure a satisfactory conclusion to the matter."

"Can you tell us the victim's name?" called a reporter with carroty eyebrows under a dark cap.

"And how he died?" asked another.

"How old was he?"

Questions were hurled at the inspector like a barrage of snowballs.

"*Where* on the premises?" shouted a pockmarked fellow at the back.

"Do you have enough experience to do this job properly?" asked a man with white hair poking out around the edges of his hat.

"Was it an intruder?"

"Have you got a suspect?"

"Is Lord Greyson a suspect?"

"His lordship is not a suspect," said the inspector. "At this time."

Hector's hand caught my wrist and squeezed, silently sharing my surprise.

At this time? Did that mean James might be a suspect at a later time?

"We heard the body was discovered by children," said a slim fellow at the front of the horde. "Is this true?"

Inspector Willard put up a hand. "The victim's name is being withheld until the family can be informed of the tragedy. Other details cannot be released. That's all for now, gentlemen. Please respect the privacy of a household in mourning and be on your way."

This was met with noisy grousing, but the inspector gave a curt wave and stepped back into the house. The reporters pocketed their notebooks and conferred with each other. Two of them waved to their colleagues and began the long march down the drive.

"They go to find a telephone," said Hector. "Or a telegraph office. The newspapers await their reports."

"*Brr*," said Lucy. "It's a mile to the village."

"He gave them nothing useful," I said. "How could they make a story out of that? Not even so much as a bucket of vinegar and a pound of salt. Poor fellows, they must be freezing."

"*I'm* freezing," said Lucy. "Let's go in."

Hector's trousers were sodden, up to the knees. He could not bear the discomfort and headed up all those stairs to the nursery to change into his second pair. Lucy and I preferred to dry out before the dancing flames in the drawing room grate. James and Marjorie sat together on the sofa. I had a notion that their conversation had stopped one instant before. Lucy filled them in on the inspector's statement. My damp stockings steamed as the fire warmed my legs. We had barely shrugged off the chill of our expedition outdoors when the butler appeared.

"Who is it, Pressman?" asked Marjorie. The sole purpose of the silver tray in his hand, I had learned from Lucy, was to carry the calling card of any visitor to the master or mistress of the house.

"A journalist, my lady." He bent slightly, though it could not be called a bow.

"We are not receiving journalists, as you know, Pressman. Send him away."

The butler hesitated.

"Was there something else?" asked Marjorie.

Mr. Pressman turned to me and proffered the card upon the tray. "The gentleman is asking most particularly to speak with you, Miss Morton, or with Master Perot. He tells me that you are well acquainted."

CHAPTER 21

A DISQUIETING SCENE

"I CAN TURN THE man away, my lady," the butler suggested to my sister.

"You needn't do that," I said, quickly taking up the card. Lucy stood on tiptoes to look.

Marjorie put aside her book. "Didn't you say, James, that we mustn't speak with—"

"Mr. Augustus Fibbley is from Torquay," I told her. "He wrote about the murder in October, when Rose's mother was poisoned."

"Ah yes," said James. "The determined Mr. Fibbley."

"Whether you know him or not, he is still a reporter," said Marjorie. "A man whose livelihood relies on the disasters of others."

I hesitated at the word *man*. But then, "Well, yes. But he does try to tell the stories readers want to hear."

Why was I defending Mr. Fibbley? In my experience, he was not a trustworthy person. However, I rather liked him. He was a writer, after all. And he'd called me a writer too. I hoped that wasn't a lie.

"I'd like to meet with him," I said. So bold! "Thank you, Mr. Pressman. Where is he?"

"I want to come with you." Lucy gazed defiantly at her uncle James. "For protection."

"I think not," said James.

"I shan't need protection," I said. Ignoring Lucy's scowl, I slipped around Mr. Pressman.

"Should we not accompany . . . ?" said James to Marjorie. "A young girl alone with a man? It isn't proper."

"Oh, he isn't a—" I stopped myself. Now was not the time to be breaking promises, especially in front of a bigmouth like Lucy. "I shall be perfectly fine. Mr. Pressman will watch."

Marjorie sighed her consent.

The butler walked ahead, his back as straight as a bookcase.

The reporter was bundled in a sailor's peacoat and a muffler, but held his hat in a mittened hand. He stood by the armored knight in the Great Hall, peering into the eye-slit in the visor as if hoping to encounter the ghost of the long-ago inhabitant.

"Hello," I said.

Mr. Fibbley turned and smiled and pushed wire-rimmed glasses up the bridge of his nose. "Hello," he said. "No barking dog?"

"Tony stayed at home to keep Mummy company for Christmas," I said. "He would have driven the servants quite mad, I think."

We considered one another. Our last encounter had been on a dark road, during a night of anguish and alarm. Memory took me there now, chilled and wet through, frightened but coming to the end of an ordeal that this odd person and I had partly shared.

"How did you know we were here?" I said. "Is Owl Park not rather out of your territory?"

"Very much so, Miss Morton. But *you* are my territory, especially when it comes to murder. My editor was notified of the connection—that your sister is the new Lady Greyson and that terrible events had occurred under her roof. So, here I am, not having Christmas. I have traveled through the night and would appreciate any details you might share. The detective inspector, as you heard, was not at all forthcoming."

I felt a bit sorry for him, traveling nearly fifty miles to stand about getting chilblains in the snowy courtyard, but I was resolved to honor my sister's wish of discretion.

"I don't have anything more to add to his statement," I said.

Mr. Fibbley smiled, a cunning, charming smile. "We both know that's not true," he said. "We both know you're the most observant twelve-year-old in the south of England."

"I'm observant too. And I'm only ten." Lucy was suddenly at my side, grinning like a cat who'd swallowed a canary. *Like Jack Horner with a giant plum on his thumb. Like a little girl who had tricked her aunt and uncle into letting her speak with a reporter* . . .

"I'm Lucy," she said, not looking at me.

I managed not to groan aloud.

"How do you do?" Mr. Fibbley gave a slight bow. "I am Augustus Fibbley of the *Torquay Voice*. Are you related to the clever Miss Morton?"

Lucy giggled. "She's my new cousin. My uncle James is married to her sister."

"Ah," said Mr. Fibbley. "I expect your uncle James is a lucky man."

He was pleasant and informal, as if we met often for a glass of lemonade and a game of Snakes and Ladders. A very friendly fellow, Mr. Gus Fibbley, up until the minute he decided not to be.

Friendly, or a fellow.

"We're not meant to speak with—" I began.

"We found the body," said Lucy. "I was first."

"Tell me about that," said Mr. Fibbley. His hat now dangled from the hilt of the knight's sword, his mittens stuffed into pockets. A notebook had appeared in one hand and a pencil in the other.

Lucy told, of course. About the dim library, the blood-soaked carpet and identifying Mr. Corker, despite his being in costume.

She might be considered as much of a barking dog as Tony, I thought.

"So, the cause of death was a stab wound?" said Mr. Fibbley.

"Yes, but the dagger—" Lucy began.

"That's enough," I said. What Lucy had said so far might have come from a servant. But we mustn't say anything we knew from spying in the hidden passage.

Lucy's look showed that she had plenty more to tell.

"Lucy," I said. "Think of James and Marjorie."

"He was in costume because he was an actor?" said Mr. Fibbley, still scratching along the page with his pencil. "Could you describe exactly what he was wearing? I heard he was dressed like a pirate."

"White shirt, orange-colored trousers," said Lucy, promptly. "Dingy stockings and no boots!"

"No boots?" said Mr. Fibbley, looking up. "Why was that?"

Lucy glanced at me and I shook my head. She pressed her lips tightly together as if they were fighting her.

"Where is the body now?" said Mr. Fibbley. "Could you take me to see it?"

"Certainly not," I said.

"They moved it," said Lucy.

I pressed the toe of my shoe upon the toe of hers.

"A peek at the crime site, then?" said Mr. Fibbley.

Footsteps thundered down the marble stairs into the Great Hall. Mr. Pressman, usually so stately, darted toward the commotion, which turned out to be two constables racing to find Inspector Willard.

"What's this?" Mr. Fibbley watched with a keen eye as the policemen jumped the last three steps. One of them carried a woman's low buttoned boot. They trotted toward the Avon Room where Inspector Willard was still conducting interviews.

"They must have found it," Lucy said to me.

"Found what?" said Mr. Fibbley.

"The emerald," said Lucy.

"An emerald was lost?" said Mr. Fibbley.

"Lucy," I said. "You are an object of tremendous vexation."

Another constable trotted toward the ballroom. Mr. Pressman strode our way, addressing Mr. Fibbley in the firmest of tones.

"I believe the time has come, sir, to say good day."

"Just as things get interesting," said the reporter, with a bright smile. "I am not dismayed, however. I have enough to get started."

A scuffle in the passage from the ballroom sent Mr. Pressman hurrying to investigate.

"Must this occur at the front of the house?" said the butler tersely. "It is most discourteous to the—"

"Most bloody discourteous, being treated like a common criminal!" shouted Miss Annabelle Day, as she was dragged into the Great Hall.

One of the constables put a hand over her mouth. "None of your barnyard language here, miss, if you please."

Miss Day wriggled her face clear of his hand and protested so loudly that the Dowager Lady Greyson may have heard her in East House. Two footmen came into the Great Hall from the service passage and stopped to gape, this not being a common scene at Owl Park. Sergeant Shaw appeared and moved quickly to assist the struggling constables.

"I never touched that emerald, as Heaven is my witness!" cried Miss Day. "And if I had—which I did not— why would I be such a fool as to hide it in my own damn shoe? This is a trap!"

She yanked her arm from the grasp of Sergeant Shaw's thick fingers. "Let go of me, you great ape! I can walk perfectly well without you pawing me."

"This way, miss," said Sergeant Shaw, quite humbly, I thought, for a great ape. "The inspector will put it all to rights, whatever right is."

Annabelle lifted her chin, set her shoulders straight and, flanked by two men, with a third behind, marched toward the Avon Room as gracefully as a doomed queen heading to the scaffold.

Mr. Fibbley was madly scribbling the whole time.

"You mustn't put in anything about the emerald," I said. "Please? Not yet. You mustn't."

"And why is that, Miss Morton? You did not breach a confidence. I've watched all this with my own two eyes."

"Mr. Fibbley, sir?" Mr. Pressman loomed over us. "Your departure will be most efficient through a side entrance. Here is Frederick to escort you."

He signaled the second footman, who strode forward and stood waiting until Mr. Fibbley had put away his notebook and pencil, straightened his muffler and retrieved his hat from the knight. He managed to wink at me before following Frederick out of the Great Hall.

"What is all the racket, Pressman?" James was here, the book he'd been reading still in his hand. "Are the girls—oh, hello, girls. What happened? Did the reporter cause trouble after all?"

"The reporter was lovely, Uncle James," said Lucy. "He winked at Aggie and said I was a clever girl."

To be factual, he'd called *me* "the clever Miss Morton," and never said any such thing about Lucy, but let her have her silly fib. I would not deny her story.

"My lord," said Mr. Pressman. "There has been an apprehension."

"Explain."

Mr. Pressman explained. James shook his head, in disbelief or dismay I could not tell.

"Has my mother been visible at all?" said James.

"No, my lord."

"Small mercies," said James. "Though I do feel an element of sympathy, since the chloroform drops for her toothache seem to have disappeared into thin air. Not that she needed any help in becoming crankier."

The doorbell rang.

Mr. Pressman glanced around to be certain that the Great Hall was as quiet and elegant as it was meant to be. Lucy and I crept closer as he unlatched the door. Outside was an elderly gentleman, accompanied only by his cane.

"Good afternoon," said Mr. Pressman.

"Good afternoon." The man touched his hat. "I am here at the request of a Mr. Lakshay Sivam. We have an appointment today. My name is Sir Mayhew Dullingham. The stationmaster was kind enough to bring me from the village in a sleigh! I am here from the British Gemological Society. I believe the appraisal of a gemstone is required?"

CHAPTER 22

AN EXPERT OPINION

SIR MAYHEW DULLINGHAM seemed as old as a tree, remarkable upon first sight because of his eyebrows. They were not sleek and agile, as Hector's were, but wiry and ferocious. His eyes were difficult to find beneath such hairy scrawls, and behind thick spectacles as well.

Mr. Pressman helped the old man out of his coat and took his hat, but was shooed away when he offered to carry a small leather valise. James sent a footman to notify Kitty Sivam. She soon arrived with Marjorie, and with a grinning Hector close behind.

"I am most excited to meet an expert of such renown," he whispered to me.

"How do you know he is renowned?" I said.

"He is a sir!" said Hector. "Rewarded for the power of his brain and not for prowess on a battlefield."

The Great Hall was populated with more people than I imagined Sir Mayhew Dullingham expected to see, and none of them the person he'd planned to meet. Inspector Willard had also appeared, looking quite puffed up and ready to make a pronouncement. James introduced himself to Sir Mayhew and explained there had been a tragic death, that the police were here, that Mr. Sivam had been called away, but here was Mrs. Sivam in her husband's stead.

"And the stone, my dear lady?" said Sir Mayhew.

"The stone—" Kitty began.

Inspector Willard could keep quiet no longer. He raised two tightly closed fists, looking like a boxer without puffy gloves.

"Officially," he said, "the stone is currently in the care of the Tiverton constabulary, as part of an investigation into the crimes committed."

"You have the—" Kitty Sivam's eyes watched the inspector's hand, as if he were a conjurer about to produce a white rabbit. "You've found the stone?" she cried. She pounced on him, pulling his fists out of the air. He stepped back and held his arms aloft.

"Madam," he said, "I must ask you—"

"Where did you find it?" she demanded.

"The stone has been lost?" Sir Mayhew's voice held a distinct waver.

"Who took it?" said Mrs. Sivam. "I want to know where it was."

"Under the circumstances," said the inspector, "the police are reluctant to allow the Echo Emerald out of our care, even for a short time."

Kitty Sivam had two spots of color high on her cheeks. "Let me see the stone!" she cried. "Have you found my husband too?"

"Have I arrived in a madhouse?" The old gemologist's eyebrows seemed to tremble as he peered at the inspector, who finally opened his left fist to offer a glimpse of the gem. I stood on my tiptoes to catch a glint of green, as did Hector next to me.

"I'd like it back," said Kitty Sivam. "Until Lakshay can be here to—"

James intervened. "I propose that we proceed with the appraisal that Lakshay arranged. Surely it will be to everyone's advantage to know precisely what sort of gem we've got here—why the actress took it into her silly head to—"

"The actress?" said Kitty Sivam, her voice high-pitched and furious. "The *actress*?"

The inspector's hand snapped shut. James realized his error in revealing the possible culprit and attempted to change direction.

"We do need to know whether it was worth . . ." He paused again.

What had he been about to say? Was it worth the risk that Annabelle had apparently taken? Was it worth Roger Corker dying for? Was it worth so much that someone (I had trouble imagining Annabelle) had become a killer? Or . . . was it fulfilling an ancient curse?

Marjorie put a hand on Kitty Sivam's arm. "It will be best for everyone, dear, if we know its value."

Mrs. Sivam swallowed hard and straightened her back, seeming to adjust her attitude along with her posture. "Of course." She nodded to Inspector Willard. "I apologize for my upset. I'm . . . on edge."

The inspector passed the Echo Emerald into Sir Mayhew's open palm. The gemologist sighed, rather like the sigh of someone given a large slice of cake. He squinted through his thick spectacles, lifted it close to his lips and exhaled abruptly. He then peered again at the jewel, his head seeming to jiggle as much as the tremor in his hand.

"Well, sir?" said Kitty Sivam. "What do you see?"

Her voice was soft, but surprising to the old man. He fumbled. The emerald fell from his fingers. All watching gasped together, and then again half a second later when Hector darted with the speed of a hummingbird and caught the gem before it hit the floor.

Sir Mayhew Dullingham jumped, and began a wheezy chuckle. "Splendid," he said.

It seemed he was about to pat Hector's head, but accepted the emerald instead.

"If you would be so kind," he said to James. "I should like two glasses of water and a private place with good light to continue my examination."

"But—" Kitty began, and stopped at once.

James signaled to Mr. Pressman to arrange for water. James himself would escort the gemologist to a private spot.

"I will have the boy to assist," said Sir Mayhew.

Excellent work, my friend! Hector shot me a triumphant smile.

The inspector himself planned to stand guard while the gemstone was examined.

Lucy poked me.

"James will take them to his study!" she whispered. "We can watch!"

Doubly excellent! We pretended to scrutinize one of the enormous urns full of festive greenery as Marjorie guided Kitty toward the drawing room. A few minutes on, we sidled out of the Great Hall, with the casual stealth of practiced spies.

How deflating to arrive at the morning room and discover James leaning against the door frame! Lucy glared. He had read our minds—and didn't he look smug.

"Hello, ladies," he said. "Going somewhere special?"

"I have misplaced my landscape embroidery," said Lucy. "I may have left it on the . . . on the ottoman."

"Do have a look," said James. "I can wait."

I did not imagine that Lucy had ever embroidered anything more than her initial on a handkerchief. I laughed.

"Come on, Lucy," I said. "We've been outsmarted. Let's go and wait with Marjorie for news about the emerald."

"But it's so deadly boring in the drawing room!"

"You could start a new piece of embroidery," suggested James.

Hector, presumably, was passing a pleasant hour of instruction in gemology, while Lucy and I sat upright on a drawing room chaise, listening to Kitty Sivam mutter and fuss as she paced back and forth across the cabbage roses woven into the carpet.

"But where is Lakshay?" she cried, every third or fourth turn. "It made sense that he might flee to protect his precious jewel, but it makes no sense at all that he should go away without taking it with him."

Marjorie invented a new soothing remark each time. Lucy yawned or retied the ribbons at the ends of her plaits. And I thought about Hector diving for the Echo Emerald and how *not* bored he must be just now.

A tap on the door and Frederick came in. He bowed to my sister and glanced over his shoulder to where I saw Stephen hovering.

"Begging your pardon, my lady," said Frederick. "Due to the police activity, the lamps have not been trimmed on schedule. If the boy could slip in now? The inspector wishes to speak with him again and we do not know when next—"

"Certainly, Frederick, send him in," said Marjorie, ignoring Kitty's raised eyebrow. "The servants' schedules are as upset as everyone else's," she explained to her guest. "Perhaps even more so. We must accommodate, for our own comfort."

Kitty sat, in a rustle of silk, as Stephen came in carrying his basket of lamp-tending tools. Frederick waited at the door, perhaps to prevent any misbehavior on the part of the boy. We sat for a few minutes, diverted by Stephen performing his duties—though if I'd been in his place, the mortification of all eyes on me would have been unbearable!

It was Kitty who cracked the silence by addressing Frederick. "Are you the boy who was acting as my husband's valet?" she said.

"Yes, ma'am,"

"And were you the one to rifle his drawers and leave the room in disgraceful disarray?"

"Kitty!" scolded my sister.

"No, ma'am!" Frederick colored scarlet. "I found the room that way! The police asked that I wait to tidy while they looked around."

"The police have searched there too?" said Kitty, disconcerted.

"Yes, ma'am." Frederick's voice was quiet but firm.

"Frederick has been with us for many months," said Marjorie. "He's becoming a fine footman, aren't you, Frederick?"

"Yes, your ladyship, I hope so," said Frederick.

Lucy turned to Stephen. "Why are *you* being interviewed again by the police? Are you also a suspect?"

Stephen paused in his task, with scissors in midair. "No, Miss Chatsworth, I am as honest as a mirror."

This made Marjorie and Kitty laugh, while Stephen flushed.

"Why then?" said Lucy.

"I expect they want to hear more about my observations on the subject of boots," said Stephen. "As I happen to be the one polishing, and I know there were no jewel in Miss Day's boot last night, because I'd of noticed if—"

"Stephen," said Frederick, sharply, from his place at the door. "Finish up."

Stephen ducked his face to his task, while his ears glowed red.

Lucy moved to the piano. "May I play, Aunt Marjorie?"

"I suppose so," said my sister.

Kitty rolled her eyes and Marjorie rolled her eyes in return, but listening to Lucy *plink-plunk* her way through a Brahms lullaby allowed us to pass the next many minutes. Frederick escorted Stephen away, and we were back to waiting for news from Sir Mayhew Dullingham.

Happily, James appeared after not too, too long. "Please come to the study."

"Oh, thank Heaven." Kitty reached for her shawl.

It was my first time being inside the study, though I had seen a slice of it through the spy-hole. The desk of burnished wood caught a trickle of winter light through leaded panes. Walls of books, a reading chair, a tin of biscuits close to hand. I could live in this one room!

But we were here on important business, and what did it mean that Hector would not meet my eyes?

"Well?" said Kitty Sivam, too eager for good manners.

"Lord and Lady Greyson," said Sir Mayhew, "and Mrs. Sivam. I shall be brief. It grieves me to inform you that the stone in your possession is not the famous Echo Emerald missing from the statue of Aditi in Ceylon."

Kitty Sivam gasped and reached for my sister's hand.

"It is not, in fact, an emerald at all," said the old man. "It is a well-composed copy, made of glass."

CHAPTER 23

A HORRIBLE SOUND

KITTY SIVAM RELEASED A cry of anguish and swayed on her feet.

Not an emerald? A lump of colored glass? The faces around me reflected many shades of disbelief and horror. Hector came to stand next to me now that the worst was said aloud, though we could not yet confer as we wished. Inspector Willard was listening closely, and watching each person in turn.

Sir Mayhew bowed to James and to Kitty Sivam.

"It dismays me to impart ill-wished-for news, my lord. If it is of any comfort, the copy is an old one, and of the highest quality." He bowed again and looked about as if wondering how he'd got here.

Hector took his arm and we led him back to the Great

Hall. Mr. Pressman was most solicitous in ensuring that the old man was seated comfortably in the station-master's sleigh.

"Cook has wrapped a pork pie for your journey," the butler told Sir Mayhew. "Along with a pot of her famous pickled radishes."

Returning to the library, we discovered that the news continued to cause an uproar. Mrs. Sivam's face was blotched and teary, like sand after a brief downpour. My sister offered her a handkerchief.

"Sir Mayhew said the duplicate was many years old," James was saying. "I expect Lakshay's father had it made for safety's sake. Were you aware that a copy of the Echo Emerald existed, Mrs. Sivam?"

She looked at him as if uncertain how to answer.

But then, "We learned of the copy when we went to the bank, thinking to collect just the Echo Emerald itself," she said. "Lakshay's father left a note to explain about the second stone. It was a . . . precaution, I believe he said? Though Lakshay wondered if it was more of a souvenir."

"Had you learned to see the difference between the two?"

"I . . . I did not ever hold the two at once," said Kitty Sivam. "I am not an expert. Lakshay kept them apart. But someone . . . that woman! She has stolen the genuine stone and put a copy in its place!"

"Refuse Worthless Imitations . . ." I whispered to Hector, recalling the motto on the bottle of smelling salts.

"Why does a thief keep a copy in her own shoe?" Hector murmured back. "Does she know the difference? Has Mr. Sivam taken the genuine stone somewhere?"

"We've been tricked!" cried Mrs. Sivam. "Annabelle Day is partners with someone who works at the bank! They tried to steal the emerald our first night here, and then succeeded on Christmas Eve! Who knows where the jewel is now?" She stared about wildly. "Lakshay has run for his life! Or else been murdered too!"

"Kitty, my dear," said Marjorie. "The police will soon learn all the answers, do not fear."

A gong sounded.

"Half an hour until lunch!" said Lucy. "I'm starving near to expiring."

James leaned in to speak with his wife. "My darling, I must go and tell Mother of this new twist in the plot. I'll bring her to lunch and join you as soon as I can. We're awfully late today, aren't we?"

"Aggie?" Marjorie's arm was around my shoulder. "Do you mind terribly much taking Hector and Lucy to eat in the servants' hall again? James's mother makes everything so difficult, and—"

"We don't mind," I said.

Hector looked away so that Marjorie wouldn't see his smile.

Lucy did not think to hide her feelings. "Hurrah!" she said. "It's much better fun below stairs."

Dot was at the table, with Archer and Stephen, and a couple of others I had no names for. The footmen, Frederick and Norman and John, formed a small parade, traveling back and forth from Cook's domain to the dining room upstairs, carrying clean plates, polished glasses and shining silverware to set the table.

"The doctor and Mrs. Sivam have asked for their lunches on trays in their rooms," said Cook. "So you'll take those up, Frederick, when you get back."

"Yes, ma'am," said Frederick.

"I'm running a hotel instead of a house," Cook grumbled.

We had just begun our turnip soup with bread and butter when Mr. Mooney came in from the service courtyard. He brought a swirl of snow and a blast of winter. His face was ruddy, hair disheveled.

"Have you lost your hat?" asked Lucy.

Mr. Mooney touched his head and shrugged, saying that yes, he must have, while moving scenery. He had not

even noticed. We revealed to him the news of the fraudulent jewel, and his jaw dropped open in astonishment.

"I don't understand," said Mr. Mooney. "There are
two emeralds? A real one and a copy?"

"That's what Uncle James asked Mrs. Sivam," said Lucy.

"And how did Mrs. Sivam answer?" said Mr. Mooney.

"She seemed to agree that there might be two," I said.
"She was very upset."

"I suppose Mr. Sivam mixed things up on purpose,"
said Mr. Mooney. "Very clever of him. Put the copy in a
fancy box and pretend it's stolen while he runs away with
the real one."

We all went silent. Who would tell him? One friend
had been murdered and now his other friend was revealed
to be—well, *appeared* to be—a jewel thief.

Admirably, it was Lucy who spoke up. "Sorry, Mr.
Mooney, but nobody knows if there really *is* a real one.
Miss Day had the copy hidden in her room."

"Miss *Day*? But that's impossible!" Mr. Mooney
looked from one to the next of us, begging with his eyes
that Lucy had misspoken. "This cannot . . . How did . . .
No! It doesn't make sense! Not Annabelle!"

"The constable named Worth found it in the toe of her
boot," said Lucy.

"Them's nice boots, the red ones," said Stephen. "I
took extra care."

"The *toe* of her *boot*?" Mr. Mooney was dumbfounded. He sat at the table and stared at the basket of bread for several minutes. Mrs. Hornby put a bowl of soup in front of him. He ate it up, but it could have been a bowl of snow for all the attention he paid.

"Tell us about Sir Mayhew," I said to Hector. "What happened in there?"

Hector told us all in rapid detail what tests the stone had failed during its examination. If one exhales on a real emerald, the fog will disperse at once rather than linger for several seconds as it does on the surface of glass. The gemologist had suspected from his first breath that he was looking at a copy, but went through several more trials before allowing himself to make a pronouncement. A drop of water on a real emerald will hold its shape, but on a fake will run off. A submerged emerald will cast a green light in water, but a copy will not. Only a false gem is clear all the way through. A genuine emerald has many interior fissures and flaws, and its facets are sharp, not easily worn away. A real emerald does not flash or cast what the old expert had called fire.

"When Mrs. Sivam held the jewel up to the light that first evening," said Lucy, "it was the flashes that impressed us all."

"Next time, I will know," said Hector. "It is glass that flashes. A genuine emerald does not."

Mr. Mooney perked up. "You've been apprenticed under the top man in his field," he said to Hector. "You can start your trade as a master jewel thief."

Hector grinned. "It is a beginning," he said. "Though, sadly, I do not think I have the nerve to be a villain." He patted his lips with a napkin and folded it tidily beside his empty soup bowl.

Frederick came in and collected the first of the lunch trays, carrying it up the men's stairs on a slight slant.

Hector was still thinking about the Echo Emerald. "If the genuine jewel still exists, where is it? Does Mr. Lakshay Sivam know, or not know, which stone is mere glass?"

"The burning question!" Mr. Mooney slapped the table with his palm. "How many ladies' necks are adorned with counterfeit jewels while crafty husbands sell the genuine items?" He took out his watch, attached on a long chain to his pocket, and looked at the time. He held it to his ear to be certain it was ticking before idly twisting the links a few times about his finger.

"Will Miss Day be in less trouble for stealing a copy?" said Lucy. "Because it's not so valuable?"

"I can't believe she did this," said Mr. Mooney. "When I think of all the treasures we've seen, in all the manor houses we've visited . . . I suppose we've learned a little about fine stones along the way . . . but why would she . . . why now?"

"The beauty of the emerald, it is irresistible," said Hector.

"And small enough to fit anywhere," said Stephen.

"Speaking of small," said Mrs. Frost to Stephen, "it's time you went up to do the bedroom lamps while they're all at lunch. Go on, you."

Stephen scooped up his tool basket and went to the men's stairs.

"When the first attempt was made to steal the Echo Emerald," I said to Mr. Mooney, "Miss Day and the rest of you had not yet arrived at Owl Park. So, I don't see how she had any part of a burglary." I was thinking of Kitty Sivam's accusations. "You were performing elsewhere?"

"We were," said Mr. Mooney. "We performed a play that night, a charming version of *Alice's Adventures in Wonderland* at Hanley House near Axminster. The daughter of the house made rather a buck-toothed Alice and could not recall a single one of her lines."

The door to the courtyard opened, hurling in another rush of cold air. Sergeant Fellowes scraped his boots on the mat, and shook the snow off his jacket.

"All is calm outdoors," he said, touching the brim of his hat to acknowledge Mrs. Frost. "I'm just doing my rounds."

"You can tell your inspector there'll be lunch for you lot in the Avon Room when his lordship's company has been served," said the housekeeper.

"That's right nice of you, ma'am," said the sergeant. "And we'll be wanting the boy for more questions as soon as you can spare him."

He went through the baize door just as the gong sounded for lunch upstairs.

"Oh, heavens, there's the bell gone," said Cook. "Where's Frederick to take the second tray?"

No one had an answer. Norman waited patiently for Cook to finish filling a tureen. The aroma was fresh, like celery and thyme. Upstairs was having a different soup.

A minute later, we heard a cry from the men's staircase. And then a crack. And then a rapid series of dreadful thumps.

Stephen lay at the bottom of the stairs, like a doll tossed down in a temper. He was more or less on his back, arms flung wide, and we could see his face, still and blank. The kitchen fell silent for a single heartbeat before Effie screamed, and the rest of us made other horrified noises.

Hector, the speedy one, was first to kneel beside him. "He is breathing."

The muslin shirt on Stephen's chest stirred with a slight but regular rise and fall.

"Heaven be praised," said Cook.

"Shall I find the doctor, Mrs. Frost?" said Archer.

"Dr. Musselman is a houseguest for Christmas," said Mrs. Frost. "Not on duty, so to speak. And he's already got m'lady's teeth to worry about. We'll pull out

Stephen's mat and let him rest quiet till he comes to."

"He's meant to be speaking with the inspector in five minutes," said Dot.

"Do not move him," said Hector urgently. "If the arm is fractured, or inside maybe . . ." He made a stirring motion in front of his own stomach. "An injury may become worse with motion."

"The boy is right," said Mr. Mooney. "You'd best have the doctor check for broken bones. And someone tell the inspector there's been a delay."

Mrs. Frost sighed. "Frederick? Where has Frederick got to? Norman, go up and tell Dr. Musselman, soft like, while you fill his glass, we've had an incident needing medical advice. No need to fuss the rest of them. Miss Lucy, you and your friends had best get up to the nursery. No need to linger about seeing this . . ." She nodded toward Stephen, whose face was swelling and turning darker.

"Shouldn't he have a pillow at least?" said Lucy.

"Do not move the head," said Hector.

"The doctor will say what's needed," said Mrs. Frost. "Off you go, children. Too many cooks in the kitchen."

Mr. Mooney went over and mounted the first few steps of the men's staircase, craning his neck to look up around the turn.

"I don't see anything he might've tripped over," he said. "What happened, do you think?"

"He's been up and down those steps like a mountain goat for half his life," said Mrs. Frost. "His feet is still little enough to fit, no matter how steep the rise. How did so nimble a boy lose his footing?"

Up to the nursery we went, as the housekeeper had said we should. But then what?

The sky was darkening already, because of the ever-falling snow, *a bruised yellow swath above the tangle of black branches. As if Owl Park itself were mourning Mr. Corker's woeful end. Nature's way of expressing disquiet over the boot boy's fate.*

It was too snowy to go skating and no one much felt like it anyway. Especially Hector. We were not inclined to play a board game, and the few nursery books were too pious to be of interest. Had James really read *Elsie Dinsmore?* Hector and I would have liked to discuss the murder, but Lucy was there—being Lucy—and that did not feel helpful to the cause. Eventually Marjorie came up to tell us that the doctor had visited Stephen, but the boy was still unconscious. She delivered to me a folded paper bearing my name, *Agatha*, in Grannie Jane's scrawl.

"Our heroic grandmother has been at Lady Greyson's side for the entire afternoon," said Marjorie. "She must now know more about James's childhood than James does himself. Dot will be up in a bit with a supper tray. Good night, darlings."

The note read:

Children in nurseries are often
more entertained than
old ladies in drawing rooms.
Sweet dreams.

TORQUAY VOICE

BOXING DAY, 1902

LATE EDITION

DEADLY SWORDPLAY!!
BODY DISCOVERED BY CHILDREN ON CHRISTMAS MORNING! VICTIM LIES IN POOL OF BLOOD WITH SLASHED THROAT!

by Augustus C. Fibbley

Horror awaited unsuspecting children as they sought their gifts from Father Christmas yesterday morning at an elegant manor outside the village of Tiverton, in Devon. The murdered corpse of Mr. Roger Corker, wearing the disguise of a pirate, lay upon the floor of the library at Owl Park. Readers of the Torquay Voice will recall the murder–by–poison that shook our town in October, a case solved, in part, through the fortitude and determination of twelve–year–old Miss Agatha Morton. Here she is again, first to arrive at another fearsome scene.

Miss Morton was accompanied by a cousin, Miss Lucy Chatsworth, 10, and Torquay resident Hector Perot, 12, a guest of the household. Miss Chatsworth revealed that blood had seeped from the dead man's wounds across the carpet all the way to the fringe. Her uncle, the young Baron, Lord James Greyson, requested that all further questions be addressed to the police. The investigation is being led by Detective Inspector Thaddeus Willard, new to the rank, and tight-lipped regarding this case. Mr. Corker's murder is the first such crime since D.I. Willard joined the Tiverton force last summer. Concern has already been voiced regarding his inexperience, and his brief statement to the press on Christmas Day was not reassuring. The family is sequestered and did not care to comment, though rumors circulate about a second houseguest not accounted for and a valuable jewel gone missing. This intrepid reporter will continue to investigate despite efforts by police and staff to close their doors to our inquiries.

DECEMBER 27, 1902
SATURDAY

CHAPTER 24

A MOUNTAIN OF WORRIES

THE NEXT MORNING, Dot rattled us awake by dropping the fire tongs.

"How is Stephen?" I said from my bed.

"Just the same, miss. He looks like death. Meaning, I'll be doing his work as well as my own. Next to impossible, it being Christmas week. Near impossible already, even without clodhopping policemen around every corner." She wiped her cloth along the mantelpiece, squinted at it and sighed. "I do forty-one fire grates every day of my life," she said. "And then I've got the soot grime and ash-dust to look after. It's a never-ending story. Not even mentioning poor Frederick's troubles with that inspector. Did he ever see the special emerald? And what was Mr. Sivam wearing? And has he got a need for money? Well, don't we all?"

She poured us each a cup of cocoa—but no tray today, she said. There was a perfectly good breakfast waiting in the breakfast room. "Master Hector is already dressed and gone downstairs."

Lucy began to count strokes as she brushed her hair. "Three, four, five . . ."

"Stephen usually sleeps on a mat near the oven," said Dot. "For now, he's been put in the butler's pantry, so's we can watch him but also keep him out of the way. Except it's Mr. Pressman's private spot, and he's an ogre when peeved, I'll tell you straight. The doctor says Stephen's got hisself concussed in the skull. No bones broken, but horrible bruises! I had a peek first thing—his eyes is all swolled up and purple, like a mask."

I shivered.

"His head is wrapped up with brown paper soaked in vinegar. He don't half smell like a jar of pickles."

"Just like Jack," I said. "And Jill. Bumped his head and went to bed."

Lucy's punishing brushstrokes made her hair crackle. "Eleven, twelve, thirteen . . . What about the prisoner?" she said.

"Oh, Miss Day's all right," said Dot. "Mrs. Frost said only porridge, as she's a prisoner, but Archer and me, we like Miss Day, she's as nice as sugar, so we take turns going up and slipping her buns and whatnot. The sergeant on guard, he don't mind. He likes her too." Dot waggled her eyebrows up and down. "I mean, he *likes* her."

Lucy tried to copy the eyebrow maneuver but she looked demented.

"I'd best be off." Dot collected our mugs. "We had a bit of an uproar below stairs last evening," she said, pausing at the door. "Lords and ladies can't have all the fun, can they? Effie—she's scullery—and Archer, they saw out the window what seemed to be some sort of hunchbacked monster, swaying against the coalhouse door, clutching his head and staggering like he were a lunatic."

"Go on!" said Lucy, eyes round.

"Lucky that Mr. Mooney happened along. He nipped straight out to investigate without a smidgen of fear. 'Stay away from the windows!' he says to us, and we ducked down giggling, but leery too. He was gone ever so long, we thought he might be doing battle. And what do you think it was?" Dot hushed her voice to a spooky whisper.

We shook our heads, waiting to hear. Lucy had stopped brushing.

Dot cackled. "He found the coalhouse door swinging open and shut, with an empty coal sack caught in a hinge and flapping. 'Here's your monster,' says Mr. Mooney, and he plunks down the sack on the kitchen table. He flashed that smile of his what Archer says could melt a block of ice."

"A coal sack?" I said.

Lucy picked up her brush again. "Fancy thinking it was a monster," she said.

"I'm hungry." I threw back my coverlet. "Time to get dressed."

Hector waved cheerily when we came in. But he was sitting with Dr. Musselman at the far end of the table, so I sat next to my grandmother. She was happily eating a kipper and listening to Marjorie read aloud from last evening's *Torquay Voice*. Mrs. Sivam held her hands over her ears. She said the only news she wished to hear was that her husband was safe and sound.

"'Miss Chatsworth revealed that blood had seeped'—" Marjorie stopped reading because James put up a hand to request a pause.

"Now that you girls are here," he said, "I may voice my disappointment."

My heart doubled in weight and turned over inside my chest. Disappointing James was a dreadful feeling. But Lucy! She wiggled herself right next to Marjorie so as to read along with her.

"Good thing I came with you yesterday," she said to me. "What I told that man was important enough to put in the newspaper!"

"That is precisely where you've let the family down," said James, in his sternest tone. "It was a mistake to let Aggie meet with him, but far, far worse that you tricked us into tagging along—and then *blabbed*! I will say this one last time, Lucy . . . We. Do. Not. Speak. With. Reporters."

Lucy paled and then flushed bright pink. I felt a tinge of empathy. I'd made the same mistake in October, starting with a thrill down my spine at the sight of my name in a news article and ending with wishing to shrivel up like a poked worm.

And the same reporter had been wielding the pencil.

"He did come from Torquay because of Hector and me," I said, clutching at a defense of Lucy's actions—even if I had tried to stop her.

"And he did write a better story than the local chap did," said Marjorie, "using a bit of ingenuity with the same lack of information."

"No one could say that Mr. Fibbley is not clever," I said.

"The point is," said James, "that Mr. Fibbley had rather *more* information than the local chap, thanks to our little chatterbox."

I confess to feeling some comfort in Lucy being the one to cause trouble instead of me. I served myself a waffle, covered with a syrup made of the sap from maple trees and imported all the way from Canada.

James gave Lucy an ultimatum after breakfast.

"You are fortunate that your grandmother does not care for the daily news—or, indeed, for any reference to our presence in the twentieth century. I will not tell her that you've been sharing family secrets. In exchange, you will read aloud *whatever she requests* until lunchtime."

Off Lucy went with her lower lip stuck out far enough to catch flies, as my nursemaid Charlotte would say. Goodness, I hadn't missed Charlotte for one minute since I'd arrived at Owl Park. I wondered whether Christmas with her mother had been the ordinary sort, with a roast goose and carol singing and no dead body in the library. Was she feverishly writing letters to Constable Beck every evening? Had she told her mother about the young man with whom she'd been walking out?

"Aggie?" said Marjorie. "Are you two coming?" She meant to the morning room, where she and Grannie and Kitty Sivam were heading.

"I suppose."

Hector and I would have much preferred to find a policeman to follow about, or to search the house ourselves for the magnifying glass and the blood-smeared shirt, but alas . . .

Back in the morning room—though it was nearly past morning—Grannie Jane was sorting through her skeins of wool. Marjorie rang for tea and sat at her desk to write. Snow continued to blow against the windows and boredom wormed its way into the room like smoke from an ill-burning fire. Grannie's needles began the clickety-clacking that accompanied most of our quiet hours. Hector turned the pages of a book, hoping to find a pressed flower. I wished for Tony's nose to be lying across my boot and his tail to thump as we listened to the familiar clicks of Grannie knitting.

Mrs. Sivam draped herself upon the chaise, her neck on the headrest, her face glowering at the ceiling. "I keep thinking of that thieving actress," she said, "making such a noise, while her victim—one of her victims, since I am the other—has disappeared without a trace and the police seem not to care one bit."

"I see that it must feel that way," said Marjorie, "while you are so distraught, but James tells me that the police from four other villages are assisting the Tiverton constabulary. There is plenty of activity beyond what we're aware of. Your motorcar is still in the coach house, rather penned in by tableaux scenery, so he has not gone off in that. Which means on foot or by train, unless he was picked up in somebody's coach. The police keep asking questions, hoping that a witness will come forward."

"So many questions, and no answers!" complained Kitty.

I leaned on Marjorie's shoulders, nuzzling her cheek with my cheek, trying to see what she was writing.

"Aggie," she said. "You're making my script go wobbly."

"Are you writing to Mummy?" I said.

"Yes."

"And you're telling her? About Mr. Corker?"

"I feel I must," said Marjorie, glancing at Grannie Jane. "Even if Mummy doesn't read the newspaper herself, most people do. Someone is bound to think it a duty to pay a call and tell her all about it."

"She'll know I wrote a letter full of untruths," I said, "and I only fibbed because you said I must."

"We did not realize that a reporter would come all the way from Torquay to make such a fuss," said Marjorie. "We thought we were protecting her from worry."

I slumped on an ottoman with a glum conscience.

Mr. Pressman appeared at the door to offer a welcome instant of anticipation. Why had he come? What might happen next?

Mummy had arrived, bringing Tony with her, unable to bear another day without us . . . The police had found another clue, this time a ruby necklace with a broken clasp . . . Mr. Lakshay Sivam had been sighted, running along the top of a train between Leeds and Durham . . . Mr. Lakshay Sivam had been arrested, a passenger in a coach carrying the post to Scotland . . .

"Yes, Pressman?" said Marjorie. "Did I hear the bell ring?"

"Indeed, my lady. There is a woman come calling, without a card. I put her in the drawing room to wait, but . . . I don't know."

"What troubles you, Pressman?" Marjorie put down her teacup and saucer. "Who is she?"

"Her name is Miss Beatrice Truitt, my lady. She is wearing heavy mourning. She is apparently betrothed to marry the corpse."

CHAPTER 25

A BEREAVED VISITOR

"OH MY." Marjorie's face paled to what in books is called *ashen. As white as fresh-fallen snow. As if visited by a ghostly apparition. As shocked as curdled cream.*

"No!" Mrs. Sivam looked every bit as dreadful. "She'll think that Lakshay killed him!"

"Grannie Jane?" said my sister. "What shall I do?"

Grannie moved stitches back and forth on her knitting needle. "You will go to greet her, my dear. Take Agatha with you, for good cheer. Ring the bell in twenty minutes and we will join you."

"Not I," said Mrs. Sivam. "How could I face her?"

"This will be your opportunity to set matters straight," Grannie Jane said, firmly.

Marjorie stood, her face a picture of woe. My poor sister! It wasn't her fault that Roger Corker had received stab wounds from two different weapons. But the stabbings *had* occurred in her library, and now she must offer kindness and solicitude to a devastated stranger. Lucky me to watch how this unfurled! With a guilty and delicious quiver of anticipation, I followed close on Marjorie's heels along the hall, while she practiced words of condolence. *We are so sorry for your loss . . . my utmost sadness that you find yourself . . . how can I express my sorrow on your grievous . . .*

"This is awful, Aggie! What words can possibly make the slightest difference? The poor woman! How do you suppose she heard the news?"

"She likely expected him to visit on Christmas Day when he returned from Owl Park," I said. "Imagine sitting down to one's Christmas tea, a nice slice of fruitcake, and having a message come that your sweetheart has had his neck pierced!"

"Aggie, stop! It's too grim to think of. And now here she is to seek solace and answers from a household of strangers! Should we not be the ones visiting *her* in her hour of despair? Though how could we know that the poor man had a sweetheart? And goodness knows in what dreadful place an actor's fiancée must live."

"Any of the phrases you've been muttering will work perfectly," I said. I imagined that Mrs. Sivam should have a few words to say as well. She might say, *It may have been my husband who made you a widow before you were even married* . . . or . . . *My sincere condolences that your betrothed seems to have been a drunkard before he died* . . . or . . . *Your dream of a happy wedding has been shattered by the ancient curse upon an emerald I carry about in a box* . . .

"Marjorie," I said. "You need only survive twenty minutes before Grannie Jane joins us. She is ever so good at visits with the bereaved."

"I shall be counting every second," said my sister. She paused at the door of the drawing room, took a deep breath, and transformed into the young Lady Greyson, in full possession of grace and poise.

Miss Beatrice Truitt stood before the fire, *close* before the fire, leaning in as if her very blood had frozen and she'd prefer to melt than shiver another moment. As Mr. Pressman had informed us, she was dressed from head to toe in mourning. A dress of silk crape, a short cloak, a widow's cap with heavy veil, all in dull black that did not reflect the light, as was the custom. One should not permit one's clothing to display a sheen during one's darkest hour.

She turned at our approach and accepted my sister's outstretched hands with gratitude, her head bent low and stifling a sob. I knew without looking that Marjorie's cheeks would also display tears. I nearly wept myself at her distress. The introductions were made, and Miss Truitt agreed to sit. Marjorie peppered her gently with questions. Had she come far? Would she take tea? Had she been long engaged to Mr. Corker? What shocking news to hear on Christmas Day!

Our guest responded sweetly, in a voice not much above a whisper. She had not come too far, only from Exeter. She would like tea, if it wouldn't be too much trouble. She had been acquainted with Mr. Corker for some two years, but engaged for only these past three months. Shocking? Yes. Far beyond shocking—and what progress had the police investigation made?

"Pull the cord, will you, Aggie? We'll order tea and have Grannie join us." Marjorie's hands, turning over themselves in her lap, betrayed her great discomfort.

"The police . . ." she said. "It is a Detective Inspector Willard who leads the case, and he is very clever, it seems to me, though these things take time, I am afraid."

"Interviews," I whispered to Marjorie as I sat, after ringing the bell. Marjorie patted my knee.

"Ah, yes, thank you, Aggie. The police have interviewed everyone in the house, all the guests and servants. And a search has been conducted, though . . ." Her voice died away as she entered the murky waters of how much a stranger should be told about the other crime committed within these walls. "Though I do not know how a search might assist in apprehending a . . . a . . ."

"A killer, Lady Greyson?" said Miss Truitt. "I must learn to say it plainly. Though I cannot begin to understand why anyone would murder my poor dear Roger."

For this we had no answer, and thus a lengthy moment of silence.

"We have been wondering the same thing," said Marjorie, finally. "How could we not?"

Another painful interlude where none of us spoke.

"Tell me," said Miss Truitt. "Is it true that one of your houseguests is suspected of the crime? Did I not read in the newspaper—on my journey—that someone else is missing? Or is my . . . my sorrow muddling my sense?"

Marjorie took in another slow breath. "It is best not to pay much heed to the newspapers," she said. "The fellows so often get things wrong. We must put our trust in the police and their steadfast endeavors."

She had deftly avoided answering the question, but there was no comfort in her words. The tea arrived at last, and a moment later, Grannie Jane and Hector came in, with Mrs. Sivam following nervously.

We had an interlude of introductions and condolences, tea-pouring and biscuit-passing. At the very moment when we might have sunk once again into the Awkward Well of

Despair, Miss Truitt lifted the veil from her face and pinned it back momentarily so that she might sip her tea.

She lifted the cup to her lips, having put in a slice of lemon, and looked me straight in the eye.

I nearly dropped my macaroon.

I'd seen those eyes before.

And they were not the eyes of a stranger named Miss Beatrice Truitt.

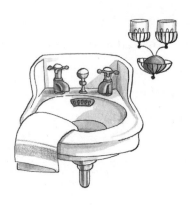

CHAPTER 26

AN AGONY OF DECEIT

MY HEART STOOD STILL and then began to tremble as if it were a mouse under the gaze of a cat. I had met those eyes a dozen times. For a moment I could not place the face, until it struck me that on other occasions there had been a pair of round gold-rimmed spectacles sliding down the pointed nose. I opened my mouth and closed it again. My eyes flicked to Marjorie, who used the tongs to put a slice of lemon into her teacup with no notice of a calamitous revelation here in her drawing room.

One does not expect to be utterly deceived by the same person twice. But here I was, a double dupe. Admittedly, in my experience, she was very, *very* good at deception, so I credited her talent more than I rued my foolishness.

Until this morning, I had only ever seen her dressed as a man. That's how Mr. Fibbley did his job, in disguise, writing about sights that most women dare not see, sights that most newspaper employers consider unhealthy for any but the hardest-hearted men to witness.

And yet, here was another version of Mr. Fibbley, a slim and pretty woman, un-spectacled and clad in mourning from hat to hemline, sniffling into a black-bordered handkerchief. So familiar, and yet never seen before!

"Miss Truitt," I said. I did not wish to expose her without knowing what game she played. For my sister's sake, I could not join the game with an easy conscience. "Perhaps . . ." I glanced again at Marjorie, but her lips were at the rim of her teacup. "Would you care to, er, wash your hands after your journey? I could show you the way."

Marjorie flushed, and smiled at me warmly. "Oh, Aggie, thank you. I should have offered at once to . . ."

Miss Truitt rose and followed me.

"We haven't much time," she whispered, her black skirt rustling along the passage.

She opened the door of the lavatory and turned back to me with a sassy grin. "This *will* be cozy." She clasped my wrist and pulled me with her into the tiny room, closing the door swiftly. We were squished together as closely as herrings in a jar.

"Have they got electric lights?" she whispered.

"In some of the rooms," I said. "Some of the time. It does not appear to be a reliable commodity." I felt her arms swatting the walls in a fruitless search of some manner of illumination. I found the switch and turned on a small lamp suspended from the ceiling.

"I *will* wash my hands while we're in here," said Miss Truitt, "if you don't mind."

My hip was wedged against the sink, but I pressed myself flat against the wall while she turned on the tap and found lavender soap.

"What are you doing here?" I said. "What if someone recognizes you?"

"Why would it occur to anyone to look for a male journalist in the clothes of a bereaved young maiden?"

"Why are you pretending to *be* a bereaved young maiden?" I spoke as fiercely as I could. "Wherever did you find a weeping veil at such short notice?"

She wiped her hands dry on her skirt and ignored my question. The hook with the hand towel was digging into my back.

"The police," I said, "will want to speak with you, Miss Beatrice Truitt. They'll be looking for a motive. Perhaps it was you who killed him, that's what they'll be thinking. They'll ask all sorts of questions—and you know nothing about him!"

"I know from the other reporters the bits they've

gathered from the servants," she said. "I know he was a harmless chap who owed a bit of money and was too fond of the bottle. Nothing to get killed for."

"Maybe he wasn't the one meant to *be* killed," I said. "There were four men dressed the same way. What if one of the others—"

"It's done now," said Miss Truitt. "I report on what happened, not what might have happened. His old mum died last year, and he'd got no one else to care about him, except these actors. I shall disappear as soon as I have gathered a bit more color. Just watch. As good as a conjurer, my vanishing act. Really, these few minutes with Lady Greyson have already given me a trove of details . . . though it would be a treat to have a quick look at the body. Only you and Hector will ever know I was in here. I'd have thought, as a fellow writer, that you would applaud my ingenuity!"

"Your ingenuity is swamping my sister with guilt," I said. "And what if a real fiancée arrives? Or an actual Mrs. Corker, with three children and genuine sorrow in her heart? What will you do then?"

"I tell you, there's nobody like that. Mr. Corker had a heart-to-heart with a footman over a bottle of ale, told him he was alone in the world, not so much as a cat to go home to." Miss Truitt grinned, her teeth gleaming faintly in the near dark.

Which footman? I wondered.

"Listen," she said. "It is not every day that a reporter has an opportunity like this, to see the inside story. Not one of those men out there could do what I have done this morning, isn't that right?"

I thought of the fellow with the pocked face and wiry black beard. Or the ginger-haired man with gray smudges under his eyes and a droopy mustache. What sort of women might they dress up to be? I laughed.

"I'm not certain that's a fair defense of your trickery," I said.

"You and Hector swore an oath in October that you would not tell the secret of my identity," Miss Truitt said. "Surely you will not break a promise so soon as this?"

"I will not," I said. Promises were to be honored, I knew that much. But could not the same be said of honesty?

"Good girl," she said. "Then poke me in the eye, Miss Morton."

"Wha—?" I began to say. But truly? There was nothing I wanted to do more right then. I followed her instruction and twisted two corners of the hand towel into points.

She leaned forward. "Go on," she said.

Without warning her as to the moment of attack, I jabbed one eye and then the other, an instant later.

"Ohh!" She blinked and winced and peered into the mirror. "That worked a charm!" Her eyes had turned pink and filled with tears. "Now you have conspired with me and must play the game to the end. Come, let us get back before my sorrow dries up!"

In the drawing room, everyone was seated as before, except for Hector, who offered around the plate of seed cake. I had such a trove to tell him! Miss Beatrice Truitt had her veil turned up and allowed her pink eyes to brim with tears. This prevented anyone from wondering why we'd been absent for so many minutes.

"Miss Truitt," said Grannie Jane. "Please sit here by me."

Miss Truitt sat, modestly shielding her face—now that her woe had been witnessed.

"Because of the investigation . . ." Marjorie spoke in a careful voice so that I guessed at once that Grannie had been coaching her. "We may not assist in making plans for a funeral as yet, but please be assured that when the time comes . . ." She paused because Miss Truitt had sobbed.

Her weeping now rang loudly of fraudulence. I wished to stamp on her toe. I waited with the others, however, for the woman to recover her calm.

"If I could just . . ." said Miss Truitt. "It would mean so much to me if I might . . . see him? To pay my last respects?"

"Would that really give you comfort, my dear?" said Grannie Jane. "It may be . . . just a bit gruesome."

A soft knock came at the door half a moment before it opened to reveal Mr. Pressman and one of the policemen.

"Constable Gillie, my lady," said the butler.

The constable stepped in and cast a quick look around the room, as if he had not entered many like it before. The ornate plaster roses, set into the ceiling to reflect the ones in the carpets, the gold-threaded draperies, the cascade of crystal blossoms hanging in the chandelier—it was all pretty grand.

"Yes, Constable?" said Marjorie. "How can we help?"

Constable Gillie cleared his throat. "Detective Inspector Willard understands there's a young woman come who might shed light on the investigation." His eyes fell on Miss Truitt, sitting with head bowed. Truly, gossip flew from one room to the next in this house, as speedily as a nervous bat. *Like a fly catching a whiff of honey. Like a bird with its tail on fire.*

"The inspector would like to have a word, as soon as it is convenient," said the constable.

Marjorie rose to her feet and smiled. "I cannot, naturally, presume for our guest, but neither will I disappoint her. She wishes to spend a few moments, now, alone with . . . with Mr. Corker. After that, she may speak with the inspector, if she has strength to do so."

"Thank you, Lady Greyson," murmured Miss Truitt. "The girl has been unwavering in her kindness. Might she lead me to view the body of my beloved?"

CHAPTER 27

AN INTIMIDATION

CONSTABLE GILLIE escorted us to visit the corpse. We could not escape that courtesy. What machinations were occurring in Miss Truitt's head to prepare herself for an interview with the detective inspector?

I led them along the route I knew to reach the service courtyard, through the baize door and into the kitchen.

Cook slapped a hand to her mouth at the sight of us there, and hearing her squawk made all the staff look up in surprise and worry. It was no common sight to see a lady in a fine mourning dress and veil come traipsing through their territory without a word of warning.

"You should be going through the side door, miss, next to the library. It leads to the terrace and a path to the courtyard."

"I do apologize, Cook," I said. "I'll remember that for next time."

Dot pulled a woolly shawl from a hook near the door and bundled it about my shoulders. "You'll need this," she said. "Snow's coming down like powdered sugar on a plum cake."

The stable had two doors. A tall double door used by the horses, closed for the moment, and an ordinary human-sized entrance. Sergeant Fellowes stood at this one, thumping the end of his baton into one palm in quite a threatening fashion. He nodded to our constable and eyed Miss Truitt up and down. He ignored me as thoroughly as if I were a sparrow on some distant branch.

"Lady Greyson was firm in her wish," explained Constable Gillie. "Miss Truitt here is to have a look at his nibs."

"She's *what?*" said Sergeant Fellowes. "Going in there?"

"Alone," said Miss Truitt, from behind her veil.

Sergeant Fellowes looked at Constable Gillie and Gillie nodded curtly. Sergeant Fellowes looked hard at me (for the first time) and the constable said, "Not her."

"I'll wait here," I said to Miss Truitt. "I've seen him already."

She made a noise that I discerned to be laughter, but she covered it smoothly with a tearful sob. Constable Gillie backed away and left us. Sergeant Fellowes opened the door, which creaked on its hinges and welcomed the grieving charlatan into a world of straw and dung.

Straw, dung and a dead body. I peered into the dark before the sergeant pulled the door shut. Was Mr. Corker on the floor or on a table? Perhaps a bench? Was he wrapped in a sheet or his own coat? Had Miss Truitt hidden her notebook in the folds of her mourning gown? What details would she be writing down, to preserve her memory of the scene? Had she seen a dead body before now?

Sergeant Fellowes stamped his feet against the creeping cold, and I stamped mine.

I could not boast that I felt proud of participating in Miss Truitt's deceit, and yet . . . her devotion to her task was wholly admirable. Certainly, the report of a murder could not be so vivid if one did not meet the corpse. I wished I could tell James or Grannie Jane the extent of her research, but I could not. My admiration was at odds with my loyalty. By assisting Mr. Fibbley to tell as true a story as possible, I was being untrue to my family.

The stable door flew open and Miss Truitt was with us again. She tugged the veil over her pale face as if to extinguish her connection to the world.

Another door banged and Mr. Mooney approached from the kitchen, arms wrapped around the enormous plaster goose from the Blue Carbuncle tableau, in which he'd starred as Sherlock Holmes. Our small company turned to stare and he stared back, with most particular attention to Miss Beatrice Truitt, head to foot in black mourning weeds. Miss Truitt's foot pressed firmly upon my toe, so surprising me that I nearly laughed.

"Good afternoon, sir," she said.

"Good afternoon." Mr. Mooney seemed somewhat puzzled to be addressed by a woman who was a stranger.

"Oh, er, hello," I said. "Miss Truitt, this is Mr. Sebastian Mooney, actor and friend of your . . . of the decease—of Mr. Corker. Mr. Mooney, sir, may I introduce Miss Truitt."

Miss Truitt extended her gloved hand. "I regret the circumstance under which we meet, Mr. Mooney. My Roger has spoken of you so often."

Mr. Mooney gaped. "*Your* Roger?" he said. "Who the devil—" He glanced at me and back again to peer at Miss Truitt, as if by gawping harder he might penetrate the crape of her weeping veil.

"Miss . . . Turret?" he said.

"Truitt," said she and I together, though how I spoke I do not know, as my heart was skittering like a rat in a trap. *Thumping like a dog's tail on a plank floor. Beating like autumn rain against a windowpane.*

"Forgive me, Miss Truitt," said Mr. Mooney. "But I have known Roger for . . . eight years? Nine? In all that time he has never once mentioned that he had a lady-friend, though there were occasions when together we dallied with—"

He looked at me and stopped his tongue, and even had the grace to flush. Surely it was discourteous to tell a young woman of the other young women who may have come before her in a man's affections?

"I was a secret," said Miss Truitt. "I still am, truth be told, on account of my husband who is still living."

Truth be told? When would that happen? A *husband*??

Sergeant Fellowes's eyes bulged, while Mr. Mooney's narrowed.

Miss Truitt hurtled on. "I have lost my dearest friend," she said. "And now that I've said farewell, I shall be on my way. No need to encumber the family with my grief a moment longer." She took in a deep breath and turned so quickly that it took half a second for her skirt to catch up. I jumped to her side, recognizing an attempt to escape.

"Miss Truitt," said Mr. Mooney. "Your hat and veil."

Her gloved hand flew to touch the brim of her widow's cap.

"Nothing is amiss," I told her.

Sergeant Fellowes stomped his feet and briskly rubbed his hands together. "Cold," he muttered. "Devilish cold."

"I recognize your hat," said Mr. Mooney. "I believe it to be part of the costume for our tableau of Queen Victoria at the graveside of Prince Albert."

I felt that devilish cold from the roots of my hair to the soles of my feet. Mr. Mooney knew Miss Truitt to be a fraud.

She did not falter. "A keen eye, sir," she said. "As an ardent admirer of the esteemed late queen, I wished to honor my dear love as she honored hers. Good day to you." She strode toward the kitchen door, which was the nearest. I trotted behind like a tipsy duckling.

"Who *are* you?" called Mr. Mooney. My foot tripped on the kitchen doorstep as I crossed. I saw the actor thrust the giant goose into Sergeant Fellowes's unwilling arms.

"He means to chase us!" I hissed.

Miss Truitt raced ahead, the length of the kitchen and through the baize door to the Upstairs part of the house. I followed in haste, apologizing to Cook as I flew past. Miss Truitt galloped—*galloped*!—along the passage toward the Great Hall. She turned a corner with a swish of her silk skirt, and disappeared.

I heard Mr. Mooney's voice booming behind me. "Hello, hello! Sorry all! Which way did the ladies travel, can you tell me? We're playing a silly game of Duck, Duck, Goose!"

He mustn't find me! I would *die* of mortification if he found me. Or certainly faint dead away as Annabelle had in the library when she saw Mr. Corker's body. I ran up one passage and down another. The constable outside the library door was thankfully dozing and didn't see me hurry past. Finally, I recognized the familiar door of the morning room and flung myself inside.

Another door opened and banged shut nearby. Footsteps, and then an even closer door. Mr. Mooney was checking every room! I prayed that Miss Truitt had made her escape. One breath later I turned the cabinet handle with a giddy tug. More footsteps. From the dark of the secret passage, I pulled the door shut with not a moment's grace.

"Hello?" said Mr. Mooney's voice, inside the morning room. And then a muffled clunk as he presumably moved on. I sank to the floor, a trickle of unladylike perspiration running down my spine. Slowly, my breathing returned to normal. All that running and I'd been wrapped in Dot's shawl. I shook it off and lay it across my knees, thinking hard. One question had been answered. Miss Truitt's clothing had come from the theatrical trunks. She must have crept into the coach house and helped herself.

Mr. Mooney had known at once that Miss Truitt was not who she claimed to be. He'd likely been Mr. Corker's closest acquaintance, he and Annabelle. He'd have met a sweetheart—or would certainly have heard news of her. Spotting familiar garments from the troupe's own collection had naturally stirred his suspicions. Did he think her guilty of murder? Then why had he not sent Sergeant Fellowes racing after us instead of coming himself? Knowing she was an imposter, who did he imagine her true self to be?

Miss Truitt had not killed Mr. Corker. But only I—and the murderer—were certain of that. Even Hector did not yet know, because her true identity was hidden behind her veil. So, why had Mr. Mooney not (thank goodness) asked the trickster to show her face? Had he seemed more afraid than angry? Did he, too, have something to hide?

I shivered. The chill of snow-damp stockings propelled me to stand and move my legs, to pull the shawl back over my shoulders. How would I explain my absence to Marjorie and Grannie Jane? My rumbling stomach told me that lunch must be well over. I surely would be missed by now. Had Miss Truitt been cornered by Mr. Mooney? I did not like to emerge until the chance of an encounter had passed. Perhaps I should remain concealed for just a little longer.

And, since I was here . . . Might I learn anything by peeking into the library or James's study? I found the torch on its hook and pressed the button. Nothing. Its failing beam on our previous excursion had now expired. Instead of light, my fingertips upon the wall would serve as guides.

The shades in the study were drawn, making it as dark as night except for threads of light outlining the windows. It appeared that James had not been there today. Peering into the library, I deduced from the evidence that someone had visited recently. The grate sparkled with embers and the curtains were pulled back. The table lamp glowed as it had when first we entered on Christmas morning, its glass shade casting a bright pool of green.

I pressed one cheek and then the other to the spy-hole, trying to see as far to the sides as I might. My chest and arms were also pressed against the wall, as snugly as a body could be. In this way, I felt a handle jabbing my stomach.

The spy-hole was embedded in a door!

CHAPTER 28

A PLETHORA OF PLOT TWISTS

LUCY COULD NOT POSSIBLY know that this end of the secret passage opened into the library—or would she not have shown us? Dare I enter? The room was empty. Had Mr. Mooney already checked the library and gone on his way?

I turned the handle ever so slowly, expecting resistance from disuse, or a creak of protest. It rotated smoothly and quietly. I stepped into the library and turned to see what sort of door I'd come through. It was disguised as a bookcase that held the complete works of William Shakespeare and other fat leather-bound books with gilt lettering on the spines. The spy-hole was well hidden in the shadow above a volume of *The Moonstone* by Wilkie Collins.

Being certain the bookcase was again firmly in place, I turned to examine the scene before me, as if it were a theatrical stage awaiting actors to enter from the wings. The carpet had been scrubbed, I knew, but Mr. Corker's final resting place was still evident, the wool now darkened with water rather than blood. A tiny crackle from the grate made me jump. I was not truly certain that the spirit of a murdered man might not linger for a time in the place where he had died. How helpful that would be! *What happened here, if I may inquire?* The cushion on the big leather chair was still squashed down. On Christmas morning, the contents of the nearby glass had been identified as rum by Inspector Willard. Reporters' gossip, repeated by Miss Truitt, lingered in my head. *A genial chap, a little too fond of drink.* It had likely been Mr. Corker lounging in the chair, squashing the cushion flat. Before or after his argument with Mr. Mooney?

And what of the magnifying glass on the other table, beneath the bright green lamp? Had Mr. Corker used it to examine some volume from the bookshelf? And then— because the magnifier had not been on the same table as the one that held the glass of rum—he crossed the room to remove his boots and fall asleep in his chair? Was he finally relaxing? Or still fuming at Mr. Mooney for scolding him?

I closed my eyes to think through Mr. Corker's final half hour . . .

Perhaps the third drink had not been a good idea, but, dash it! Mooney had no right to boss him about! The weary actor pulled off his boots and rubbed a hand across the stubble on his chin, his head a little foggy. Where was his partner in this crime caper? Had that nervous young footman encountered trouble during the burglary? Had he run into Mooney on the stairs?

Or, was Frederick alone in this endeavor—and the author of a terrible mistake?

The nervous young footman entered the library with his heart pounding. He had taken the emerald from the foreigner's bureau in a moment of daring and now . . . Oh, horror! The man from Ceylon was here before him, still clad in pirate garb, and at any moment would turn to catch him red-handed. He took up a weapon and struck, realizing too late that he'd been fooled by the costume and attacked the wrong man!

Or had Mr. Corker been waiting for Miss Annabelle Day?

The actor pulled off his boots, with a sigh of anticipation. He rubbed a hand across the stubble on his chin, his head a little foggy. An irresistible opportunity had presented itself here at Owl Park, tied up like a Christmas package. Even if Annabelle encountered the scowling Mr. Mooney on her way downstairs, she could handle him easily. In her pocket would be a chance to leave the fickle world of theater. She'd pulled off the jewel heist of a lifetime!

Or had Miss Day been working alone, and Mr. Corker only an unhappy witness?

The actor's earring flashed in the candlelight as he looked up, surprised, when the library door opened. Miss Annabelle Day did not notice him, but strode purposefully toward the single lamp glowing in the darkened room. From her pocket she withdrew . . . the Echo Emerald! But how did this infamous gem come to be in her possession? Roger Corker lurched to his feet with a grunt and stumbled toward his friend. "What have you done?" he cried.

Suppose he had wrestled her for it? Neither of them realizing that the stone they battled for was merely a copy?

Merely a copy . . .

What if . . . Oh! What if the magnifying glass had been used—not to peer at a book, but at the Echo Emerald instead? Who, other than the Sivams, might have discovered that the gemstone was a copy before Sir Mayhew arrived?

The man from Ceylon crept into the library and took up the silver-handled magnifying glass from where it lay next to the pens and inkwell on the desk. Mr. Corker, in a fog of rum, watched as the owner of the infamous Echo Emerald carefully examined his own precious jewel under the light cast by the green-shaded lamp . . .

But, how would that lead to murder?

Mr. Corker, in a fog of rum, crept into the library and took up the silver-handled magnifying glass from where it lay next to the inkwell on the desk. With a trembling hand, he withdrew from his pocket his newly stolen prize, the beautiful Echo

Emerald. The door swung open with a bang, and in strode Mr. Sivam, his hair tousled and the cord of his dressing gown trailing. "You dunderhead!" he thundered. "How dare you! Return my gem at once!"

And then a tussle, where Mr. Corker tried to frighten Mr. Sivam by drawing his dagger, but dropped it, perhaps . . . and Mr. Sivam, seized with fury, stabbed the actor, and . . . sat calmly down to examine his jewel?

I could hear Hector's voice inside my head: *This is not logical.*

None of my storylines made sense all the way through. It was most disheartening. I sat on the chair at the library desk and looked in the drawer for paper, but found none. I should not go anywhere without my notebook. I needed to have a Detection Consultation with Hector. We might scavenge some biscuits and cocoa at the same time. I rolled one of the pens back and forth, my fingertips tracing the delicate owl embossed in silver.

Surely Mr. Mooney had given up his chase by now.

And Miss Beatrice Truitt safely gone away?

Miss Truitt.

I had put her out of my mind for a few minutes, but now she waltzed back in. Not Miss Truitt herself, really, but the reporter who had used her as a disguise to gain entry to Owl Park. The reporter longing to uncover the true story of Mr. Corker's demise, to tell it from a unique vantage point.

That's what she'd said while we were squished together in the lavatory. *Not one of those men out there could do what I have done.* And was that not what real writers looked for, to write about? A part of the story that had so far gone unseen.

I laid my hand across the row of pens and tools, the silver owls cool beneath my palm. My fingers rested on the paper knife. The sharp, narrow blade was meant to cut the edges of new book pages, as common in a library as books themselves. A shiver ran down and up my arms.

"You dunderhead!"

The actor pulled his dagger from its sheath at his waist, fumbling slightly as he wished away the rum that fogged his head. His foe looked about for a weapon and seized the silver-handled paper knife from the desk. One urgent swipe and the deed was done, the artery severed, the man's blood spilling to the ground . . .

I went to the window and held the knife under the light. This was not a time for fancy, I told myself. I must see only what was there to see. And so I did. The merest smear of black near the hilt could perhaps be ink, but . . . might also be something far more ominous.

I turned with a jolt to the door that masqueraded as a bookcase. I must take the knife to Inspector Willard right away. I untied the ribbon from one of my braids and wrapped it several times around the sharp edges of the paper knife. I slid the blade down the side of my boot, where it bulged uncomfortably. No matter. It would not be there for long.

Certainty surged through me like fresh air through a newly opened window. I had uncovered the missing murder weapon! I stood before the complete works of William Shakespeare, patting and shifting the volumes with ever more frantic fingers. Where was the latch to open the door?

Where was the latch??? I recalled the handle on the inside, digging into my stomach, but search as I might, I could find no handle or knob on this side, nothing to aid my departure. Only one person, I supposed, knew the secret to opening this secret door, and that person was James. But for now, I had a knife to deliver and an urgent wish to speak with Hector.

Only one person, I thought, knew how to enter and exit the library without being seen. I felt a rush of cold so harsh it brought tears to my eyes. Was I truly considering James as a killer?

CHAPTER 29

A Determined Duet

Ridiculous! Impossible! Absurd and out of the question.

Just because a person knew something that no one else knew, did not mean that he used his secret to kill people! A killer must have a *reason* to kill—or to steal a valuable gemstone. James did not have reason to do either of those things. And yes, he had access to the paper knife with the silver owl on its handle, but so did everybody else in the house! It was sitting right there on the desk!

"Aggie."

My name, quite clearly spoken, made me clutch my chest in fright. I looked to the door, but no one was there.

"Aggie, here." Accompanied by tapping. From the bookcase right in front of me. "Are you alone?"

I peered carefully, and yes! I could distinguish a bright green eye peering back at me from the spy-hole above the novel by Wilkie Collins!

"Hector! Let me in!"

Obeying my instructions, he found the handle on the other side and opened the door. I did not let him exclaim or enjoy the new find, but dragged him quickly through the secret passage to the morning room.

Back in the light, he laughed. "You have the smudge," he said.

I rubbed at the spot.

"Now it is worse." He led me to a gilt-framed mirror mounted on the wall.

I had a grimy smear under my eye, from all my spying. Hector offered his pocket handkerchief which I used with vigor. Despite its grubbiness, he folded it neatly and returned it to his pocket.

"And your hair," he said. "It is . . . loose."

Half of it, anyway, because I'd used the ribbon elsewhere.

"I have so much to tell you," I said, the paper knife digging into my calf.

"Miss Truitt is gone," said Hector, at the same moment. "She leaves before the police can speak with her. This makes the good detective inspector most disconsolate. I am puzzled where you might be. Mr. Mooney is looking in every room. From a window, I see the bereaved lady hurrying toward the woods. A most irregular enterprise, but I say nothing, as you are not here to share counsel. But where, I ask myself, is Aggie most likely to be hiding that no one finds her?"

"Good," I said. "You found me!"

"The inspector and his constables go chasing down the drive and have not yet returned."

The knife would have to wait a while longer.

"What was Miss Truitt wearing?" I said.

"There is a logical reason to ask such a question? She is wearing the same dark and cumbersome ensemble as when last we met."

He went to the window and pulled aside the drape. Outside, the afternoon met dusk with snowy yellow light that dimpled the blanketed gardens. Plump flakes quite sedately continued to fall.

"Where the low wall divides the garden, you see?" Hector said. "That is where Miss Truitt is running. In such ugly weather! She will be cold."

"I expect she has hidden her other clothes," I said, "under a rock or behind a tree, though I suppose they'll be heavily dusted with snow."

Up went his eyebrow. I told him as much as I knew. Miss Truitt was Mr. Fibbley in disguise. Or, Mr. Fibbley was Miss Fibbley in disguise (not believing for a moment that

Fibbley was her real name), who was briefly pretending to be Miss Truitt. In any version, she had no intention of speaking with Inspector Willard, nor could she provide any insight or information about the murder. She was merely a sly reporter, fulfilling what she believed to be her duty to report the news. She had failed the test of Mr. Mooney's scrutiny and made her getaway as speedily as she was able.

"She borrowed clothing from the trunks already packed in the coach house," I said. "That's how Mr. Mooney knew she was a fraud. She'll be a man again by now. And we have pledged to keep her secret, remember?"

"I am—how do you say in English? Étonné?"

"Astonished," I said.

"Also, I am an idiot," said Hector.

"Not at all," I said. "I only realized because she looked me straight in the eye and *dared* me to realize."

"But, as you say, this escapade does not tell us what happened to Mr. Corker, or why."

"I think I know more about that than I did an hour ago." I pulled the paper knife from its odd sheath and put it into his hands. "What do you think of this as a murder weapon?"

"Ooh la la," he said.

"You see, there?" I pointed at what I'd swear to be blood.

"I wonder," said Hector, "if we might find a room with a fire?"

It seemed a small request in a house so grand but each firelit room we peeped into seemed also to contain a person. When we passed the footman, Norman, I asked him to tell Marjorie I'd gone upstairs to wash my hands— to keep her from worrying that I'd not reappeared after escorting Miss Truitt to see the corpse. That gave us the idea of going to the nursery, where we found a fire burning and some shortbread biscuits in a tin.

I pulled my notebook out from under my pillow—at the same time sliding the paper knife beneath my quilt, halfway down the bed.

I wrote the heading: <u>Things That Seem Odd</u>. And below that I made a list:

1. disappearance of Mr. Sivam
2. "wrong boots"
3. missing pirate shirt
4. false Echo Emerald
5. genuine Echo Emerald?
6. disappearance of the magnifying glass
7. false murder weapon
8. probably true murder weapon
9. chloroform missing from Dr. Musselman's bag

"Ready?" I said. "It's a terribly long list. And we must speak with Stephen to discover anything more about boots."

"I believe we may also dismiss for now the pirate shirt and the magnifying glass," said Hector. "These items we must locate, but what is there to say?"

"Well, I've had a thought about the magnifier," I said. "What if someone used it that night, not to look in the dictionary, but to examine the Echo Emerald? Or to examine *two* Echo Emeralds? Identifying the true one and leaving the copy behind? Would knowing a jewel was true or false be a reason to kill someone?"

Hector's eyebrows did a small dance while he considered. "There may be a circumstance where this is so," he said, after a while. "As we continue, such a reason may become clear."

"The more I think about it," I said, "the more certain I am that both stones were brought to Owl Park. Mrs. Sivam knew that. Her only surprise was that the one stolen from the box was the copy. If Mr. Sivam made the switch without telling her, he probably still has it with him."

"Why does Mr. Sivam leave without writing a note for his wife," said Hector, "or asking a servant to deliver a message? Or alerting his old friend, Lord Greyson? It is a puzzling lapse in manners for so genteel a man."

"It does seem very strange," I added, "that he left by some means other than his own motorcar. Especially as he so dislikes the cold. But how could a person be missing inside a house? On the other side, if he has *not* departed from Owl Park, he must either be dead—or he is the villain! He's hiding in the wine cellar, wearing a bloody shirt. Or lurking on the servants' stairs, ready to push innocent boys to their doom."

"We know he is not wearing a bloody shirt," said Hector. "He is perfectly clean and well-attired on Christmas morning."

"Unless he'd already had a bath to wash off Mr. Corker's blood," I said. I looked at my notebook, and wrote: *the matter of Mr. Sivam, to be pursued.*

"Chloroform is on the list because it is missing from Dr. Musselman's bag, one more item that is not where it should be, causing great misery for old Lady Greyson."

"Possibly the doctor, he is forgetful, does not bring the bottle he imagines?"

"He gave her a dose when he first got here, so he did bring it. But his bag was in a terrible jumble," I said. "It took three of us to find the smelling salts. Perhaps the chloroform has been there all along. I don't see how toothache medicine is connected anyway, do you?"

"Chloroform is not only for the aching tooth," said Hector. "It is used to remove pain by permitting the patient to go to sleep. But let us worry another time about that. We have still the mystery of killing a man with two blades."

"Do you suppose Mr. Corker was the object of such loathing that two different killers crept in and stabbed him?"

"The second killer is awfully foolish not to notice that he is plunging his dagger into a dead man," said Hector.

"I'm afraid none of our suspects can be described as foolish," I said, "though Frederick, I suppose, is a teeny bit thick. Wouldn't it make a deliciously morbid story, though? If there were a despicable millionaire with lots of enemies, and they all took turns killing him in different ways, not realizing?"

"This plot is not believable," said Hector. "And meanwhile, we have no solution to the puzzle before us."

"The one puzzle we do have a solution for," I said, "we can never tell the police or anyone else. The identity of Miss Beatrice Truitt."

Hector grinned. "I predict," he said, "that when the actors next create a tableau that includes a mourning widow, the meticulous Miss Day will find that her gown and veil are not folded to her liking."

"Or she won't find the costume at all, if Fibbley leaves it in the wood," I said. "Buried under snow until spring! And perhaps Miss Day will be in prison for theft and murder, and a rumpled weeping veil won't matter at all."

"Another gong!" said Hector. "What now?"

"It's the dressing bell, for dinner. Aren't we lucky not to be dining down tonight?"

Lucy arrived one minute later. James had allowed, in gratitude for her hours of attending to her grandmother, that Lucy could have dinner with the grown-ups. Hector went to his room while Lucy changed into a peacock blue velvet frock—and filled my ears with gossip.

The blizzard had prevented Detective Inspector Willard, his team of sergeants, and Constables Gillie and Worth from driving or riding back to the village. There were not enough snowshoes to go around.

"Poor Aunt Marjorie has to sort out where they'll all sleep. Uncle James came to warn Grandmamma so she'd have time to adjust her mood, he said, because the detective inspector will be at table with us. Grandmamma is even more vexed than usual. What a surprise. Uncle James said the police are performing a noble service and the least we can do is to feed them and find them beds. Grandmamma said they were only here because Aunt Marjorie thinks that theater was a suitable entertainment, and that actors always mean trouble, especially ones who ended up being murdered. Uncle James was furious that his mother was being narky about his wife, and that's when Grandmamma sent me to find her barley water so I wouldn't hear more. Will you do my ribbons?"

I did her ribbons, which were lovely and wide and matched the dress, but very fiddly to keep tied properly. Especially as my mind was fiddling with a different puzzle. If the police were remaining in Owl Park all night, might

I have an opportunity to speak with Detective Inspector Willard about the paper knife?

Lucy went off downstairs and Hector came back just as Dot delivered our suppers. Hector was transported with happiness at the taste of macaroni with cheese sauce. I composed a couplet while we ate:

You never feel groany
When you eat macaroni.

Then we had chocolate cake for pudding and were utterly sated.

When Dot came back to clear our supper things, she brought the news we'd been longing to hear. Stephen was awake! He looked like a mushroom, Dot said, with his head still swaddled in layers of brown paper. Cheeky as ever.

Hector and I must visit right away. We had two important questions to ask.

CHAPTER 30

A Happy Awakening

IT WAS LONG PAST the time when adults were accustomed to seeing children upright, but Dot led us down through the kitchen, where Effie and another girl were tackling a heap of washing up.

"A visit will cheer Stephen's spirits, that's what matters," said Dot. "If he's not working in the morning, I'll twist his nose."

"You won't be the only one," said her brother, appearing with more dishes from the dining room. "I've been stuck doing all the shoe polishing tonight, in his place, the little dunderhead."

I froze. Hector froze beside me. Of all the words in the English language . . .

"I've got a bump the size of a turnip!" Stephen was still on a mat in the butler's pantry. He pushed away his head-wrapping to reveal matted hair on the back of his skull. "Go on, touch it!"

Hector allowed Stephen to guide his fingers to the afflicted spot. I imagined what it must feel like and shivered, finding it spongy and horrible.

"Did they catch her?" said Stephen.

"Catch whom?" said Hector.

"The woman, what pushed me down the stairs." Stephen's earnest eyes darted back and forth between Hector and me.

"*Who?*" I said.

"I been puzzling why she were after me."

"A woman?" said Hector. "What woman?"

"I didn't see her, did I?" said Stephen. "She got me from behind, just where the landing takes a turn. I hears a footstep, I hears her murmuring sounds, then hands on my back and *whoomph!*"

"Ouch!" I tried to bat away the memory of Stephen at the bottom of the stairs, lying as still as a scrubbing brush.

A pot clattered in the kitchen and we heard Cook's voice scolding Effie.

"Miss?" said Stephen.

"We thought it was an accident," I said.

"It's an accident my neck weren't broke," said Stephen. "I'd like to break *her* neck, that's what."

I looked to be sure the door was shut between us and the rest of the kitchen staff.

"You're certain you were pushed?"

"By a woman?" said Hector.

"As certain as my name is Stephen."

Who would do that? One of the servants? But why? Marjorie? Ridiculous. Mrs. Sivam? Because even if Annabelle had stolen the jewel and killed Mr. Corker—not yet proven—she'd been on the third floor under guard when Stephen fell . . . and why would she hurt a harmless boy? Had bumping his head filled his brain with nonsense?

"What did she say?" I asked him. "This mysterious woman?"

"No words," he said. "Just a sound, really."

Perhaps only imagined. Should we again consider Frederick as the fiend we were looking for? Had he been in the kitchen when the accident happened? Mr. Mooney certainly had—sitting right there next to us, slurping his soup. But no, Cook had been calling for Frederick a few minutes before and not finding him.

"Who knows you're awake?" asked Hector.

"Everyone, I suppose." Stephen tugged his paper bandage back into place. "Mrs. Frost has been right kind, considering I'm only lamps and boots."

"Did you tell them all you'd been pushed?" I said.

"I suppose I did."

"I do not like this." Hector's eyes strayed to the closed door.

Stephen looked miserable, thanks to his bulging violet-rimmed right eye.

"The voices you overheard in the library," I asked him. "What did they say?"

Stephen shrugged. "Only word I heard was *dunderhead*, thrown like a curse. I put meself out of the way, quick as quick."

"Did you *see* anyone on Christmas Eve when you collected the boots?"

"Someone female, perhaps?" said Hector. "A servant? Anyone?"

"I didn't see no one," said Stephen. "Nobody caught her?"

"They're looking for a murderer and a jewel thief," I said. "Not a person who pushed a boy down the stairs. We all thought your tumble was an accident."

Stephen's face crinkled in disgust. "I'd never've stumbled, not ever. It weren't no accident."

"What did you mean when you said *the wrong boots*?"

"Mr. Corker's boots was upstairs in the passage next to the ones what Mr. Sivam was wearing. Only Mr. Corker's feet were lying dead on the library carpet with some other toff's boots next to him. Mixed-up, see?"

"But weren't all the pirate boots the same?" I asked.

"That's what I was waiting to explain to the police," said Stephen. "They weren't the same. Because of the bumps."

The bumps, Stephen told us, were bunions, a pitiable affliction that happens sometimes to old feet like Mr. Corker's. Bunions pushed the bones into painful bumps beside each of Mr. Corker's big toes. His regular shoes and his costume boots had the sides stretched out to make room so the bunions would not pinch or chafe. His boots could only be his, and they were *not* the ones next to the body in the library.

"No wonder you were confused," I said.

"The owner of the boots found next to Mr. Corker may also be the villain," said Hector, "and wants to keep you quiet."

"You keep yourself safely hidden away in here," I said. "We'll spread the word that you're sleeping again. Try not to wake up, no matter who comes in, unless it's us, or Lucy, and we're alone. You understand?"

"I does," said Stephen. "You just find that woman afore she finds me." He closed his eyes and curled up under his blanket.

In the passage beyond the baize door, I kept my voice low, though the servants had all retired and light in the kitchen was dim.

"Bunions!" I said.

"A happy discovery," agreed Hector. "Though not, alas, for poor Mr. Corker."

"How did Mr. Corker's boots arrive on the mat outside Mr. Sivam's room?" I said. "And whose boots were next to his corpse?"

"I think not the boots of Annabelle," said Hector. "They were the size for a man."

"But hers were too, remember? The toes stuffed with newspaper?"

"We must investigate," said Hector. "Compile the facts. Activate the friction of the brain cells."

"My investigation," I said, "will take me to visit Annabelle before I go to bed. We must be absolutely certain that she was locked up during the time of Stephen's fall, not sneaking about or bribing the guard."

"It seems that the servants and also Mr. Mooney must now be in their beds," said Hector. "I will visit the coach house and examine the boots returned to Miss Day by the police, tied up with string."

"Let's hope the police are also sleeping," I said, realizing I had no idea which rooms Marjorie had assigned the inspector and his men.

"We shall confer shortly," said Hector.

We shook hands and went our separate ways.

Sergeant Shaw sat on a chair directly in front of Annabelle's door, his big feet planted on the plank floor.

"No visitors," said Sergeant Shaw, standing up. "Except with the inspector's approval." His head nearly met the low ceiling of the servants' hallway.

"Who's out there?" called Annabelle's voice from behind the door.

"He approves," I lied. "Annabelle, it's me, Aggie Morton."

"Let her in," said Annabelle. "I've got a few things to say."

"I need to see a note," said Sergeant Shaw, "from the inspector."

"Aw, Sergeant, honey?" said Annabelle. "This would be one of those times when you can use your intuition and your generosity in the same action. Let the child in. She will not assist in a daring escape."

The sergeant's ears went pink. He glanced at the chair. Moving it, we both knew, meant an admission that his authority on the third floor of Owl Park amounted to nothing.

"Charley?" said Annabelle.

"Oh, dash it," said Sergeant Shaw. He shifted the chair and tapped on the door. He turned the handle and let me into the room. There wasn't a lock. That's what the chair was for.

Annabelle Day gave me a squeeze and the sergeant a wink. "You see?" she said to him. "Not a threat to my person or yours. Leave the door open if you must. Then no one can accuse you of shirking your official duty."

His hand lifted in the beginning of a salute, but he caught himself and flushed, tripping over his own boots in leaving the tiny room. There was space for a cot, a small bureau, a washstand, and two people standing close together or both sitting on the bed, which is what we did.

"What are you doing up and about at half past ten at night, young lady?"

"You sound like Grannie Jane," I said. "I'm already twelve."

She laughed. "Well then, Miss Twelve, what are you doing visiting an accused-and-imprisoned-but-entirely-innocent person?"

"I've come to check your alibi," I said.

Now she really laughed. "That'll rankle the handsome sergeant," said Annabelle. "He's stuck up here guarding the wicked Miss Day, and they've replaced him with a girl detective! My alibi for when, ducky?"

"To you, it might sound silly," I said. "I don't know if you stole the emerald, but we don't think you did. And something else bad has happened, so we're checking where people were at a particular time."

Annabelle lifted an eyebrow the way Hector often did, a question and a comment with the same flick. "Who is 'we,' exactly?"

My turn to blush. "Well, Hector and I," I admitted. "We have this idea, and—"

"What else bad has happened?" she said. "Inspector Willard didn't mention anything when he questioned me yesterday."

"The inspector may not have been told," I said. "Everyone thought it was a kitchen accident until Stephen woke up this evening." I told her about the fall, and how Stephen said he hadn't fallen. I did not tell her that Stephen claimed a woman had done the deed.

"When was this?" said Annabelle.

"Yesterday afternoon."

"I'm a prisoner," she said. "I've been up here, not lurking about on staircases."

"Yes, but we wanted to be certain."

"What time did it happen?" She glanced at the thin towel hanging on the bar of the washstand.

"Just after lunch in the kitchen," I said. "About two o'clock."

"Charley?" she called.

Sergeant Shaw poked his head around the door frame.

"Do you remember what time it was yesterday when your kind heart allowed me to take a bath?" said Annabelle.

"It'd be after the lunch tray," said the sergeant. "'Round about two? Half past?"

"There's a little bath chamber along the passage," she explained to me. "I took my time, I can tell you. First wash in nearly a week. What were you doing while I was in there?" she asked her prison guard.

"I went to stretch my legs for a bit," said Sergeant Shaw. "Out for a smoke with those reporters. Had a bit of a laugh with Fellowes about him guarding a corpse while I watched you." His face reddened again. "Came back upstairs while you were still in there. Singing," he said.

"There you go," said Annabelle, sliding an arm about my shoulder. "That's my alibi. An officer of the law."

"Thank you," I said. "That seems watertight, if you'll excuse the pun."

She laughed. "Shouldn't you be getting off to bed?"

I said good night and hurried away. Annabelle had not been the mysterious woman to push Stephen. She'd been in the bathtub.

But if not Annabelle . . . then who? Was Stephen mistaken about the muttering he'd heard? Or was it done by a man who made himself sound like a woman? Had

Stephen even been pushed? Maybe he was the sort of boy who made things up. We'd only known him a few days. Could we base our theories on someone who might not be trustworthy?

I crossed the landing that separated the servants' quarters from the nursery rooms, wondering whether Hector had news to trade with mine. But no light shone beneath his door. I guessed he wouldn't like me to knock if he were in his nightshirt or already sleeping. We would consult in the morning.

Lucy pounced the instant I came into the nursery and closed the door.

"Where have you been? It's nearly eleven o'clock! Grandmamma would faint dead away if she knew you were roaming the halls at this time of night."

"I was not *roaming*," I said. "I was on a mission, to the kitchen."

"You saw Stephen? Dot said he woke up."

"Just for a short while . . ." If I put about a rumor that Stephen was still loopy, perhaps it would help to keep him safe? "He was awake, so we rushed down, but he was talking wildly and then *ffft*—back to sleep, like a candle being guttered."

"Oh dear," said Lucy.

"I'm sure he'll rally," I said. "Eventually. Was there any excitement at dinner?"

"Grandmamma was still cross with James for inviting the policemen to stay but couldn't behave crossly with Inspector Willard chomping on duck two places over. She was also cross with Dr. Musselman for losing her toothache medicine. Mrs. Sivam was cross with Uncle James for not permitting Mr. Mooney to join the civilized company, as she called it, rather than being banished to the kitchen. She said if Frederick was allowed to serve—being a murder suspect—then surely Mr. Mooney deserved to eat a hot dinner. Frederick took away the soup plates and never came back. Your Grannie Jane did her best to be merry with the inspector, asking him about a Dr. Palmer who was hanged as a poisoner—but that set off Dr. Musselman defending his profession." Lucy paused to plump up her pillow. "Also, the first course was snails, which is never a pleasant thing."

"Goodness, Lucy, you could write the gossip column for a ladies' magazine!"

"I could, couldn't I?" she said, but soon enough, her vigor subsided. She snuggled under her quilt and went to sleep.

I brought notepaper into my bed and wrote to Mummy, using a pillow for my desk. I shared a little more truth than in my first report, but, admittedly, not all the truth I knew.

December 27, 1902

Dear Mummy,

I hope this letter finds you well and not too lonesome. Tony is an excellent companion and never sassy.

You'll have had news from Marjorie and may also have seen the <u>Torquay Voice</u>. Now you know that I was not all the way truthful in my previous letter. Please forgive me, Mummy? Grannie Jane said my fibs were for a good cause as I was trying to preserve your calm.

The police have put Miss Day, the actress, under guard. They think she stole the emerald, though she claims that someone else is trying to falsely implicate her and that she is innocent. Mr. Corker's killer has not yet been discovered, but <u>please</u> do not worry about me. I am well and safe and most admiring of Marjorie being Lady Greyson in such a way as to make you (and Papa) and James, and even herself, quite proud.

I shall write again soon with every detail.

With many kisses to you and Tony,

Your loving,

Aggie

Only after folding the letter, and then losing my pencil over the side of the bed, did another scenario creep into my head . . .

The wily actress wore a pink blouse and a gray gabardine skirt, a little shorter than considered proper and revealing a glimpse of shapely calf from certain angles. Seated on the three-legged stool next to the tub, she swirled her hand in the bath-water, splashing noisily and humming a beguiling tune. As the prison guard's bootsteps receded, the woman dashed to the door. She pressed her ear against the crack to confirm that the passage was empty. Wiping dry her hands on her skirt, she hurried to the men's staircase to await in desperation her chance to silence the boy who knew the terrible truth . . .

Annabelle's alibi was a little shaky after all.

TORQUAY VOICE

DECEMBER 27, 1902

CHRISTMAS CORPSE KEPT IN A STABLE!!!

by Augustus C. Fibbley

Two days after the luckless Mr. Roger Corker was brutally stabbed in the neck, there is speculation that he was a victim of a tragic case of mistaken identity. Mr. Corker wore the costume of a pirate, one among four men so clad, following the performance of a tableau of *Treasure Island* on Christmas Eve. Was one of the other men meant to receive the mortal blow? According to an inside source, the actor's body has been ignominiously placed in the stable at Owl Park near Tiverton, accessible only across a snowy and windblown courtyard. Stall number 5 still bears the label of its previous inhabitant, a bay mare named Captain's Lady.

Lady Greyson was surprised yesterday by a visit from the victim's fiancée, Miss Beatrice Truitt, arrived from Exeter after being informed of Mr.

Corker's demise. It was reported that the young lady was received with heartfelt condolence and permitted to see the body of her beloved to bid farewell.

Miss Truitt, demented with sorrow, agreed to speak with this reporter in the hope that public attention might bring justice upon the head of her sweetheart's killer. Asked if she knew why someone might kill Mr. Corker, the heartbroken woman replied, "He never did anyone wrong. It must have been a grievous mistake—unless he saw something that put him in peril. I hope the wicked murderer meets the hangman." Miss Truitt was further dismayed upon encountering one of Mr. Corker's colleagues, a Mr. Sebastian Mooney. This actor's erratic behavior must be attributed to the tragic loss of his friend, as nothing else could explain why he chased the bereaved Miss Truitt off the premises with words of anger and abuse.

When will the police report success in the Case of the Christmas Corpse?

DECEMBER 28, 1902
SUNDAY

CHAPTER 31

A WORRISOME ABSENCE

I STRETCHED AT THE sound of Dot striking a match. I did not think about the paper knife until I rolled over and my knee touched it. Then, *boing*! I sat up faster than a rubber ball bouncing off a brick wall.

"What time is it?" I said. Hector had not come to wake us as he had on other mornings.

"I went in to light his fire," said Dot. "But he's already gone to breakfast. I never saw a boy so deft at making his own bed. Tight and smooth as a drum."

I brushed my hair in eight strokes and did not wait for Lucy to do her usual hundred. A dedicated sleuth does not waste time on primping. I tidied my own bed with care, keeping the probable murder weapon tucked out of sight. I would report to Inspector Willard as soon as

Hector and I had exchanged our news from last night's excursions.

But Hector was not in the breakfast room.

Grannie Jane had the *Torquay Voice* spread open, last evening's edition, but her attention was turned to Inspector Willard sitting next to her. It was entirely peculiar having him at the breakfast table, demonstrating that inspectors liked to eat oatmeal and ham and eggs just as the rest of us did. (His eggs were poached, mine scrambled.) Despite wishing to see him, this was not the ideal occasion. One thing I mustn't do is mention a bloodied blade in front of Grannie.

"Has anyone seen Hector?" I said.

"Good morning, Agatha," said Grannie Jane. The edge to her voice suggested that my manners had lapsed.

"Good morning, Grannie. Good morning, Detective Inspector. Has Hector been here?"

"We have not yet had the pleasure of Master Perot's company this morning," said Grannie Jane. "Inspector Willard and I have been considering the most recent offering from your friend, Mr. Fibbley."

The policeman's genial expression became instantly inquisitive. "Your friend, Miss Morton? You have friends among the press?"

A flush crept up my neck. Grannie had put me on the spot. "Mr. Fibbley is, um, the gentleman who wrote about certain events in Torquay during the autumn." Why not tell the whole truth? I might rise in his esteem.

"I was able to assist in the solving of a murder, you see. Mr. Fibbley's account acknowledged my endeavors."

"Is that so?" The inspector eyed me with what I liked to imagine was admiration. "You are one up on me, Miss Morton. This is my first murder case."

"And you are doing just fine, Detective Inspector," said Grannie Jane, kindly. "But I am curious . . ." She tapped the newspaper. "When precisely did Mr. Fibbley have the opportunity to interview Miss Truitt? Did he waylay her as she fled from Mr. Mooney?"

"Astutely noted, Mrs. Morton," said Inspector Willard. "I was puzzled by the same question. We did not encounter the reporter during our hunt for the young woman."

"May I please read the article, Grannie Jane? In order that I might follow your conversation?"

She passed me the newspaper. They both waited in silence while my eyes galloped down the page.

Miss Truitt, I read, *demented with sorrow, agreed to speak with this reporter in the hope that . . .* Agreed to speak with this reporter?? She *was* this reporter! My goodness, but Mr. Augustus Fibbley had more twists than a skein of wool.

"Perhaps I may ask you a few questions, Miss Morton?" said Inspector Willard. "To confirm yesterday's timeline?

You and Constable Gillie accompanied Miss Truitt during her visit to Mr. Corker yesterday, did you not?"

His brown eyes were as sharp as I imagined those of a fox might be, if presented with the open door of a chicken coop. How much more brightly they would burn when presented with the knife now hiding beneath my quilt!

"We neither of us went *into* the stable with her, sir." That was a safe chunk of fact. "She wanted privacy for her, uh, farewell."

"Was this reporter in the vicinity at the same time?"

How to answer *that* in a truthful manner?

"I did not see Mr. Fibbley anywhere about, sir."

"But you and Miss Truitt met the actor, Mr. Mooney, when the woman had finished in the stable?"

"Yes, sir."

"And what was your impression of their exchange?"

Had Mr. Mooney already expressed his view to the inspector? Or was Mr. Fibbley's article the only version of the story?

"I would say . . . prickly, sir. But, sir?"

"Miss Morton?"

"My friend, Hector. This disappearance is most unlike him."

"Perhaps he's having a little lie-in," said Inspector Willard. "Have you thought of that?"

"He is not in his bed," I said. "He may have been missing all night."

"Hush, pet." Grannie Jane reached out a hand to soothe me. "He could be off exploring."

"Without me?" I said. "That's an absurd idea."

Constable Gillie poked his head around the door of the breakfast room.

"Miss Day is expecting you upstairs, sir, when you're ready for that interview. We've got Mr. Mooney coming into the Avon Room after that. And three servants to fit in, between their duties."

"Thank you, Constable." Inspector Willard took a last gulp of his coffee. The white shock of hair over his forehead blazed in the light of the chandelier.

"It may have been a miscalculation on my part," he said, "to put the servants on alert for small oddities or alterations within the household. I have received all manner of unrelated reports, most to do with petty grievances against one another. I now must sort through who saw what, where and when." He chuckled at his own tangle of words.

"Like the magnifying glass?" I said.

The inspector's look sharpened. "Precisely," he said. "We have only the word of you children that it was on the table near the corpse, and your word is not to be disregarded. As of this morning, however, the magnifying glass has been discovered in its regular place among the accessories on the desk. It appears your concern about its whereabouts was exaggerated by circumstance. Quite a simple thing to happen."

In its regular place? But it had not been there yesterday when I'd examined the . . . the accessories on the desk! Who had replaced it? This was all too confusing!

"But what about the blade that dealt the deadly blow, sir? I, uh, wondered . . . um, since there were two wounds, were there perhaps two weapons?"

Inspector Willard stood up. "I realize, Miss Morton, that you may feel you are practiced in the business of detection, but we are concerned here with a violent act of murder. I would ask, for your own safety, that you and your chums refrain from snooping and sleuthing. Ours is a serious business and not an entertainment."

"Thank you, Inspector," said Grannie Jane. "I believe Agatha understands your suggestion perfectly clearly."

My cheeks burned as I ducked my head.

The inspector made a courteous bow to Grannie and then paused before leaving. "Do let me know if your friend has not turned up in time for luncheon," he said.

Lucy came in just then, hair beautifully braided, and sang out cheery good mornings without being reminded. The inspector repeated his stern look at me and left us.

"Where's Hector?" said Lucy, putting pancakes on her plate.

"Not here," I said. "Grannie, I'm really worried. His bed is made as if he never slept in it."

"But what harm could come to a boy in a nursery bedroom?"

Lucy stopped chewing and looked at me. Hector had not been in a nursery bedroom last evening. We had been doing precisely what we'd just been forbidden from doing—snooping and sleuthing.

A sound at the door made me turn in hope.

Not Hector. Marjorie collected a slice of toast at the sideboard and slid into the seat next to me. "Good morning, dear ones." She poured herself coffee from the silver pot on the table.

"Have you seen Hector?" I asked her. She shook her head no, cup to her lips.

"Don't be offended, Marjorie," I said, "that I am leaving the moment you come to breakfast. I must go up to the nursery."

"Today is Sunday," said Marjorie. "We're to be in the chapel at nine o'clock. All of us. Absolutely no choice, you understand?"

"Grandmamma," said Lucy, with a sigh.

"I understand." I folded my napkin and put it beside my plate. "Though it might be all of us minus one boy from Belgium. I am hoping that Hector left a note in his room, or some other clue as to his whereabouts."

"I'll come with you." Lucy's chair squeaked as she pushed it back.

It took Lucy and me under five minutes to search Hector's room. His sailor suit and two shirts hung on hooks. His dress-up trousers and jacket were on a hanger. The drawers held socks and underthings. His nightshirt was folded under the pillow. The book on his nightstand was *Kidnapped* by Robert Louis Stevenson, the same author who wrote *Treasure Island*. That made me feel sick. First Mr. Sivam, and now Hector. Unexplained absences in the middle of a blizzard.

"Nothing here," said Lucy. "It's the barest room in the house."

No note. No clever instructive clue. I let my eyes roam, certain I had missed something. *Put to work the friction of the brain cells!* Hector said in my head. *Use the logic!*

I did not believe for a moment that he was strolling through the rooms and passages of Owl Park with complete disregard for the time. Nor that he'd been thunderstruck with a theory so urgent that he would not wait to have me dissect it with him. However early he'd come down from the nursery, he would have wanted breakfast. Hector Perot was the most eager eater I had ever met. He would certainly have encountered a servant—or two or three or nine—because Owl Park had nearly as many servants as a centipede had legs. But, according to Dot's quick ask-around, no one had seen him.

Because he wasn't here.

Something was terribly wrong. Had he encountered one of the two men on our list of suspects? We had assumed, in the quiet kitchen last evening, that Frederick had gone to bed with all the other servants. We had assumed that Mr. Mooney would be in his room, giving Hector a chance to poke about the coach house in search of clues. We had assumed that Hector's knitted pullover and woolly socks under his button-up boots would be snug enough for crossing the courtyard.

"Lucy," I said. "The clothes he was wearing yesterday are not hanging tidily or folded away. His woolly jumper isn't here. Hector never came back last night."

Lucy's hand flew to her mouth. "Mr. Sivam has got him!" she said. "It's the curse of the Echo Emerald!"

"I don't think so," I said. "I think Mr. Sivam might be in trouble too."

In trouble meaning "dead," which seemed far more likely.

As Marjorie had reminded us, it was Sunday. We were obliged to attend service in the private chapel nestled on the far side of East House. Lucy and I joined our grandmothers in the front pew. Boughs of beribboned greenery were laced to the railings, emitting the rich scent of a pine forest after a rainfall. Marjorie and James sat behind us, with Mrs. Frost, Frederick, Dot and a couple of others in the third and last pew. James's grandfather had overseen the construction of this little place, especially for his wife, one hundred years ago. He had commissioned the stained-glass windows from a solitary woman who'd lived in the hills a few miles away. Rather than scenes from the Bible, her panels depicted the wildflowers and birds that she saw during her daily rambles across the downs. Bluebells, buttercups, teasel and tansy. Sparrow, goldfinch, dunnock and robin.

The curate arrived on snowshoes. Reverend Barrell was a chubby fellow with a lovely voice who made the readings sound like poems, quite unlike the bellowing Reverend Mr. Teasdale at All Saints church in Torquay. Had it been any other Sunday, I might have perched in the pew to pass a pleasant hour. As it was, a corpse lay in the stable, a boy with a bandaged head insisted that a woman had pushed him down the stairs, a villain lurked somewhere close by, and my dearest friend was nowhere to be found.

After the chapel service, I sneaked away, unkindly but deftly, from Lucy, and hurried toward the main part of the house. I had half a plan, or, rather, two plans. Which to pursue first?

I opened the door to Hector's room with a tiny flame of hope that he'd be calmly sitting on his bed, reading a book. But no. So, I went to collect the paper knife, as well as my notebook, from under the quilt on my bed. It wouldn't do, I realized, to be seen with a six-inch blade in my fist. Yet how to carry it about without stabbing my own ankle? I slid the knife into the foot of a stocking and tied it snugly to the sash about my waist. It made an odd-looking accessory, but not obviously a murder weapon. Marjorie and Kitty Sivam were just back from the chapel and settling themselves in the morning room as I passed. I opened my mouth to say *Hector's still missing*, but stopped to consider. Kitty Sivam's husband was also missing. Not just overnight, but for nearly three whole days! I felt a rush of empathy with her. She must be every bit as frightened for her husband as I was for Hector. To be fair, possibly more so.

I gave my sister a deceitful, cheery wave and returned to my quest.

And what exactly was my quest? Should I be looking for Hector? Or presenting my discovery to Inspector Willard? Did I have the nerve to interrupt the inspector during an interview? He'd likely finished with Annabelle while we'd been listening to Reverend Barrell, and had moved on to speak with the servants. Might one of them have uncovered a reason to show Frederick or Mr.

Mooney as even more suspicious? Oddly enough, Hector's disappearance had pushed Annabelle off the suspect list for me, making her shaky alibi more solid. It seemed much likelier that one of the two men had waylaid my friend. If the pirate boots next to Mr. Corker's body had belonged to either of them, Hector's exploration had put his life at risk. Why had I let him go off by himself?

What if Hector had crossed paths with a thieving, murderous footman when he crept through the kitchen? Or, even more probably, what if Mr. Mooney had not been safely in his room on the third floor as we had guessed? He had admitted that he'd argued with Mr. Corker in the library. What if he'd been inside the coach house when a curious boy appeared to poke through his belongings? Hector not returning after a mission to sleuth on Mr. Mooney's territory put the actor on top of my list. Number One Most Suspicious Character. My lungs seemed filled with wet mud, so drenched was I in dread. My suspicion grew and festered, like mold on cheese. *Like a stench in hot sunshine. Like maggots on a dead badger.*

While I'd been pursuing my own endeavors last evening, chatting with Annabelle and Sergeant Shaw, hearing the news from Lucy and writing to Mummy . . . all that time, Hector must have faced a crisis that swallowed him up and not released him. My breakfast egg rose in my throat, threatening to reappear. I tapped on my forehead, trying to banish my vigorous imagination. It could carry me too swiftly to dark and dreadful places.

Be logical, I said to myself.

But what if he's dead?? myself screamed back.

There was only one way to find out, and it was the last thing I wanted to do.

Hector being missing made Annabelle's bath seem . . . like only a bath.

Hector being missing let awful, scary thoughts creep into my mind.

Hector being missing meant that I could not tell my best friend about what scared me.

Hector being missing was the only reason on earth that could propel me out to the coach house, knowing that Mr. Mooney might be waiting . . . and not in a friendly mood.

CHAPTER 32

A Cause for Alarm

I crossed the busy kitchen as if I hadn't a care in the world, dodging the staff carrying platters for the upstairs luncheon. I pulled one of the servants' shawls from a hook by the door, to use for the same reason they all did—an extra layer around neck and shoulders when going out to collect coal or eggs or bread or whatever next was needed from one of the outbuildings. I hoped to be collecting Hector.

Sergeant Fellowes, on guard duty for the corpse inside the stable, was chatting with three reporters who clustered at the doorway of the bakehouse.

Mr. Blake Cramshot from the *Tiverton Bugle*, Mr. Pockmark Dented Hat and . . . Mr. Augustus Fibbley of the *Torquay Voice*. Well, hello. Back so soon? Mr. Fibbley wore his dark peacoat and cap. His spectacles shone like twin mirrors in the glare of light from the snow.

"Have you seen my friend Hector, by any chance?" I asked them.

They shook their heads and shuffled their feet. I couldn't bear to think how cold their feet must be. I hoped that Marjorie had given the baker permission to feed them warm bread. Should I pause to speak with Mr. Fibbley? Tell him how frantic I was about Hector? Should I say, *Please help*?

I thought back to what happened in October when I'd chased a villain by myself, and the frightful night that came as a result. A wave of icy recollection washed over me, sweeping away the notion that I might stand toe-to-toe with an angry man. Lucy was right. This was a task for the police. Hector would surely agree with Lucy. He wanted to *be* a policeman when he got older, so they could do no wrong in his opinion.

I glanced over at Sergeant Fellowes. I did not wonder that guarding a dead man might be boring, but he was now singing a duet with Mr. Cramshot, and was not the policeman in whom I wanted to confide. Inspector Willard had said I might inform him if Hector had not appeared by lunchtime. I'd sat next to him at breakfast and not mentioned that the murder weapon was in my bed. My fingers strayed to the bundle at my waist. I'd found the paper knife yesterday, and not yet told anyone.

The time had come.

I marched back inside and straight to the Avon Room. Constable Gillie stood at attention beside the door.

"One of the maids is in there just now," he said.

Did that mean Mr. Mooney was in the coach house where I'd just been headed? Luck was on my side.

I'd found something the inspector would want to see, I told the constable. He followed me through the door and parked himself, straight and tall. I waited next to him. Our own Dot, under-parlormaid, was in the chair opposite Inspector Willard. On the table in front of him sat a plate from the kitchen holding a heap of gray muck. From where I stood, it looked like a macaroon gone terribly wrong.

Dot was in the middle of her story.

"Well, I says to her," she said, "'Scoff you might, Mrs. Frost,' I says, 'but of the forty-one grates I cleans each day, this be the only one with ashes what've got threads and bits of fabric and not just paper scraps and coal ash.'"

"I hope you did not sass the housekeeper so much as that," said Inspector Willard, "but do go on, Miss Bolt. I'm listening."

Dot's shoulders rode up to her ears. "Well, anyway," she said, after a moment's sulk, "I showed her what I found, and she said that after all the police might want a gander. We put a sampling on this plate, what's usually used for scones, and up I come to see you."

Dot used the hem of her apron to wipe her face. "I've gone all perspiring."

"Take your time," said Inspector Willard. "We are keenly interested in what you have to say."

Dot blinked two or three times, the freckles standing out on her cheeks.

"Whose grate were you cleaning, Miss Bolt," said the inspector, gently, "when these threads and bits of blood-stained fabric emerged from the ashes?"

A day ago, Dot's answer would have made the blood freeze in my veins, but now I guessed the name before she opened her mouth.

"Didn't I say?" said Dot. "These bits has come from the grate in Mr. Mooney's room. He hasn't let me in there since Christmas, being ever so messy. It'll take me all afternoon to scrub and tidy once he's gone."

"You won't be expected to clean it," said Inspector Willard. "The police will take care of that."

"I've got the murder weapon," I said, unable to wait another moment. "And Hector is still missing."

Inspector Willard looked abruptly in my direction. The light sparked in his eyes as if I'd lit a match.

"Thank you, Miss Bolt," he said to Dot. "You have been a great help. I shall commend you to Mrs. Frost." Dot stood up and smoothed her apron. She smiled at me, a smile of triumph. *A great help!*

"Constable?"

The constable stiffened in anticipation of new orders. "Sir."

"You will escort Miss Bolt to the kitchen. You will then locate Mr. Mooney and tell him that I'd like another word. If he objects, you will thump him. Go!"

As Constable Gillie hustled her out, Dot shot me another grin. This was the sort of action she could tell the servants' hall!

Inspector Willard indicated that I should sit. I willed myself to meet his eyes.

"You are persistent," he said. Did I discern the faintest twinkle or was that wishful thinking?

"Sir," I said. My fingers closed around the lump inside the stocking at my waist.

"Please proceed," he said, "even knowing that my focus is needed elsewhere."

Goodness, yes. What was I hesitating over? Hector's safety was in peril! I fumbled to untie the clumsy knot in the stocking and withdrew the paper knife. I placed it on the table between us. He picked it up to take a closer look.

"It's from the desk in the library," I said. "Sir."

"Yes," he agreed. "I recognize the owl." The black streak caught his attention. His eyes darted to me and then back to the knife. For one-tenth of a second, he allowed a grin—but replaced it quickly with a wooden face.

"I will not ask how you came by this item from a guarded room during a murder investigation," he said. "I'm beginning to suspect there is a secret passage in this old house. We have no time for that now. There is a chance that you have just presented a critical clue. One that you should not have. Having it means you are putting yourself in danger. I cannot allow—"

"But, Hector!" I said. "He's still—"

He picked up the knife while shaking his head. "Please find your sister or your grandmother—or a book—and sit quietly for just a little while. We will get to the bottom of this."

There came a tap at the door and Constable Gillie put his head in.

"We've got Mr. Mooney, sir. Sergeant Fellowes is here too, in case of trouble."

"Thank you, Constable," said Inspector Willard. "And thank *you* for your contribution, Miss Morton. Good day."

Grrrrr!

The two policemen and Mr. Mooney filed into the Avon Room with no struggle, while I was marooned on the wrong side of the door. I'd delivered the murder weapon right into Inspector Willard's hands! How could he be so cruel as to prevent me from watching its effect on the killer? If only the secret passage reached this far!

But wait!

A short bark of glee escaped before I clapped a hand over my mouth and pursued my brilliant idea. Lucy had shown us the wood cupboards that allowed the servants to resupply the log pile in each room without disturbing the family members within. And was I not standing in front of the Avon Room wood cupboard this very minute?

I checked that no one was in the passage before yanking open the tall narrow door. There were only a dozen logs stacked at the bottom, mostly against the other door, leaving enough room for a person to hoist herself up and *squeeeeze* sideways into the cupboard. I managed to shut the door but had to bend my neck rather awkwardly. The logs were knobby underfoot, but tightly packed and not at risk of rolling noisily about. It was the definition of uncomfortable, but I could hear nearly every word being spoken!

"Yes, he was drunk," Mr. Mooney was saying. "But worse than that, he had in his hand the jewel that Mrs. Sivam had shown us all a few hours earlier."

"Had he indeed?" said the inspector. "I'm sorry you did not provide this crucial detail during our first conversation, Mr. Mooney. How did you react to seeing that?"

"I confess I was very angry indeed," said Mr. Mooney. His actorly voice carried nicely through the cupboard door. "There'd been a matter of a mislaid bracelet at another manor house we visited a few months ago. As roaming actors, we came under suspicion—a cloud we cannot afford to carry. I was furious that here seemed to be proof that my old friend was guilty of such low dealings."

A moment's pause.

I'd never thought to wonder whether the Echo Emerald was the first or only theft. Was our calamity just one in a chain of events?

"I'm afraid," Mr. Mooney said, "that I used harsh words. I called him an idiot, and a dunderhead."

But hadn't he said last time that it was Mr. Corker who'd called *him* names?

"I told him," said Mr. Mooney, "that his ongoing presence with the troupe was impossible. He'd put Annabelle and myself in a terrible situation."

"And how did he respond?" asked Inspector Willard.

"He . . . he . . ." The actor paused again. "That's when he hit me. My nose began to bleed."

"This is the first I've heard of a bloody nose," said Inspector Willard. "Another point withheld during our previous encounter."

"Did I not mention that? I suppose I was embarrassed that a man ten years my senior managed to land a punch."

"And did you hit him back?" said the inspector, coaxing.

"I did not." Mr. Mooney sounded offended. "I gave him a push toward the chair. I had no intention of hitting a man so much the worse for drink. I told him again that we were finished and that he should be gone by morning. I didn't care that he'd have to walk to Tiverton, is what I said, and maybe it would sober him up."

Nearly a minute passed. I tried to turn my head to ease the crick, but my nose met the wall.

Then came a gulping noise before Mr. Mooney continued in a voice of deep regret. "I left the library. Because of the late hour, I went up the staircase from the Great Hall instead of using the servants' steps. I heard a door open but hurried on, afraid to be noticed where I should not be. Thinking back, I assume it was Mr. Sivam, coming out of his room. He must have discovered the missing gem and gone to confront the thief."

"Mr. Mooney." The inspector's tone was soft, almost confiding, meaning that I stopped breathing in order to hear properly. "Put yourself in my position for a moment," he said. "What would you think if confronted by an intelligent man who lies to the police during a murder inquiry?"

No answer. Inspector Willard posed his next question.

"Why did you burn your shirt, if the blood was merely from your nose?"

I heard the clink of a dish and guessed that the plate of ashes had been pushed forward for Mr. Mooney to contemplate. I was impressed so far with Inspector Willard's probing technique. His wording was careful, his pacing sure-footed, and his manner aloof but congenial.

I had expected Mr. Mooney to be caught off-guard by the question about blood, but instead, he laughed!

"Ha! It saddens me to realize there is no woman in your life, Inspector! I live in fear of my colleague, Miss Annabelle Day. Of worrying or vexing her. Give her a bloodied shirt and confess the cause to be a dispute between her two best friends? I shudder to think of the outburst. Reason enough, I promise, to tear my shirt to shreds and burn away the evidence."

We'd seen with our own eyes how particular Annabelle was about the costumes. Mr. Mooney's wish to avoid making her cross was entirely wise. I paused to reconsider the whole of his testimony. What if everything he'd said was true, rather than false? How would that color our investigation? If only Hector were here to—

Hector!

Hector was *not* here! And this was my chance—while Mr. Mooney was occupied in police company—to have a quick look around the coach house! I backed up slowly on the uneven logs, pressing my perspiring palms against the sides of the cupboard. I bounced my heel against the door to nudge it open and eased myself to the ground. I had been confined for only a few minutes, but my joints seemed as creaky as Grannie Jane claimed hers to be. I smoothed my hair, shook wood chips from my skirt and set off at a run toward the kitchen.

CHAPTER 33

A MARVELOUS FIND

AGAIN I BORROWED one of the servants' shawls as I tore
through the kitchen door and hurried past the reporters, still
loitering in the courtyard. No one stopped me from dart-
ing in through the stable door, because Sergeant Fellowes,
I realized, was with Mr. Mooney in the Avon Room.

A shape lay beneath a chilly linen sheet in stall number 5.
I worried for a moment that pulling back the covering
would reveal not Mr. Corker, but Mr. Sivam . . . or
Hector. How unkind it felt to be relieved at the sight of
the actor's face.

His skin did not look human, but like a waxwork version, a film of frost glistening upon his features, as if he'd
been exhumed from a prehistoric ice cave. The hole in his
neck was puckered and nearly black, crusted with dried

blood. I might have stayed to examine him more closely, an endeavor of scientific research, but I had a more pressing search to pursue.

I paused in the archway that divided stable and coach house. It was *freeeezing* cold. Mr. Mooney had been interrupted in his labors when summoned by Inspector Willard, and the big door to the courtyard was only partway shut. A shaft of light cut across the floor and bent its way up the side of a packing case. Several large and awkwardly shaped pieces of painted scenery were stacked against the side of Mr. Sivam's motorcar.

I stepped in—and tripped over a rope on the floor. "*Ouch!*"

Instantly, I heard a thudding noise. *Whump. Whump. Whump.* Dull and steady.

"Hello?" I whispered, scarcely daring to call out, though I knew that Mr. Mooney was not here.

"Hector?" Full of fright, my voice had not enough air to make noise. I tried again.

"HECTOR!"

The thumping stopped and then began again with a frantic pulse. *Whump, whum-whump, whump-whump-whump.* The packing case before me shook with every *whump.* Until *cr-raack!* The wood on one end splintered open from the force behind it, revealing that the hammer was the sole of a boot.

For an instant, my legs would not move. But then I heard a voice along with the thuds, a thin, furious keening. I nearly dove across the straw-covered dirt to land on my knees next to the shaking crate.

"Hector!" My fingers were trembling twigs not performing as I required. "Hector, I'm here! Stop thumping!" After several tries, I unfastened the tight-fitting latch and yanked open the lid.

"Hector!"

He was lying on his side, legs bent and arms wrapped across his chest. One foot was caught partway through the smashed end of his tiny prison. His eyes were livid and bruised, his face strained, and pale, and oh, so dear.

"Hector!"

He tried to sit up but his foot was trapped, or perhaps the ordeal had left him weak. When I wiped the tears from my eyes, I saw that he was crying too. I pulled aside the splintered wood from around his shoe. Gently, I put my hands under his arms and helped him to sit.

But, could he stand?

Eventually, he could, trembling terribly. "I am wishing and wishing that you will come."

"Oh, Hector."

"I am very much cold," he said.

I rubbed his arms fiercely, the way Mummy rubbed mine when I came in from a winter walk with Tony.

"Who did this to you?" I whispered.

"I cannot say for certain," said Hector. "He conks me from behind when I am considering the boots. When again I am conscious, I am lying in what I think is to be my coffin."

I shuddered, sliding an arm around his back. He seemed not to know how to proceed. I lifted his knee over the side of the box while he held my shoulder to steady himself.

"Take it slowly," I said. "You might not be ready to walk yet."

He took one step and then another. One step and then another, as wobbly as a baby.

"I have a revelation about the boots," he said.

We had reached the open door. In the bright light outside, Hector's skin was nearly blue with cold. One eye was circled with the gray of fatigue, the other swollen and purple, making him look like an exotic monkey.

"LUCY!" I bellowed. She was across the courtyard, talking to Mr. Fibbley. She spun around at the sound of my voice and galloped over.

"Hector!" she cried. "You're back! Where were you? You look horrible!"

"Lucy," I said. "Run to find Marjorie or James, will you?" She was gone before I could add *please*.

"Aggie." Hector clutched my arm, swayed and crumpled into the snow like a broken doll.

Reporters flocked around us, each tugging Hector in a different direction. His swoon lasted only a few seconds. He was not hurt, just woozy and embarrassed. Lucy hurtled out of the house with James on her heels. James hollered at the reporters to skedaddle, and most of them did, delighted with a new story to be filed at once. James scooped Hector off the ground and held him like an infant. Hector barked a laugh of surprise as James spun around and went straight back through the kitchen door that Lucy held open for him.

"Come, Aggie!" Lucy dragged on my arm. "Aunt Marjorie is bringing blankets for a chaise in the conservatory. She says he needs the warmth and humidity in there, like an hour in Africa. Also, no stairs. Cook is making him a posset."

After much fussing, tucking, cosseting and sipping, we three were finally alone.

"Well?" I said, as the conservatory door closed on Marjorie's swishing skirt.

"Who did this?" said Lucy.

"As I am saying already," said Hector, "I never see him and he does not speak to me. Occasionally there is muttering or moaning. I am deducing Mr. Mooney. Because of the boots."

"I gave Inspector Willard the paper knife," I said, "but I was asked to leave and then I came to find you. Mr. Mooney had a sensible explanation for every question, so I don't know if he has been arrested or freed."

"What boots?" said Lucy. "What knife?"

Hector's eyelids fluttered and his pale face looked even paler.

"Wait!" I said. "Don't you dare go to sleep or faint again before you've told us. What about the boots?"

Hector had the strength to tilt half his mouth into a smile.

"Are you warm enough?" said Lucy. "Aunt Marjorie said you need to stay warm."

"Ssh, Lucy, he's under two feather quilts! Hector, the boots?"

"Six pair of pirate boots," said Hector. "One pair is Mr. Corker's, altered for the affliction of bunions. One pair belongs to Annabelle, stuffed in the toe with newspaper so her feminine foot will fit."

I nodded. So far, not news.

"When I go to the coach house," said Hector, slowly, "we wish to identify the person who wears the boots that are in the library next to le pauvre Mr. Corker. Is it Lord Greyson? We think not. Mr. Sivam? This also is unlikely."

I trusted Hector to be leading somewhere, so I listened patiently to what I already knew.

"We know all this," said Lucy.

Hector closed his eyes, and licked his cracked lips.

I lifted the porcelain invalid cup to his mouth so he could sip from its spout. I caught a whiff of the contents. Hector's favorite, chocolat!

"Two remaining pair," he whispered.

"Frederick and Mr. Mooney," I said. "Identical with the ones worn by James and Mr. Sivam."

"Not identical," said Hector. "I look at the heels." His eyelids were still closed, one the color of a rotten plum.

I wanted to shake him. *What about the heels*?? But he'd spent the whole night in a trunk with his bones turned to ice. Didn't he deserve some rest?

"Don't sleep yet!!" said Lucy. "What about the heels?"

"One is worn down," he murmured. "But the other is barely scuffed, almost like new."

"What does that mean?" said Lucy.

Hector made a sound like a cat purring. He was asleep.

The door behind us opened with a polite click.

"Grannie, hello," I said, pointing at Hector. "Ssh."

Behind her was Inspector Willard, both their faces showing grave concern.

"He'll recover," I said. "But he was awake all night in a packing case as cold as the icehouse." I furtively wiped a hot tear from my cheek. Grannie pulled me close. The next few tears were not so furtive.

"There, there," she murmured, into my hair. "There's a pet. I admire you greatly, Agatha, for the persistent friend you've been today."

"And I apologize," said Inspector Willard, "for not heeding your alarm to the extent that I should have."

Or at all, I thought.

"If it weren't for Aggie," said Lucy, "Hector would be dead."

I shivered, despite the drenching humidity of the conservatory. "He was about to tell us something important," I said, "about the boots."

Another *purrr* from Hector. Lucy giggled.

"Boots?" said the inspector.

"The boots found beside the body," I added. "He had a revelation."

"Surely the police can take things from here, Agatha?" Grannie Jane was about to be an obstacle to justice, I could feel it.

"Perhaps, Mrs. Morton . . ." said the inspector. "Would you be so kind as to sit with the boy, while I borrow Miss Morton for a few questions about the particulars of his rescue?"

"I'll stay," said Lucy.

"As shall I, Inspector," said Grannie Jane. "And I firmly recommend that you not put my granddaughter in peril, unless you are prepared to duel with a very angry old woman."

Inspector Willard bowed his assurance. I followed him out of the conservatory, not caring what questions he might have for me, as I had many for him.

"Did you arrest Mr. Mooney? Did he confess to anything? Did you ask him about the paper knife?"

Inspector Willard sighed heavily. "Mr. Mooney gave a satisfactory answer for every question," he said. "He laughed when I showed him the paper knife, and reminded me that dried ink is very similar to dried blood. Until I have a microscope at my disposal, I cannot say which it is. Without some piece of proof, I have no reason to take the cocky fellow into custody."

I stared at him, trying to swallow the rock of disappointment in my throat.

"I know this is not the answer you wished for." He wiped a hand over his face. "I wonder if *I* am wishing too hard for success with this case, to prove my ability to those who belittle me, rather than being more meticulous in my thinking . . ." He tapped the side of his head.

"Simply wishing for success does not make it happen." Didn't I sound like Grannie Jane? I peered through the glass door to see her needles flashing, while Lucy sat by Hector with her hand covering his, something he would only tolerate while unconscious, I was certain.

"You can't just let Mr. Mooney drive away in his caravan," I said, "when he's the one who probably captured Hector and killed Mr. Corker."

"What has Hector said about all this?" Inspector Willard wanted to know.

"Hector never saw his captor. He could not say for certain it was Mr. Mooney."

"But how and where did it occur?"

Oh dear. Here we were again, at a place where I knew more than I should and had hidden more than was wise. Loyalty and safety were both being strained.

"Hector went to the coach house last night," I admitted, "expecting it to be empty. He meant only to confirm certain points about the pirate boots. Someone attacked him from behind and he was suddenly a prisoner. Can you not detain Mr. Mooney on *suspicion* of theft and murder, just as you have with Miss Day? And hope to find some vital evidence before you must let him go?"

"Mr. Mooney has been asked to remain at Owl Park until our investigation is complete," said the inspector. "Two officers have taken him up just now to see Miss Day. We wish to observe the encounter. Our suspicion is that he has used her as an accomplice, possibly against her will."

An accomplice? Had hers been the voice after all, heard by Stephen before his catastrophic fall? But against her will? How could Mr. Mooney force her to commit such a heinous act?

"Perhaps he'll slip up," Inspector Willard continued. "We'll have him under watch until . . . Well, until I can find *some*thing against him. If only the boy could swear it was Mooney who abducted him! What did you want to tell me about that pair of boots?"

I peered again into the conservatory, in case Hector was awake and could tell us his idea.

"Hector said that the heels were different," I began. "One was worn down and the other . . ." I paused to look at the soles and heels of my own boots. They had matching signs of wear—the back rims of both heels were softened and slightly eroded by the hundreds of ordinary steps I walked each day, up and down the hills of Torquay and the stairs inside our house.

What Hector had described was a pair of boots *not* worn in an ordinary way. Boots that had apparently *not* taken the same number of steps . . .

"Eureka!" I cried. What Hector had described was a pair of boots owned by—"Someone *who does not have two feet!*" I said aloud. "Inspector Willard! I know whose boots were left in the library!"

CHAPTER 34

AN AWFUL ORDEAL

"INSPECTOR WILLARD, sir?"

Before I could say anything more, Constable Gillie had appeared, accompanied by Sergeant Fellowes and Mr. Mooney. "The prisoner wants to know, is he actually a prisoner? Or merely requested to remain on the premises pending the outcome of the investigation?"

Mr. Mooney smiled in such a way that showed he did not for one moment imagine himself to be a prisoner.

The inspector glanced at the conservatory door, and tugged on his odd shock of white hair. "Were you not paying a visit to Miss Day?" he asked the actor.

"She wouldn't see him, sir," said Constable Gillie.

"Your persistent hounding has turned her against

me," said Mr. Mooney. "Clearly part of a police scheme to divide and conquer the innocent."

"Perhaps," I said, as boldly as I have ever spoken. "Perhaps she wonders why your boots were found next to Mr. Corker's body while his were upstairs next to those of Mr. Sivam?"

Four grown men stared, causing my courage to dive back down my throat. I turned my attention to my own boots for only a moment before I thought of Hector crying, of his swollen-shut eye. It was up to me, in Hector's absence, to explain his theory.

"Inspector Willard, sir? May I clarify my supposition?"

"Please do," he said.

I took the deepest breath my lungs could hold and let the words stream out. "The heels were worn away at very different rates, indicating that one of the boots had been less active than the other. I suggest that Mr. Mooney, in the guise of Long John Silver, has reason to wear one boot most of the time, and the other boot only occasionally. When appearing at a Christmas Eve supper, for example, in the company of his hosts. The result is a marked difference in the erosion of his boot heels."

Inspector Willard laughed, and patted my shoulder, as if in happy pride. The two police officers looked a bit baffled. Mr. Mooney put on a face of agreeable puzzlement.

"But if you wanted to know whose boots were in the library," he said, "why did you not simply ask?"

He might have dashed a cup of cold water into my face. Why had we not simply asked?

"You knew I'd been in there," continued Mr. Mooney. "How can it be of import that I took off my boots? What of it?"

"Why did you not mention that you had removed your boots?" Inspector Willard said.

"I suppose I did not consider it a matter of importance, what I might or might not wear on my feet. I have a right to take off my—"

"*When* did you take them off?" asked the inspector, calmly and quietly.

Oh, he was clever. Because he did not add, *Before you snatched the Echo Emerald from Mr. Corker's hand? Or after he'd given you a bloody nose?*

Mr. Mooney's mouth opened, and then it closed. He had stepped into a trap and, for the first time, was not ready with a clever answer. There could be no sensible reason to remove his boots during the scene that he had described to Inspector Willard.

Something about the boots was wrong, just as Stephen had said.

"You have confessed to handling a stolen gemstone," said Inspector Willard, "and to wearing a bloody shirt in the same room where a blood-soaked corpse was discovered a few hours later. I will ask you, Sebastian Mooney, to return to the Avon Room while we re-examine the timeline of your actions."

"Really, Inspector," said Mr. Mooney. He pulled out his pocket watch and glanced at the time. What was he so impatient to be doing elsewhere? "I'm getting a bit fed up with the implication that I—"

A *tap-tap* sound made our group turn as one to see Lucy's face through the glass of the conservatory door. She waved urgently, begging me to come inside.

"A stolen gemstone," repeated Inspector Willard, "a blood-soaked corpse, and the abduction of a young boy . . ."

I heard their departure rather than watching it, as I hurried to find Hector awake, with a faint pink glow in his cheeks.

"You look much better," I said. "But I expect you wish you were at home in your own bed. In Belgium, I mean, with your own mother."

Hector turned his face away, so I knew that I was right.

I quickly shifted direction. "The inspector has just taken Mr. Mooney for more questioning."

Grannie Jane tucked away her knitting and rose. "I will alert Marjorie that Hector is awake," she said. "She will no doubt ask Dr. Musselman to attend."

Hector bugged his eyes at me in horror.

I shrugged helpless shoulders in return. "Thank you, Grannie Jane," I said.

"Are you needing another drink, Hector?" asked Lucy. "We may ask Cook for anything our hearts desire while you are an invalid."

"Merci, non," said Hector. "I require nothing."

"Orange juice!" I jumped at the chance of a few minutes alone with Hector. "Mummy says freshly squeezed oranges are best when you're feeling low. Thank you, Lucy. If Cook has any."

There would be no oranges during a snowstorm in December. How long would it take to come up with an alternative refreshment?

"I'll ask for a pitcher!" said Lucy, rushing away.

Hector's eyebrow made its comment on my mode of Lucy removal.

"Tell to me all that has happened since I am gone," he said. "I am missing many chapters, am I not?"

"I don't think Annabelle's a suspect anymore," I said, "except that the inspector just suggested she might be an accomplice. But she was having a bath when Stephen fell down the stairs, unless she was just pretending."

"You are saying that Annabelle may, or, perhaps, may not be guilty," said Hector. "How is this news?"

"If what you say about the boots is true, which it likely is, then Frederick is innocent too, even with that dunderhead remark, though I suppose he could have carried Mr. Mooney's boots to the library just as easily as Mr. Mooney might have carried the dead man's boots upstairs, so, really . . ."

Hector was looking at me, shaking his head. "Another shaky solution." He pushed off one of the quilts that covered his legs and then kicked off the other. "I am . . . too confined."

"Snug as a bug in a rug," I said.

He sat up awkwardly, tipping off the side of the chaise. As he landed, something rolled out from his pocket and across the floor.

"Oh," he snatched it up. A small glass tube.

"I find this in the coach house," he said, his voice more vigorous with every word. "I put into my pocket and then I am attacked and I forget." He waved it back and forth. "You see what it is? You see?"

"Stop waggling your hand and let me look!"

He passed it over. Not a tube but a medical vial with a cork in one end and a label stuck to the side: CHLOROFORM. Old Lady Greyson's tooth medicine. Just a few drops left.

"But why would it be in the—?"

Hector struggled to his feet. "We must hurry!" he said. "Zut! Hector Perot needs a new brain!" He clasped my arm. "Come, come!"

"Where are we going?"

"Mr. Sivam!" said Hector, dragging me through the door and along the passage. "The moaning and muttering! I am thinking it is Mr. Mooney making such noises, but I am wrong. Dépêche-toi!" He was limping but moving quickly enough that I must trot to keep up. "We must rescue him just as you rescue me."

"You mean . . ." We'd reached the side door and hustled through it, meeting winter wind without coats or hats. "You mean Mr. Mooney used the chloroform to put Mr. Sivam to sleep?"

Hector nodded, his eyes streaming from the cold, his lips quite blue already. How foolish to let him come outside while still recovering from his ordeal. At least he was wearing his woolly pullover. I was not. We skittered along the path toward the courtyard.

"But *why*?" I said.

Why keep someone imprisoned and asleep? Unless . . . that person had something you wanted. Or knew something that you wanted to know.

"The emerald," I said. "Oh, my goodness, Mr. Mooney has been trying all this time to find out where the real Echo Emerald is hidden."

Hector was breathing in noisy little huffs as we entered the snowy and nearly empty courtyard. The stable was unguarded and only one stoic reporter stood outside the bakehouse door. He came right over when he saw us, aglow with his usual eagerness.

"You're moving very quickly," said Mr. Fibbley, trotting along. "Is my persistence about to pay off, while my colleagues have departed to file their stories and celebrate in the pub?"

"You may not come in," I told him. "Not yet."

We stepped from the bright, blustery courtyard into the gloom of the coach house. Hector glanced at the splintered panels of his recent prison but then hurried past. The actors' caravan looked to be almost packed and ready to go, with little room to spare. The basket of pirate boots sat beside the caravan's open doors.

The Sivam motorcar sat in the same place it had all week, quite near where Hector had lain through his ordeal. The familiar plaster goose sat on the bonnet. We climbed up to the running board and peered inside. The luxurious bearskin blanket lay across the back seat, covering a lumpy form. My hand moved from the smooth, icy metal of the car door to pull on thick, soft fur that seemed to be alive and faintly groaning. Beneath the blanket, hands clutching his head, was Mr. Lakshay Sivam.

The man we sought and the man we found were not the same. Who would match this sorry creature with the fine and handsome guest who had arrived at Owl Park only four days earlier? The bearskin about his shoulders—which then had seemed like a regal garment—now dwarfed a bleary-eyed man, hunched in pain and weeping. His hair was not sleek and shining as it had been during our first evening together, but tangled and awry. His skin, normally such a warm brown, was now a peculiar shade of gray, closer to the color of beach sand at twilight. A livid welt across his jaw suggested that he had been struck with a wrench or some other tool. Further wounds and bruises we saw later, but for now we were most concerned that we might assist him into the house.

Inch by inch, we helped him turn in the seat, that we could coax his legs to take his weight. He seemed not fully conscious, but nor was he afraid. Had the chloroform dulled his mind? I supposed he knew we were of best intent and not in league with the brute who had tortured him.

Hector, ever so gently, put his arms under Mr. Sivam's shoulders and encouraged him to lean. His teeth bit into his lower lip so fiercely I saw a drop of blood.

"Aggie," he whispered. "Will you call someone? I do not believe I have the strength . . ."

I had been foolishly gaping, but now I ran.

"Help!" I cried to Mr. Fibbley, who had loitered by the door, probably trying to eavesdrop. "Help Hector inside!" The reporter slipped past me and I dashed toward the house.

"Aggie!" Lucy burst through the kitchen door. "Hide, Aggie, *hiiiiiide!*"

"I need . . . to get . . . help!" I panted.

Lucy ran toward me, waving her arms. "Where's Hector? Get Hector! Mr. Mooney is coming! He kicked Constable Gillie so hard that he fell over, howling. Mr. Mooney has escaped from the police!"

CHAPTER 35

A FIGHT TO THE FINISH

ALERT HECTOR? Or call for James and a constable? I turned one way and then the other, slipping in the snow, not knowing what to do. But shortly I had no choice about the matter, for Mr. Mooney was upon us. I felt my hair wrenched nearly from its roots as the villain grabbed my braids and used them to haul me backward. I would have toppled but for the menacing grip on my hair. Pain like a hatful of pins pierced my head. I clawed and batted but could not reach the eyeballs I wished to gouge out.

Lucy stared, eyes round in horror. She spun in a circle but no one was here to save us. She closed her eyes and screamed, the same astonishing scream she had used in the library on Christmas morning.

Mr. Mooney cursed and jerked me hard again. I vowed

to myself I would cut off my hair if I were still alive tomorrow. In the two heartbeats following Lucy's scream, nothing happened. And then, *oof*! Mr. Mooney let go of my head and I dropped to the ground. I rolled out of his reach in the snow, and scrambled to my feet. Mr. Mooney had fallen also, had been knocked down! And now was fighting his assailant. Mr. Fibbley, astride the actor, punched him hard on the nose. Blood spurted in an arc, staining the snow with a spray of scarlet drops.

All at once, the police were there, and Frederick and Norman, and a furious Mrs. Hornby wielding a soup ladle. Mr. Mooney was soon subdued with handcuffs locked about his wrists, but even then, he glared at Mr. Fibbley.

"You punch like a girl," he growled. A trickle of blood seeped into his mustache.

"Are you speaking from experience?" said Mr. Fibbley. "I have no doubt that plenty of girls would love to do what I just did."

"Starting with Annabelle," I shouted. "Because of *you*, Annabelle has been locked up for days! Because of you, Mr. Corker is dead!"

Mr. Mooney's eyes fixed on me, the way an eagle's might, if I were a rabbit. I wasn't afraid, because Inspector Willard was there, but it felt as if my whole insides had the hiccups.

"I would never do Annabelle harm," he said, very quietly. "Not on purpose. I wish you'd tell her goodbye from me."

"You . . ." I began. And then began again, just as quietly. I hadn't planned what to say, but it poured out. "Everything you told us about that night in the library really happened, didn't it?" I said. "Except you changed the actors. It was *you* who stole the jewel. *You* who took off your boots and looked at the emerald through the magnifying glass and realized it was only a copy, because you know a thing or two about jewels, don't you? I'd guess you pocketed the magnifier when you saw it out of place on Christmas morning and sneaked in later when the constable wasn't looking, to put it back on the desk. You didn't expect we'd notice. It was Mr. Corker who saw *you* holding the stone and called *you* a dunderhead for stealing from the other manors and ruining everything."

Mr. Mooney was watching me so closely, it seemed as if he were reading my thoughts as they unscrolled. He took a breath and released it slowly.

"You've made up a story," he said, sounding very tired. "But maybe . . . some of it . . . is close."

"You and Mr. Corker had a fight," I said. "He was drunk and angry, and you picked up the paper knife, and—"

I stopped. When I said *paper knife*, the inspector and Mr. Mooney both stiffened. What had I said wrong?

But, I was thinking, what about the *dagger*? How did Mr. Corker's dagger become part of the action? My imagined scenario had all made unexpected sense up to that

333

point, but now I had bumped up against the second weapon and could not think what to say next.

"I think we've heard enough," said Inspector Willard. He gave a curt nod to the sergeant, who pulled the chain attached to the iron cuffs binding the prisoner's wrists.

"I did not kill Roger Corker," said Mr. Mooney, at last allowing himself to be tugged away.

He was transported to town within the hour and we never saw him again.

"God's teeth," said Lucy. "You are so brave!"

"Lucy!" I couldn't help but laugh. "Your grandmother would keel over to hear you swear like that!" I looked about, a little surprised to find myself still standing in the court-yard with a small crowd of onlookers. My scalp tingled.

"That was quite a punch," I said to Mr. Fibbley. "Where is Hector?"

"I can hardly flex my fingers," he said, with a crooked smile. He cocked his head toward the coach house. "Your friend is still in there. I'll wait with him until you bring someone. That man needs serious medical attention."

"What man?" said Lucy.

"Mr. Sivam," I said. "Lucy, you get the doctor, and I'll get James."

We barreled through the kitchen, startling Effie so badly that she dropped a pot. An empty pot, luckily, but it made a tremendous clang.

"Uncle James went to fetch Grandmamma for lunch, once Hector was settled," said Lucy. "He probably doesn't know what's happened, even though the gong was late."

"Because Cook was outside," I said, "armed with a soup ladle!"

Lucy giggled. "Well, anyway, I'm guessing they're all together by now. And if the doctor has finished mending Constable Gillie, he'll be eating lunch as well."

We skidded to a stop outside the dining room and inspected each other head to foot. Tousled and grubby, wrinkled and damp, we looked a fright!

"We just rescued someone," I said, shuddery and gulping in air after our frantic run, "for the second time today. Who cares if we're not groomed and proper?"

"Grandmamma cares." Lucy, too, was breathless. But she pushed open the door and in we went, bumping smack into Frederick holding a platter of fish.

We met a circle of stares. Old Lady Greyson, Grannie Jane, Marjorie, James, Dr. Musselman and Mrs. Sivam.

"A little more decorum," said Lucy's grandmother, "when entering a room?"

"Lucy?" said James.

"Aggie, what has happened?" Marjorie rose to her feet.

"Do you need to sit?" Grannie Jane shifted the empty chair next to her. I shook my head, no thank you, still panting slightly and even giggly. Lucy poked me to speak.

But, to whom should I deliver the news?

Mrs. Sivam. She would want to know first.

"Your husband," I said, "has been found."

I was scolded later for announcing the alarm this way. I had not been thinking of tact or discretion.

"Is he alive?" said Kitty Sivam.

"Almost," I said.

Dr. Musselman came out of the Juliet suite carrying a hand towel, drying his hands as if he'd just washed. Mrs. Sivam nestled under Marjorie's protective arm, while James kept an arm about Marjorie. Hector, Lucy and I sat in a row against the wall with our curiosity burning.

"When may I speak with him?" said Mrs. Sivam. "Does he remember anything?"

But the doctor shook his head. "He'll not be properly conscious for some time. He's had a nasty time of it. That Mooney ruffian stole the chloroform from my bag and administered too much for too many days. A dose should never be more than a drop or two." He turned the towel over and patted the back of his neck.

"I will sit with him," said Mrs. Sivam.

"I won't stop you," said the doctor. "But I advise that you rest tonight and let the servants keep watch. You'll be wanted tomorrow when he's awake. Bedrest only until we can get him to a hospital. He may be incapable of speech for a while, even when the drug has worn off."

Mrs. Sivam gasped as James said, "God's breath, man, why not?"

"One of the perils of the drug. It can burn a man's throat as sore as if he'd swallowed tacks. He can barely croak. I suspect he was gagged whenever Mooney left him alone, in case he woke up to cause a ruckus."

"Mr. Mooney kept checking his watch!" I murmured to Hector. "Pulling it from his pocket, remember? To be certain he was present when a dose was wearing off."

"Altogether, a nasty business." Dr. Musselman shook his head, attempting to roll the towel into his medical bag. "A very nasty business."

"When do you think Mr. Sivam will be recovered enough to speak with the police?" said James. "The inspector is eager to ask a few questions."

"Possibly by morning," said Dr. Musselman, "if he answers with a pencil and paper, I suppose. Every man's body recovers differently from an overdose. So, who's to say? Who's to say?"

Old Lady Greyson had gone to her room as soon as Lucy and I interrupted lunch, asking that this evening's meal be brought on a tray as well, and insisting the same be done for Grannie Jane. Grannie Jane would far rather be nattering with us than over there in East House behaving like an old woman, but was too polite to say so. Mrs. Sivam insisted on sitting with her husband, no matter what Dr. Musselman's advice had been. Marjorie understood—for what if it were James?—and kept company with her guest.

Thankfully, Lucy reminded James that we had not eaten, *since forever*. He said to come to the dining room to be fed whatever we wished. And so it was that we ate fried potatoes and crispy battered fish (and ignored the stewed tomatoes), while telling James every detail of Hector's miserable night, and the battle with Mr. Mooney, and the discovery of poor, pitiable Mr. Sivam.

"It is most enlightening, the English Christmas," teased Hector. "You provide much entertainment, Lord Greyson."

"Your mothers will be vexed with me," he complained, "for I have failed in my charge to supply a safe and merry Christmas."

"Mummy won't mind," I reassured James. "Marjorie was here to watch over me. Over all of us."

"The story will be made more gentle in my letters," promised Hector. "I will be certain to report that Stephen and Constable Gillie are both back on their feet . . . though the policeman is using a crutch."

"My mother may never let me come again," said Lucy, her voice full of woe. "I leave it to you, Uncle James, to fix everything with her before my summer visit."

"She'll be coming too," said James, "with your new brother, Robbie, or Bobbie, or whatever we end up calling him."

Mr. Pressman came into the room and bowed to James.

"The actress, my lord," he said. "She has been released from confinement, but it is too late at night to consider a train."

"Poor woman," said James. "She'll loathe the name of Owl Park for the rest of her life. Is she hungry?"

"Ask her if she likes stewed tomatoes," said Lucy.

James instructed Pressman to please invite Miss Day to join us for supper. She must have been close by for she appeared within a minute, dressed in a lovely sea-blue gown with a lace jacket of the same color. She tried to apologize for interrupting us, but James was apologizing to her at the same time, about her being wrongfully detained. Eventually we moved on.

"I believe, madam," said Hector, "that you and I have something in common."

Annabelle lifted an eyebrow. "Explain yourself, Master Perot," she said. Hector lifted one eyebrow in reply, and they both laughed.

"Every day I am adapting to the customs in a new land," said Hector. "I must alter myself to suit the wishes of others, to be less foreign. But for you—"

"For me, it is what I do for a living," she said. "Every time I put on an old apron or a ballgown, a crone's wig or a pair of pirate boots, I am becoming a person that I am not."

"I'm a bit bewildered too," said James. "Truth be told, learning to be Lord Greyson instead of Lord Greyson's son. Not so harsh as you must find it, Hector, far from home and navigating in a new language, but still a struggle to find my way some days. And Lucy has also entered a new world, though she may not realize the challenges just yet."

Lucy looked perplexed. "This is still England," she said, "last time I looked out the window."

James reached over to tousle her hair. "You have become a big sister," he said.

"Oh, that," said Lucy. "I suppose the baby might muck things up a bit, though I expect him to be jolly some of the time. I suppose I'll wait and see."

"You have no choice," said James. "Life-altering events are often thrust upon us."

"Like mine," I said. "The world without Papa."

James got up and came around the table to put his hands on my shoulders. "Marjorie and I are both in that world with you," he said. "Though it must still feel very lonely at times."

I blinked hard to keep the tears inside my eyes.

"Wasn't there meant to be peach crumble for dessert?" said Lucy.

"I'm too tired for dessert," I said. "This day began a long time ago."

"At the beginning of this day, I am imprisoned in a packing case," said Hector.

"I was imprisoned by a man in a chair," said Annabelle. "But at least I had a pillow."

"As lord of the manor," said James, "I decree that we have arrived at bedtime."

We paused on the nursery landing to say good night.

"I have a few unanswered questions," I said to Hector. "Mr. Mooney was eating turnip soup right next to us when Stephen fell down the stairs. So, who pushed him? And why were Mr. Corker's boots outside the Juliet suite instead of with Mr. Corker? And when did—"

"Tomorrow," said Hector. "Now, I am already sleeping."

TORQUAY VOICE

DECEMBER 29, 1902

CHRISTMAS KILLER CAUGHT!!
MANOR GUEST ABDUCTED,
TWO CHILDREN HARMED!!
HEARTLESS VILLAIN MURDERS FRIEND!!

by Augustus C. Fibbley

Perilous events continued yesterday at Owl Park manor near Tiverton. The leading role was played by an actor with blood on his hands—or certainly upon his shirt cuffs. An arrest has been made after a near escape, a physical scuffle and the enterprising actions of two young girls. This reporter was an eyewitness and has since interviewed all parties. Detective Inspector Thaddeus Willard made a statement to the hardy reporters who have lingered near the manor house of Lord and Lady Greyson since December 25. On that day, the body of Mr. Roger Corker was discovered in the library by three children seeking their gifts from Father Christmas.

The heinous criminal is named Mr. Sebastian Mooney, also known to use the alias of Sebastiano Luna when employed on the continent. He does not speak Italian.

The final act of the Christmas Corpse drama unfolded in an enclosed courtyard outside the service wing of the grand house. Mr. Mooney will be charged with murder and with child-snatching, as he brutally held a boy captive for a period of many hours. Also imprisoned in the coach house was a longtime friend of Lord Greyson, owner of a valuable gemstone stolen on Christmas Eve. Mr. Mooney has yet to confess or explain his crimes, saying only that he is innocent of murder. He is detained at the Tiverton Jail to await formal sentencing and trial.

Mr. Corker's body will be removed tomorrow, weather depending, from the stables at Owl Park. He will be buried in the churchyard of St. Aidan's church in Tiverton. Lord and Lady Greyson have commissioned a commemorative headstone. Miss Beatrice Truitt, betrothed to the deceased, has thanked them for providing the memorial marker for her fiancé and intends to visit this resting place when it is complete.

DECEMBER 29, 1902

MONDAY

CHAPTER 36

A SERIES OF CONCLUSIONS

MARJORIE CAME INTO the breakfast room fresh from a bath and smelling like chamomile.

Sturdy horses had just pulled the police wagon slowly into sight from behind the manor, trundling sedately over the shoveled drive.

"Here you all are," Marjorie said. "As if you're in a theater box, watching a melodrama."

"Have a seat," said Grannie Jane, patting the chair next to her.

"James and his mother are here as well," said Marjorie, gently warning us before they appeared.

"I have come to witness the end of this miserable episode for myself," said Lady Greyson.

We fussed and quickly rearranged chairs in front of the wide windows, so as not to miss the farewell.

Swaths of black crape had been draped from the corners of the wagon's roof, to alert onlookers to the solemnity of the vehicle's contents. Dr. Musselman sat up front with the driver, wearing a top hat. He had offered to accompany the deceased on his final ride, as Miss Truitt was nowhere to be found. Old Lady Greyson and Hector stood up out of respect, so the rest of us did too. It was not a funeral cortege, but it was the best poor Mr. Corker would get—especially as his fraudulent sweetheart, in her reporter's guise, was striding behind the moving wagon, scribbling notes.

"Has anyone noticed," said Lucy, when the sad parade had disappeared from sight down the long drive, "that four days have gone by and we have yet to open our socks from Father Christmas?"

"Goodness," cried Marjorie. "Do you suppose the stockings are still sitting where they were stashed a week ago?"

"The mice will have eaten all the sweets," James said.

"I wish you wouldn't tease, Uncle James," said Lucy. "Where were they stashed?"

"I believe the rule is," said old Lady Greyson, in an almost-kindly voice, "that you need to find the next clue."

"Will you please just tell us?" said Lucy.

"Certainly not," said her grandmother. "The stocking

hunt is a treasured tradition at Owl Park and must not be disregarded."

"Who do you suppose made the hunt for your mother and me when we were little?" James asked Lucy.

Lucy cocked her head to inspect her grandmother with closer interest.

"Where did you leave off?" said old Lady Greyson.

Beside a pirate lying in a pool of blood, I thought, catching Hector's eye.

"In the library," said Lucy.

"We are about to look at the letter *C* in the dictionary," said Hector.

Lucy's eyes lit up. "Please excuse our rapid departure, Grandmamma, Aunt Marjorie?"

A rapid departure ensued.

The dictionary waited on its stand as if nothing unusual had ever occurred nearby. Lucy flipped through the pages so eagerly there was a risk of tearing. Between *celebrate* and *ceremony* was a paper the size of a visiting card with a new poetic clue.

Perhaps you are thirsty
And want a hot drink.
Will you fill a small trunk,
While you have a good think?

"A small trunk?" said Hector. "I am having enough of small trunks, no thank you."

"Not that kind of trunk, silly," Lucy said. "It has to do with hot drinks."

"Follow me!" I cried. I led them straight to the morning room, and across the carpet to the cabinet where the teapots were kept.

"Perhaps you are thirsty?" I said. "And want a hot drink?"

"Aggie, you're brilliant!" said Lucy.

"Very clever," said Hector.

Inside the elephant teapot to the left—rolled into his small trunk—was the next clue.

In here it is gloomy.
Spiders frolic and spin.
When chilled from the Avon,
let the fire begin.

"There is only one Avon in Owl Park," said Lucy, leading the way.

"Spiders?" Hector's brow crinkled in distaste.

"It can't mean real spiders," I said. "Can it?"

Inspector Willard's table and chairs sat waiting to be moved away by the footmen. There had been no fire in the grate since yesterday's arrest of Mr. Mooney, but a tower of firewood sat on the tiled hearth.

"When chilled from the Avon," repeated Lucy.

"Let the fire begin!" I cried. "We should have known at once, with all the logs heaped outside the cupboard." I stepped over to my old hiding place and pulled open the door. "Voilà!"

Barricaded from the passage side by a carefully laid camouflage of kindling—I'd been lucky not to tread on them!—were our wonderful, lumpy, knitted stockings.

We had just rejoined the others, exclaiming at the cleverness of their clues, when Pressman appeared to alert my sister that Miss Day would be departing shortly and wished to have a word. She was waiting in the morning room.

"Come with me, Aggie," Marjorie said. We left the others and went along for another goodbye.

"Thank you for seeing me, your ladyship," said Annabelle. She looked at me with the glimmer of a smile. "Good morning, Miss Morton."

Her face was scrubbed clean, her hair swept back in a low knot. She wore a plain gray dress as if she were playing the part of a nurse or a nun.

"I understand that Mr. Sivam is regaining his health more quickly than the doctor expected. That is good news, and perhaps due to the good care you seem to offer all your guests," said Annabelle. "I want to thank you for your kindness to me, and your patience with all of this, Lady Greyson. And for making arrangements with the school in Tiverton to accept our caravan full of props and costumes in the new year. And for feeding me! Even when you all thought I was crooked, and—"

"Oh, Miss Day," said Marjorie. The injustice of Annabelle's situation was like a fishbone in her throat, I knew. "You were wrongfully accused and kept confined. I would not be so gracious in the same circumstance."

"I have a confession to make," said Annabelle. She wrung her hands and looked at the fire and took an *age* to continue. "I had a horrible suspicion about Sebastian from the first moment I saw Roger lying there in a pool of blood. I *pretended* to faint, so that I could talk to him before I said or did anything in public that might lead to more trouble."

"Goodness," said Marjorie.

"That was acting?" I said. "You were very convincing."

Annabelle shot me a half-smile. "Sebastian carried me upstairs, where I meant to learn the truth. But then Mrs. Sivam was there too, so I had to keep pretending that I was conked out."

She sighed. "None of it seems real. We came as a merry band of troubadours, playing make-believe for our livelihood. I'm leaving with one friend dead and the other suspected of his murder. How can I . . ." Her poise faltered as her eyes welled. She shook her head so hard that tears flew, one landing on my hand. Marjorie and I both put our arms around her to make a warm and awkward embrace.

"The thing is . . ." Annabelle pulled away. "I've been thinking about Mrs. Sivam pacing about my room while I lay on my bed, pretending to be in a dead faint—"

A tap at the door and the butler spoke. "Sergeant Shaw is here to accompany Miss Day to the rail station, my lady. She's catching the four fifty to Paddington and the snowy road will make the going slow."

"Thank you, Pressman," said Marjorie.

Annabelle used a hankie to dry her eyes. "I wish I'd met Miss Truitt," she said. "It's dreadful that Sebastian chased her off, while she has no one to share her anguish."

"Goodness, I feel the same way," said Marjorie. "Please let us know if you locate her! We'll provide a stone for the poor man, but I'd like to give her—"

"I expect Miss Truitt has gone away," I said. *And will not be seen again.*

"My lady," said Pressman. "The train."

Annabelle left. Marjorie stoked the fire and settled down to think about tomorrow's menus.

I went to find Hector and Lucy, who were playing Schoolmaster in the conservatory. Lucy was keeping score using the pencil and notebook from her stocking. Hector wore a stupendous false mustache, which I knew Marjorie had ordered for him especially from a theatrical costumer, at my suggestion.

Grannie sat knitting on a bench, apparently ignoring them.

"Who was Henry the Eighth's third wife?" said Lucy.

"Jane Seymour," said Hector. "In what country is invented the saxophone?"

"How would I know *that*?" said Lucy. "Awful, squawky thing. Hello, Aggie. How did it go, saying goodbye to Miss Day?"

"It was sad," I said.

Hector tugged off his mustache. "It tickles," he said. "I will trim for better comfort."

"Where *was* the saxophone invented?" I asked.

"In Belgium, naturellement," said Hector. "Also, roller skates and cricket—though the English, they argue with this claim."

"I should think so!" said Lucy, hands on hips. "It is *our* national sport!"

"Hector knows everything," I reminded her. "Not wise to play Schoolmaster with someone who has all the answers."

"Alas," said Hector, "I am occasionally confounded by certain matters, such as the mystery of the Echo Emerald."

"Stop worrying," said Lucy. "Mr. Mooney has practically confessed to stealing it!"

"And yet," said Hector, "we do not know where it is. How does he steal a jewel and still not possess it?"

Grannie's needles stopped moving for an instant before continuing without quite the same racket.

"I agree," I said to Hector. "We have too many wrong-shaped pieces in this puzzle."

"Mr. Mooney is eating soup when Stephen is pushed," said Hector. "Who does the pushing?"

"Mr. Corker's boots fly magically away from his body," I said, "and land upstairs. He is killed with one knife and stabbed with another."

"Mr. Mooney is not arrived at Owl Park when a thief in the night attempts to steal the emerald," said Hector. "Who is this thief?"

"Frederick?" said Lucy. "But didn't the police decide he couldn't have?"

"*Maaay*be," I said, "Mr. Sivam woke up in a strange house and decided—just the way Mr. Mooney guessed—to put the fake emerald in the fancy box and keep the real one in his pocket. Only he accidentally disturbed his wife while he was creeping around and she began to scream. He was too embarrassed to tell the truth. What do you think of that idea?"

"There was a boy in my church choir," said Grannie Jane, "whose name was Arnold Hollow." She peered at the row she was knitting. "Quite an apt name, if you had known him."

She pushed stitches along her needle and got distracted counting them.

"Grannie?" I nudged. "You were telling us about Arnold?"

"Yes," she said. "I was going to mention the imaginary bully."

We waited.

"It suited Arnold very well to be the victim of an aggressor who had always just departed or who was waiting by the bridge out of our sight, you see? The bully often took the paper sack containing his sandwich, or threatened to make off with his cap after lessons."

"But he wasn't real?" I said.

"It took a long while for us to realize," said Grannie Jane. "We would share our lunches, or walk him across the bridge all the way to his lane, and he would go his merry way until the next time."

"He was hungry," said Lucy.

"It is the boy's method of having an extra portion of food?" said Hector.

"It was the boy's method of having more than his share of attention," said Grannie Jane. "Though why he elected to cringe for the sake of momentary pity, I do not understand."

"Maybe he was lonely," I said.

Grannie smiled and nodded. "Yes. A lonely boy who wanted so badly to have people care about him that he invented a threat."

"Madame Morton," said Hector. "This is a most useful observation."

"I'm not certain I . . ." I said.

"If we think back . . ." He rubbed his temples with his fingertips. "If we look at only the facts, I believe there is *no attempt* to steal the jewel on the first night of our visit."

"But that's—" I caught myself before using the word *impossible*. Hector waited for me to catch up.

"If there was no attempt to steal the emerald . . ." I said, "that means Kitty Sivam was mistaken. She awoke from a nightmare and fancied there was an intruder lurking in the shadows of an unfamiliar room . . ."

"Or . . ." said Hector.

"Oh dear," said Grannie Jane. The clicking of her needles had slowed down considerably. "Arnold Hollow."

I closed my eyes, remembering what Marjorie had told me about a girl named Oinks who squealed and squalled about an intruder in the greenhouse who no one else had seen—so that she might feel the warm glow of attention.

"Or," I said, "Kitty Sivam is a liar."

CHAPTER 37

AN UNEXPECTED TURN OF EVENTS

THUNDER RANG IN my head. "Does this mean . . . that Mr. Mooney and Kitty Sivam were . . . *accomplices?*"

Mr. Mooney's last words to me suddenly took on a different color. *I did not kill Roger Corker.* What if that were true?

"Do you suppose . . . ," I said, "that Kitty Sivam is also a murderess?"

"Kitty Sivam?" said Lucy.

"The men, they are having an argument," said Hector, "but not expecting it to become deadly, as they are long-time friends . . ."

"Except that Kitty doesn't know or care about Mr. Corker," I said. "To her, he is merely an obstacle. She stabs him with the paper knife and a heart of ice."

"Mr. Mooney puts Mr. Corker's dagger into the back," said Hector, "because he wishes to disguise the real weapon and to confuse the police."

"The wrong boots were upstairs," I said, "because Kitty put them there! Was she trying to make her husband look guilty? And then, moments before he is to speak with the detective about seeing boots in the wrong place, Stephen is pushed down the stairs by a *woman* . . ."

"Kitty and Mr. Mooney are adorned with blood," said Hector. "So Mr. Mooney kindly burns such evidence in his little grate."

"He leaves his own boots with Mr. Corker," I said, "not thinking about bunions, because wouldn't it look odd to have a sock-footed corpse with no boots nearby?"

"Very odd," said Lucy.

"He uses the magnifier," said Hector, "and discovers that the jewel is false. He wishes so much to know where is the true emerald that he abducts Mr. Sivam, but does not tell the wife."

Grannie Jane stopped knitting altogether and put her needles and wool back into their bag. "I wonder . . ." She squinted down at the watch pinned to her bodice. "Is Mrs. Sivam assisting her husband to heal while we sit here discussing her motive? Or is she extracting from him the location of the real Echo Emerald?"

Hector and I, with Lucy following (for a change), raced to find James and Marjorie, who were drinking tea with Inspector Willard in the drawing room.

"Please excuse that we are intruders," said Hector. "But it is an urgent matter."

"Listen! Listen!" Lucy hopped from foot to foot.

"We have a dire idea," I said.

"Whatever can it be?" Marjorie plunked down her teacup.

"You must come with us," I said.

"Now, Uncle James," said Lucy, pulling on his arm.

"Is this a game of some sort?"

"Non, non!" said Hector.

"You mustn't let Kitty leave," I said. "She is part of the plot."

"She *what*?" Inspector Willard rose from his chair as if its seat were suddenly alight.

We told them the quickest version we could manage.

Marjorie's eyes got wider and wider. James's eyes narrowed almost to slits.

They both began to mutter, "Of course! You're perfectly right! It all makes horrible sense!"

The inspector was already at the door. I galloped after him, heart a-pounding, as Marjorie said she would go to sit with Grannie Jane. Hector and Lucy and James pursued us toward the Juliet suite.

Inspector Willard and Constable Worth were the only policemen who remained at Owl Park after the departure of Mr. Corker this morning. The constable stood at the top of the stairs and came to sharp attention at the sight of his hurrying superior.

"He seems to be awake again, sir," murmured Constable Worth.

Indeed, as we approached in stealthy silence, I heard Mr. Sivam speaking—or rather, growling, for his voice was not yet his own, still having a rasp to it. We now were a clump of five, hovering just beyond where the Sivams could see from inside the room.

"Only you and I knew where the two stones were hidden," Mr. Sivam was saying. "This confuses me, Kitty. If I had not been inspired to exchange one for the other—"

"I don't know what you mean, Lakshay," came Kitty's voice, higher than usual, brittle almost.

James shooed us down the passage, where we stood beside the door to the second bedroom of the Juliet suite, Kitty's door. This turned out to be a fortunate banishment.

"May I have a word, Mrs. Sivam?" The inspector tapped abruptly on the door frame. "Out here, if you will, to let your husband rest?"

We heard her say, "Certainly, Detective Inspector, I'll be right with you." We heard her footsteps click across the floor. We heard the connecting door between the two rooms whine slightly as she went through it.

Inspector Willard politely greeted Mr. Sivam, with James close behind.

"Lakshay, my friend!" cried James. "It does my heart good to hear your voice."

The door beside us, *right* beside us, flew open. We startled; she flinched. Our presence was a nasty shock for Kitty Sivam. She pushed Hector aside in a desperate sweep, and stomped on Lucy's foot so hard that Lucy fell over.

For half a moment, I could not move. But then—using a reliable villain-snaring technique—I put out my foot and tripped her. Hector pounced on her legs and held on while she kicked. I sat on her bottom until Constable Worth and then Inspector Willard stepped in to complete the arrest. James staggered away carrying a howling Lucy, to inform Marjorie that all was well.

All was not well, of course. Frederick and John were rallied to help the police contain a hissing, scratching Kitty Sivam. She was eventually put in the Avon Room and guarded by three men, tied to a chair with her own silk scarf, because her wrists were too delicate for the heavy handcuffs.

We were not permitted to witness the interview, but Inspector Willard was quite generous afterward with the grisly tale that Kitty Sivam had been provoked into telling.

Kitty Cartland first knew Sebastian Mooney five years ago, before she'd met Lakshay Sivam. They acted together in *The Taming of the Shrew* and then a musical piece where they sang romantic duets. They had a romance, but, as work in the theater meant separation at the end of every production, they eventually said goodbye. Their next encounter was a surprise, last spring, at a weekend party in a manor house near Lyme Regis.

"One of the houses," Inspector Willard told us, "where a diamond bracelet was reported missing. Not the first in a series of jewelry thefts that coincided with the engagement of a theatrical troupe."

Kitty was now married but already unhappy, a misfit in the cultured and elegant life that her husband was used to. She and Sebastian were delighted to find each other again, and began to meet whenever they could manage. When the Sivams traveled to Ceylon to visit Lakshay's dying father, Kitty wrote to tell Sebastian of the priceless family emerald, and her intention of possessing it—with his help.

She staged a robbery attempt before the actors arrived, to avoid their being suspects. The next night, while Lakshay was sleeping, she took the emerald from its box and passed it to Sebastian, waiting at her door. He was set to depart with his theatrical companions the next morning and could easily remove the stolen gem from Owl Park before Lakshay knew it was missing. Her plan had gone exactly as Kitty had imagined, until she went downstairs to say goodbye to Sebastian in the library.

Roger Corker, snoozing in a chair with his boots off, had awoken to find Sebastian holding the emerald, and had challenged him. Kitty came in to find the men wrestling, and saw her careful plan fall apart at the hand of this drunken old actor. In a fury, she scooped up the paper knife from the desk and plunged it in, unknowingly accurate in severing the artery in his neck.

Her nightdress was heavily splashed with blood, her dainty bedsocks ruined. Sebastian handed her the dead man's boots to wear upstairs, so as not to leave smears of blood on the floor. They made a hurried arrangement, and he came a few minutes later to receive a bundle of her bloodstained clothing, thrust into his hands before the door snapped shut. Her things were burned, she assumed, along with his shirt.

It had all gone so terribly, terribly wrong. She avoided a morning encounter with her husband by sitting in the conservatory, wondering whether these were the last flowers she would ever see. When the screams began, she prepared to act her part, of a concerned and loving wife.

Sebastian had pushed the emerald into Kitty's hand right there in the library, with everyone arriving at the scene of the crime. *It's a fake*, he'd whispered. *Put it back.*

A fake! *The* fake. Kitty was livid. Her husband, vexed with her for exhibiting the stone at the party, must have taken the precaution of secretly switching the stones—and accidentally outwitted her! It was too late to obey Sebastian's instruction to return the copy to its box. Lakshay had already announced that it was missing! Putting it back would call attention to herself.

And then Lord Greyson asked her to assist the swooning actress. The moment Kitty entered the dingy little bedroom, she thought to hide the emerald there. She slid the jewel into the toe of Miss Day's boot, not concerned with what happened next. Worthless to her, the fake gem might cause distracting trouble for Miss Annabelle Day—and so it did!

Kitty did not confess to Sebastian that she had hidden the gem. He was too fond of Miss Day and would object to using her this way. Let him be surprised. Far worse, in Kitty's opinion, was that Sebastian had abducted Lakshay without telling her. After a day or two, when her husband had not been found, she began to suspect that Sebastian might be responsible. But had he gone so far as murder? There'd been no opportunity to meet privately. She could think of no reason for Lakshay to disappear—except to protect his precious emerald. But from whom? It occurred to her to fear his return, in case he now suspected her of trying to steal the gem. She had to keep up a show of worry for Lakshay, but she had been a professional actress. She was an excellent liar.

She was far worse than only a liar.

Late in the afternoon, a fresh team of constables arrived from the village to take Kitty Sivam away in the police wagon. The prisoner requested a chance to say goodbye to her hostess, and my soft-hearted sister agreed—on condition that I be with her. Oh, happy me, to see the ending!

After only a few hours in custody, Mrs. Sivam seemed to have paled and thinned the way a rose bloom fades when deprived of water.

"I suppose this will be the end of our friendship," she said to Marjorie. "As it is the end of so much else."

"I do not believe we ever had a friendship, Kitty." My sister's voice held such bitterness that it scarcely sounded like her. "You killed a man. You tore Lakshay's life apart and exposed us all to dreadful wickedness. You hurt a child! This is all unforgiveable."

"Hurting anyone was never part of the plan! We were to take the emerald and travel to some distant place and—"

"That there was a plan of any kind is enough to sicken me," said Marjorie. "Even at school you were not to be trusted. If only I'd remembered that, Mr. Corker would not be dead."

Kitty winced.

"Marjorie!" I cried. "The blame is not yours for a moment!"

Marjorie turned abruptly away. "Please take her, Inspector Willard. I do not wish to see her again."

I kept watching, though. Hurt and fury passed over Kitty's face like storm clouds across a meadow. I would cherish this memory of her, brought low and rejected.

I followed into the Great Hall where Grannie Jane, Hector, and Lucy, of course, gathered to watch Kitty Sivam walk to the police wagon, as if to the scaffold itself. Inspector Willard paused to shake our hands, Hector's and mine, and to thank us for bravery and cleverness.

"I say *cleverness*," he said, "but the word *conniving* also springs to mind. I hope—for your sakes—that your wits are never again tested on such a puzzle as this . . . and yet I wish for you a path that keeps those wits sharp." He leaned a little closer. "Do send word when you uncover the Echo Emerald, as I have no doubt that you shall. I'd like to have a look at something so famous, before it leaves the country. I'll be back to check on Mr. Sivam in a day or two."

"Goodbye, Inspector! Goodbye!"

The villainess and the policemen had scarcely reached the end of the drive when Frederick appeared.

"Miss Morton? Master Perot?" he said. "Mr. Sivam would be obliged if you could come to his suite? He wishes to confer."

"To confer, Frederick?"

"That is what he said, miss." Frederick's eyes flicked in the direction of Grannie Jane, who was making her way toward the drawing room. "I hope that is not an improper suggestion?"

"Only a surprising one," I said. "Come on, Hector!"

"He must be pretty shaken by having his wife dragged away," I said to Hector, as we climbed the stairs. "What do you suppose he wants from us?"

"Before the dragging," said Hector, "he is telling her, 'only you and I know there are two stones'—"

"It did sound like the start of an accusation," I said. "So, you think he'd realized that she'd—"

"His brain cell friction is reduced to sluggish bumps, but still he is seeing the truth, and—"

"And despite the heartache it must cause, he knows that his wife is a thief and a murderess," I said. "Ouch."

"The question now," said Hector, "is whether he knows also the location of the Echo Emerald."

"I was wondering," I said, "whether anyone had looked in his pockets?"

"His pockets?"

"Isn't that where you put the vial of chloroform when you found it? Isn't that what I made to carry the paper knife to Inspector Willard? A pocket is for—"

We had arrived at the door of the Juliet suite.

Mr. Sivam was sitting in a high-backed chair beside a tall diamond-paned window, a steaming porcelain cup on a table by his elbow. His fingers drummed the doilies that decorated the armrests and his feet bounced in agitation on the footstool.

"Ah!" he whispered, when we tapped. "The young detectives. Please come in."

He looked . . . like a man bearing a heavy weight. *As a tiger might, with an injured forepaw. Like someone whose world had suddenly splintered.*

"We're so sorry for your . . . for your . . ." *Loss* did not seem the right word, though he *had* lost his duplicitous wife. "For your circumstances," I finished lamely.

Mr. Sivam appeared to drag his small smile out from somewhere deep within, and for that it was all the kinder. "My circumstances are much improved, thanks to you both," he said. "But we mustn't linger on past misery.

Mr. Corker's death is a terrible shadow. Not, as you well know, the result of a curse, but of greed. Greed itself is the curse! Will you assist me in recovering the gemstone that prompted such a brouhaha?"

"Yes, yes," we agreed, and, "Where is the Echo Emerald?"

Mr. Sivam took a swallow from the cup. I caught a faint whiff of warm honey.

"After Kitty's lamentable act on Christmas Eve," he said, "of exhibiting what she did not realize was the copy, I took the real one from its hiding place—in a pouch with my razor—and slipped it into my trouser pocket. To keep it close."

"Your pocket!" I cried.

Hector grinned at me.

"After the grievous discovery of the actor's body next morning," said Mr. Sivam, "I went to my room to compose myself. I knew the emerald must in some way be the cause. I remember holding it, inside my pocket, wondering whether I should throw it out the window into the snow. Within minutes came a knock at the door. Mr. Mooney stepped inside the room and before I could puzzle what he might be doing there, he had struck me and held a cloth against my face with surprising force." He paused to wipe a hand over his eyes. "When next I awoke, my hands were tied, my mouth gagged, and my thoughts as scrambled as if I'd drunk two bottles of whiskey by myself. Most often he was there to bully me, but occasionally I was alone. My head was heavy, my thoughts so slow . . . My legs would not carry me far. I made it to the door one time, out to the yard, but then he appeared to push me back inside . . ."

Dot's courtyard monster! He'd nearly escaped.

"Mrs. Sivam, she searches your room," said Hector.

"But Mr. Mooney never checked your pockets?" I asked. "Is it still there?"

Mr. Sivam shook his head, no, and allowed a twinkle of mischief to light his eyes.

"This is where I need your help," he said. "Imagine that your plight is reckless. You have a valuable jewel in your pocket . . . And on Christmas Eve you watched a tableau depicting the hiding of a valuable jewel in a most unusual place . . ."

Without another word, Hector and I were hurrying— yet again—to the coach house at the far end of the service courtyard. Inside, among the actors' bins and crates, we easily retrieved what we'd come for, and soon were back in the Juliet suite, presenting Mr. Lakshay Sivam with the plump and painted plaster goose.

He opened the compartment in the bird's gullet and withdrew the Echo Emerald. For a moment, he shut his eyes and exhaled, a deep breath of gratitude. Then he laid his palm flat to let us gaze at the deep green loveliness of the mesmerizing stone.

JANUARY 1, 1903
THURSDAY

An Epilogue

"CAN YOU EVER forgive me?" said Marjorie to James, on the first day of the new year, 1903.

"What have you done that must be forgiven?" James embraced her as she pressed her cheek against his chest.

"For allowing the wicked Kitty Cartland to manipulate me into inviting the nearly as wicked Sebastian Mooney to Owl Park! Our first Christmas together! What a dreadful way to start." When she lifted her face, it displayed the indent of one of his jacket buttons.

"I should have seen it!" cried Marjorie. "She tricked me."

"You wanted to think the best of her," said James. "How could you have known? Didn't you say 'Poor Kitty,' and 'Who could ever imagine that awful Oinks would grow up to be so lovely'?"

"She made me *almost* think that she'd changed," said Marjorie. "But frankly, Kitty was always pretty awful. I expect I was a bit of a pill myself. I suppose I thought if I'd grown up and become nicer, she likely had as well."

"You became very nice indeed," said James, kissing her on the button spot.

"But will your *mother* ever say out loud that she forgives me?"

James laughed. "My mother has much higher standards than I do," he said. "As all mothers seem to have." He kissed her again. "As you must now remember."

Marjorie hugged him and turned sly eyes to me. "We meant to tell you on Christmas morning, Aggie, but our plans went awry. We have wonderful news. You are to be an aunt! And Hector an honorary uncle, naturellement!"

An aunt! A baby! Could anything be better than this?

"Does Mummy know? And Grannie Jane?" I said. "Oh! But Grannie was knitting something very small and white!" Of course she knew!

"Grannie knows and so does Mummy," said Marjorie. "She is the happiest mummy in England."

"Or possibly the second happiest," said James. "We told *my* mother this morning, and she smiled so widely I was afraid her ears might pop off the sides of her face. That smile is quite out of practice, you may have noticed."

"You'll be happy to hear, Aggie," said Marjorie, "that I told Lady Greyson I hoped I could turn to her for help. I said that her own record of motherhood is stellar, what with James being the loveliest man on earth . . ." She stopped there because he kissed her again.

"My sister's all right too," said James.

"I think she was tickled," said Marjorie, "that she might be useful, instead of simply *old* Lady Greyson."

"We will have a nanny too, of course," said James.

"And an aunt," I said. "A supremely, divinely, ecstatically happiest aunt."

"Perhaps you don't want to talk about this," I said to Hector, later, "but I have a question . . ."

I'd been fiddling with a poem in my notebook. He was using the new pencils from his stocking to draw the new torch from my stocking.

"Oui?" said Hector.

"Our guess was that Mr. Mooney put you into that terrible packing case because you appeared unexpectedly, and he was afraid you'd notice Mr. Sivam imprisoned in the motorcar."

Hector was nodding. "This is true."

"So . . . logically speaking . . . what do you think he was going to do next?"

Hector colored in a beam of yellow light coming from the torch in his drawing.

"Why does he not kill me?" said Hector. "I spend much time considering this question. I believe that he is merely a thief, not a killer. When all this begins, he loves Kitty and he loves jewels. He hopes to take both these loves and find a new life far away. Perhaps he plans for the packing case to fall from the caravan in a distant town. Inside is a confused foreign boy who will not say anything sensible to the person who finds him."

"That might have worked," I said. "Keeping two prisoners must have been a wearying enterprise . . . But killing you would have been so much harder. What to do with the bodies?"

"Indeed, bodies are troublesome," said Hector. "This is likely the reason it does not occur so often, to have multiple corpses in the same house."

"Not in an ordinary house . . ." I said. "But it nearly happened here. First Mr. Corker, and then Stephen so badly hurt, even though he is himself again. And you, and Mr. Sivam . . . I can't bear to think of it." I shivered.

"It would make a good story, though," I said, after a few minutes' consideration. "A houseful of people trapped together with a murderer because of a snowstorm, or on an island, maybe. The guests are all invited to a weekend party because the host carries a grudge against each of them. And one by one they die horrible deaths, not knowing who to blame . . ."

"This host you describe is demented," said Hector. "Not, I think, a good description of Lord Greyson."

I laughed. "The only person James gets cross with is his mother. But only cross, not actually *murderous*."

We were quiet for a moment. Perhaps Hector was thinking of his own maman. I certainly was thinking about Mummy and had a surge of longing to see her.

Luckily, we would travel home tomorrow.

I turned back to my notebook. "I am trying to think of a rhyme for *sanguinary*," I told him. "For *bloody*, there's *muddy* or *ruddy*. For *knife*, there's *life*. For *blood*, there's *thud* or *flood* . . . or *cud*, but how to fit a cow into a blood-thirsty poem?"

"*Sanguinary*," said Hector. "Must it be used at the end of the line?"

LATE EDITION BREAKING NEWS!!!!
CHRISTMAS CORPSE UPDATE!!!!
A SECOND ARREST!!!!
KITTY SHOWS HER CLAWS

by Augustus C. Fibbley

Further to the Case of the Christmas Corpse, a second vile person has been arrested. Yesterday this newspaper reported the violent yet successful apprehension of the actor Mr. Sebastian Mooney at the manor house of Owl Park, accused of murdering his former friend and colleague Mr. Roger Corker. A further confession has made clear that it was not he who performed the assassination. Mr. Mooney's troupe, recommended by a friend of the family, was hired by Lady Greyson, formerly Miss Marjorie Morton, to perform tableaux for the household on Christmas Eve. This friend is now revealed to have been no friend at all, but a partner-in-crime with the notorious Mr. Mooney.

Mrs. Lakshay Sivam, née Katherine Cartland, known to her intimates as Kitty, used her claws to lacerate the fabric of the Owl Park family holiday celebrations. She appears to have masterminded the theft of the legendary Echo Emerald, and when her plan went awry, viciously attacked Mr. Corker with a paper knife and left him to bleed on the carpet. The bronze-handled dagger, discovered in the victim's back, was placed there merely to confuse the police— morbidly symbolic of the villains' betrayal?

Mrs. Sivam's estranged husband, Mr. Lakshay Sivam, was also a victim in this mendacious game, being drugged, bound and robbed. His rescue was devised by the enterprising children, Miss Aggie Morton, Master Hector Perot and Miss Lucy Chatsworth, guests of Lord and Lady Greyson. Mr. Sivam is once more, though temporarily, in possession of the stolen gem.

The temple from whence the jewel was removed, early in the last century, has gratefully acknowledged Mr. Sivam's mission of restoring the statue of the goddess Aditi to her original glory. The monks have no intention of prosecuting Mr. Lakshay Sivam, as he is acting immediately and honorably to return the missing property upon learning of its existence. A copy of the emerald will remain in Mr. Sivam's private collection.

This woeful episode has been brought to a close by the dogged resolve of Detective Inspector Thaddeus Willard and his team. D.I. Willard has proven to his detractors that creative thinking as well as tenacity and reason are essential elements to the successful outwitting of crime.

A happy footnote to the central story is that Miss Annabelle Day [third member of the beleaguered acting troupe so blighted by its time at Owl Park] has announced her retirement from the stage as a result of this harrowing episode. She is to be married in April to Sergeant Charles Shaw of the Tiverton constabulary and will remain in the vicinity.

January 1, 1903

Dear Miss Morton,

I am writing to thank you for your understanding on my recent visit to your sister's
home. Although the circumstance—the murder of
Mr. Roger Corker—was unspeakably distressing,
your kindness and discretion turned a difficult
time into a rewarding one. I do not know what
my future holds, but I will hope our paths may
cross again.

With affection,

B. Tru~~itt~~

January 3, 1903

Dear Marjorie,

This is to tell you that we arrived home safely. Mummy and Tony are both delirious to see us. Tony wagged his tail for an hour, and Mummy would have too, if she had a tail.

Thank you for inviting us, including Hector, to your lovely home at Owl Park. I had a marvelously stimulating holiday. I am very, very, very happy to become an aunt. I hope your baby will grow up to like teapots and owls and macaroni in cheese sauce and good stories.

I have written for her (or, I suppose—2nd choice—for him) a poem to tell about our week.

ODE TO CHRISTMAS, 1902

Outside, the snow fell soft and white
Near magical in pale moonlight

Within the walls, another mood
An actor slept, his feet un-shoed

A villain lurked with vengeful heart
And soon did play her wicked part

Vicious wielding of a knife
Robbed the actor of his life

He fell a-bleeding with no sound
Lay 'neath the bookshelves, on the ground

The sanguinary scene was fraught
A peaceful Christmas it was not

But when the evil crime was solved
A sweeter tale of love evolved

Owl Park's now home to splendid news
This aunt shall have a darling muse!

With love,

Your Best sister,

Aggie C. Morton

Sources

MANY OF MY SOURCES for this book, second in the Aggie Morton series, are the same as for the first. I re-read and listened to dozens of Agatha Christie's detective novels and stories, as well as mysteries by other crime writers, especially those who had created young sleuths, like Alan Bradley and Martha Grimes. I read Christie's autobiography another time, spent one million hours online, and looked at hundreds of pictures, building a landscape of mischief and murder. I visited Charles Dickens' house and Dr. Samuel Johnson's house, both in London, and Chawton House in Hampshire. While in London, I saw performance number 28,057 of Agatha Christie's *The Mousetrap*, the longest-running play in the world.

Some of the books I found useful are listed here:

Christie, Agatha. *An Autobiography*. London: Collins, 1977.

Curran, John, ed. *Agatha Christie's Complete Secret Notebooks*. Glasgow: HarperCollins, 2016.

Flanders, Judith. *Inside the Victorian Home: A Portrait of Domestic Life in Victorian England*. New York: W.W. Norton, 2004.

James, P.D. *Talking About Detective Fiction*. New York: Alfred A. Knopf, 2009.

Lethbridge, Lucy. *Servants: A Downstairs View of Twentieth-century Britain*. London: Bloomsbury Publishing, 2013. Kindle.

McDermid, Val. *Forensics: What Bugs, Burns, Prints, DNA, and More Tell Us About Crime*. New York: Grove Press, 2014.

Moran, Mollie. *Minding the Manor: The Memoir of a 1930s English Kitchen Maid*. Guildford, CT: Lyons Press, 2014.

Thirkell, Angela. *Three Houses*. London: Moyer Bell, 1998.

Tinniswood, Adrian. *The Long Weekend: Life in the English Country House, 1918–1939*. New York: Basic Books, 2016.

Acknowledgments

NEVER-ENDING THANK YOUS to Lynne Missen, Tara Walker, Margot Blankier and Shana Hayes for invaluable insight, relentless nitpicking, countless catches, and apparently true love.

Rhapsodic thank you to Isabelle Follath for the lovely, spooky cover, the perfect chapter illustrations, and a new gallery of highly suspicious characters. One of the best days of my year was the one spent with you.

Thank you to my dedicated agent, Ethan Ellenberg, and to everyone at Tundra Books who has worked so hard to introduce Aggie Morton to the world.

Thank you to Dr. Lee Myers and Dr. Andrew Hussey for medical guidance—any errors concerning stabbing and blood spatter are my own.

Thank you to Mahtab Narsimhan for your careful reading.

Thank you to my beta readers. You know who you are.

And thank you to Agatha Christie, for an endless source of murderous inspiration.

More adventure,

more mystery,

more murder . . .

COMING SOON IN THE NEXT

AGGIE MORTON
MYSTERY QUEEN